Elizabeth Podsiadlo

THE LAST ARIA

A Cooking Novel

by Elizabeth Podsiadlo

Order this book online at www.theoperasingingchef.com
or email ekitchen@san.rr.com.

Book design and layout by Evelyn Alemanni, www.allea.com.

Printed in the U.S.A.

ISBN 1-4392-5823-6

"Don't wait for opportunity, create your own."

The Last Aria

*This book is dedicated to my mother Elisabeth Duda
in gratitude for all the beautiful music she exposed me
to and all the hours we spent singing, playing, cooking
and crafting*

and

*to my stepmother, Patricia Anderson, for her example
of just how much one woman can accomplish when she
puts her mind and soul to it.*

FOREWORD

It has nearly been a year since I published my first book, "Talking Pictures." To date, and with the help of some local, and not so local shops, lots of book signings, cooking classes and your spreading the word, I have sold more than 500 hand-signed copies.

The reaction I got from "Talking Pictures," was a good one. Lots of folks loved the recipes and the fantasy of the story, but the comment I got the most from everyone was that it was too short. I have to admit that my main goal for the first book was simply to finish it. Also, I do not like a book that "takes you all the way around Robin Hood's barn" to get a simple thought or action across. I am a "get to the point" kind of writer and did not want to waste my readers' time by adding superfluous fluff. However, I learned from my readers that they don't mind a diversion taking them a little out of the way. Seeing the wisdom of their words, I took their advice and created what I think is a very lovely world to escape to.

In July 2008, I traveled to Romney, my hometown in West Virginia, with my husband and daughter. We visited my stepmother, Patty Anderson and played in her jewelry and gift shop, Anderson's Corner. This quaint shop is a special "oasis" right in the center of Old Town Romney. It is filled with West Virginia artisan-made products like original fine jewelry pieces, hand-blown glass, pottery, local gourmet products, wines and the list goes on. My stay was going to be a short one. We visited with old acquaintances, made arrangements for a December book signing and just for fun, had a realtor take us around, as I have a fantasy of owning a home there someday.

The day we were scheduled to leave, Patty recommended we go out to Mechanicsburg Gap to see one more house. She said it was the second oldest house in the area, built in 1791.

My interested was piqued, but I remembered seeing a photo of this place on the internet and was truly not impressed; but at Patty's insistence, I decided to go and check it out. It was about five miles from town on the right side of the road, tucked into a beautiful thicket of trees and against the base of a large West Virginia mountain. I have to clarify the mountain as being from West Virginia, because West Virginia mountains are not jagged like Colorado mountains. They are rounded and can be as high, or higher than 5,000 feet. They are totally covered with many kinds of trees and from a distance, look blue in the evening. Thus the name - Blue Ridge Mountains.

We pulled into the circular gravel drive of this old West Virginia home and came face to face with history. At the walkway leading up to the front porch was an iron pole with a horse head and ring in its mouth - a hitching post for your horse.

The first floor of this long building is made with local river stone. The second story front is wood, painted white and there are several windows. It has a rusty tin roof and a front porch that extends the entire length of the house. Above this porch, a balcony to the second floor extends the length of the house. Once inside, it became quite apparent that no one had lived there in a while. Lots of dead flies in the windows and layers of dust and cobwebs on everything. There is a dimness that a house takes on when it's been left to itself for a while, and it was this very dimness that set my imagination soaring.

Dark walnut floors covered the entire first floor and square, varnished beams stood where walls had been pulled down. The kitchen was large, but pretty torn up. Located at the right end of the house, its surrounding walls of river stone and fireplace oozed with potential. Rustic beams cross the ceiling and two deeply- set, long windows allowed the spider-webbed, diffused light to stir my imagination once again.

I fell in love with the house starting with the kitchen. I felt a connection that I couldn't explain. Perhaps I also felt a little sorry to see this wonderful historic dwelling falling into ruin and felt compelled to help it if I could. I looked at my husband with pleading eyes to which he responded with, "Save your pennies." To which I responded by pouting.

I kept fantasizing about what I would do with "the Berg," were it mine. Turn it into a bed and breakfast. Turn it into a brewery. After all, the property has a natural spring on it and folks really do stop every day alongside the road and fill their jugs from a pipe that extends there. I could just imagine turning one of the outbuildings into a brewery. I could even bottle and sell the water. My imagination was churning all kinds of ideas, but my husband was not amused, nor was he going to budge on his decision. It was then I realized that the only way I would be able to spend time at the Berg would be in my head.

Another place that sparked my imagination was the Whaley House in Old Town San Diego. It is said to be "America's most haunted house," by the Travel Channel's program, America's Most Haunted. However, it was not the history of its haunts that inspired me as much as the beauty of its interior. Each room is beautifully frozen in time, by the "Save Our Heritage Organization" in San Diego. Their careful restoration of the Whaley House helped me to visualize "the Berg" as it might have been in the late 1800s. But even this was not what really lit my fire. What set me spinning was the upstairs theater inside the Whaley House. It was built by a man named T.W. Tanner in 1867 who was renting the space for $20 in gold. He died 17 days before opening night. The original theater was filled with benches and could seat 150. Currently, there are about 50 captain's chairs in the theater and the stage has been restored in detailed authenticity. "Now with woodwork faux-grained, raked stage, authentic painted backdrop, curtains and period lighting."

I knew without knowing that these two places put together would be the ideal setting for my next story. Even if I couldn't own them, I would make them mine and yours to visit each time you open this book. Photos of both of these places can be found on my website; www.theoperasingingchef.com. Click on The Last Aria.

The inspiration for "*The Last Aria*" came from several different happenings and things I had seen this past year. The Berg and the Whaley house were huge influences but there was more to it. I missed my characters from the first book, and missed writing. I was hankering for another project but didn't have a story. In my first book, "Talking Pictures" I commented that you should "write about what you know." I took my own advice and included music in this project. When I learn a new operatic aria, I am not sure what I am singing about as they are typically in a foreign language. However, guided by the melody of the piece, I imagine the theme, and while it may not always be accurate, it's usually very close. It was this habit of mine that allowed me to see the arias included in my story in a new light. Essentially the feeling of each aria says what needs to be said, and if you look closer into the translations, there are always several lines that communicate exactly what was meant to be conveyed. One morning while showering I got the entire concept. You see, I get some of my best ideas while showering, and it was this shower that gave me the story line that I would write my next book around. So now I had the concept, the location and two very good, albeit fictional, friends who were willing to make the journey with me. Essentially, I had all the ingredients necessary for a wonderful adventure-filled story.

The story is set in the town of Romney, West Virginia. This is my hometown and was a wonderful place to be a kid. A lot of historical people came through Romney: George Washington, Robert E. Lee, Andrew Jackson, Lord Fairfax. There are battlefields just outside of town toward "the Berg" that are still visible today and open for the public to see. During the Civil War, the Berg exchanged hands more than 50 times from the

North to the South and was used as a headquarters by both sides during that war.

The town of Romney is in Hampshire County, West Virginia. It is a quaint town with a main street and two stoplights. Folks from all over visit here. Some have a second home here and some stay at the beautiful bed and breakfast called "The Hampshire House," which is totally furnished in the style of the late 1800s. Lots of "out of state" folks keep stereotypes of what kinds of folks live in West Virginia; and in a way, this stereotype has kept this little town a secret which, in my eyes, is a good thing. However, I think anyone who has visited there can tell you that Romney, West Virginia really is almost heaven, and like the mythic "Avalon," a place not everyone will be privileged to see. There is a link for the Hampshire County Department of Tourism on my website.

For the Musician, Chef and lover of a good story

There are several scenes in this book where well-known operatic arias are used to communicate, or to color the scene. If you are an opera buff and know these arias, you will immediately understand why the aria was chosen. However, if you are not familiar, you can rely on the translations made available within the text of the story to help you. That, along with the companion recording, will add a richness to your reading experience, making it a multisensory one. You will also gain a more in-depth understanding of the story line as well as the arias used.

A companion compact disk recording has been made to accompany this book. This very-clear recording was produced by me and recorded by Patricio Pickslay of Rhythm Coalition Recording Studios in Hillcrest, California. I am joined by accompanist John Danke; Soprano Jaimie Korkos, who sings Lilly's arias as well as the "damsel in distress;" and Tenor Jef Olson, who sings as the fictional, long-dead tenor, Giuseppe Ruscello. The recording contains arias and piano compositions by Puccini, Handel, Canteloube, Donizetti, Wagner, Ponchielli, Chopin, Verdi and Schumann. In keeping with the story, a few of the arias on this recording were intentionally made to sound as though they are coming through an old Victrola player.

The companion recording contains all of the arias mentioned in the story along with a few extra at the end. For a richer experience, I recommend playing the appropriate tracks where indicated. This will not only bring you closer to the story, but illuminate your imagination even more. If you did not purchase this charming recording but would like to, you can do so by going to; www.theoperasingingchef.com and clicking on "*The Last Aria*."

The recipes in this book are from my collection. Some of them were invented by me and some handed down from my mother. They are all suited for the cooler months of the year and perfect for holiday entertaining. My recommendation as a teaching chef would be to read through each of the recipes before trying them out. There are photos of some of the recipes from this book on my website. Click on "*The Last Aria*."

The Last Aria Webpage

In this day of computer wizardry I cannot resist the opportunity to share photos and anecdotes from the recording sessions and the photo shoot for the cover. There are photos of both locations as well as of the people who inspired me. As a reader and fan, you will have access to more recipes and a look into the world of Elizabeth's Kitchen. It is what I call "adding value" to your purchase. So, please be sure to visit "*The Last Aria*" page on the website to see photos of Anderson's Corner, the Berg, Old Town Romney, and the surrounding woods. Visit the site often, as I will be adding and changing the recipes.

www.theoperasingingchef.com click on "*The Last Aria*."

Acknowledgements

Acknowledgements are such an important part of a book, because a book is an accumulation of energies, ideas and inspirations harvested by the author from all those around her. So, I thank God for surrounding me with so many positive, talented and generous people.

I would also like to thank the following people for their friendship and support in this labor of love.

To my husband, David Podsiadlo and my daughter Betsy, for listening to me read a chapter here and a chapter there. For finding humor where I hoped they would, for their good ideas and for their continued supportive interest in this project.

To Pandeli Lazaridi, my voice teacher, who uses his talent as a singer and teacher to grow and complete my voice. Like an artist with a paintbrush, he colors my voice and my interpretation of the arias on the companion recording. His patience and ability to teach are unparalleled. I have never in my 25 years as a vocal student met a teacher - and I have had many - who could bring a voice to its full potential in so many people.

To John Danke, my music coach, who has exposed me to hundreds upon hundreds of arias, be they obscure or very familiar. Loaded with this arsenal of songs, I was able to easily pick arias appropriate for my character, Lilly, to sing. John spent many hours working with the music for the companion recording to "*The Last Aria*". If a piece was too high for my voice, he would transpose it; if another instrument was needed, he would add it. He put a lot of himself into this recording and into our sessions and for this I am very grateful.

To Jef Olson, a very talented tenor, for being so interested in reading early chapters of my book. For being so willing to be a part of the companion recording and so willing to allow his beautiful songs to be corrupted by the distortion of a Victrola sound. Also for allowing me to see his image when I thought of

William … but in truth, he would make a great Garrett.

To Soprano, Jaime Korkos, who is off to Boston. She has been accepted to the New England Conservatory of Music as a Graduate Diploma student. Sometimes Jamie would work with Pandeli in my home. When I heard her sing I knew I wanted her voice to be that of Lilly's. Thank you, Jaimie, for taking time to participate in the companion recording. Lending your voice's beautiful color and spirit to Lilly's arias really brought them to life.

To my stepmother, Patty Anderson, who made time in her busy life to read my early chapters and offer intelligent criticisms and suggestions. Thank you for being so supportive and caring. Thank you for buying and selling so many copies of my first book in your shop, for hosting so many book signings and for opening your home to me and my little family for an entire month this summer.

To Gene and Nancy Williams, the new owners of "The Berg" (the B&B where the story is set) and long-time friends of my family, for allowing me to visit "The Berg" with them this summer to get re-acquainted with all I had imagined. For sharing their vision of restoration and offering their new home, "The Berg" for my book release party in November.

To the folks at the "Save Our Heritage Organization" of San Diego for allowing me to use photos of their beautiful little theater on my website.

To photographer Tina Cockburn, costume designer Beverly Libby and the model for my cover, Kristina Cobarrubia. These three ladies are long-time friends and very talented, too. I am grateful for their help and for their talents and for sharing their ideas for the cover photo.

To Dana Munkelt for his sharp editing eyes and generosity in taking on the job.

To Michael Anderson, for his gift for creating special effects in turning our cover photo into an oil painting.

To Patrick Anderson for taking a very fine tooth comb through the manuscript.

To Evelyn Alemanni, my editor, layout artist and cover designer, for her vision and patience, for her firm hand at setting a task and for her gift of project completion. Thanks for the many hours spent in your lovely gardens and for sharing so many beautiful bouquets, delicious veggies and herbs. A working friendship is a rare thing, but it has been wonderful working with Evelyn.

To my cooking students these past 10 years. Thank you for your continued support and for buying so many books. Thank you for cooking the dishes I taught and for making these dishes a part of your family's traditions. I love that!

No successful person got to where they are without the support of friends and colleagues. A performer is nothing without an audience. A book is nothing without readers. That said, I would like to thank all those who purchased and read my first book, "Talking Pictures." Without your positive acceptance and love for the characters there would not be a reason to write another.

Thank you all,

Elizabeth Podsiadlo

PROLOGUE

Barbara Kinder and her mother were very close, even though they lived more than 1,000 miles apart. They shared a passion for cooking and would compare recipes every day on the phone. Barbara, a technical writer and consultant, was determined to write a cookbook. Her culinary skills were the envy of her friends and the pride of her small community.

As a joke, Barbara's mother sent her a digital talking picture frame for an early birthday present. It displayed humorous photos of Barbara's mother and played recordings of motherly advice like "Chew your food" and "Floss your teeth", all in her mother's voice.

Sadly, Barbara's mother passed away before she could share a secret that she kept hidden from Barbara her entire life.

With the help of the digital talking picture frame and through dreams, Barbara's mother tries to convey what she couldn't in life. A message too painful, but too important not to tell. During this journey, Barbara meets her new neighbor, William. It turns out he too loves to cook.

William, a talented young chef, acquired his culinary degree from a very prestigious school in France. There he met and became friends with Chef George Rossignol. Chef George had a habit of getting himself into trouble, and William, more than once, bailed him out. They remained friends until William moved back to New York, where he built his own culinary reputation.

It didn't take long for Barbara and William to become fast friends, as they both shared a passion for culinary adventure and writing. It was during this time, with the help of Barbara's mother's spirit sharing missing photos and visiting dreams, that Barbara and William came to realize the reason they were brought together.

Barbara and William cook together almost every day and entertain many local folks with their culinary experiments. They wrote a cookbook together called "Soulful Soups" and with William's help and connections the book has become very well known and sold so successfully that Barbara is able to dedicate more of her time to the culinary arts. Barbara and William's cookbook collaborations have taken them on many culinary adventures where they meet the most interesting people and taste many wonderful foods. The story of the last aria is one of those grand adventures and holds within its heart mystery, beautiful music, delicious recipes, tragedy and a love story.

THE DREAM

It was nearly dawn and the air was wet with fog. The darkness was lifting to a shade of gray that could only be associated with dreams.

As the fog from the evaporating frost seeps into his bedroom through a small open window, William lies sleeping in his antique mahogany bed.

In the stillness of this predawn, a bird sings out, piercing the silence with her lilting song. Over and over she calls out and waits for a reply only to start again and again…. The lonely night bird's song echoes through the woods behind William's house, into his room and into his dreams where….

William crouches beneath her window completely hidden by two thick boxwood hedges. A breeze blows the lacy Victorian curtains out the window and they flutter above his head. His eyes are closed and he is listening very intently to her voice. It is a voice he has always loved and heard all of his dreaming life. She is singing the *Song of the Nightingale, La maja y el ruisenor* by Granados and the lament and beauty of this piece holds him.

The song ends and she goes to the window looking out. As she does, he looks up, and as is always the case, she calls for him and he answers, but she does not hear. He sees her, but she never sees him. And, as is always the case, he wakes from his dream and stares out the window feeling the loss he has felt a thousand times before.

CONTENTS

RECIPEſ

Throughout this book, you'll see symbols like the one above. The box with a bird and number indicate the track on the companion recording where you can listen to the arias mentioned in the story. Hearing the music, as well as cooking the recipes at the end of each chapter, will make this book a unique and memorable experience.

The companion recording contains all of the arias of Puccini, Granados, Canteloube, Verdi and Handel mentioned in the story and a few extra at the end. It features the voices of the author, Elizabeth Podsiadlo, Tenor Jeff Olson and Soprano Jaimie Korkos.

If you didn't purchase the CD with your book, you can still order it online at www.theoperasingingchef.com.

A FRIEND IN NEED IS A FRIEND INDEED

The morning was golden and beams of bright, diffused light streamed into William's bedroom and across his face, causing him to pull the covers over his head. Outside there was a frenzy of birdsong as hundreds of finches, larks, cardinals and sparrows chirped in jubilation of the new day. William rose from his bed and slipped into his flannel housecoat and leather slippers and headed downstairs into the kitchen.

The house was cold. He stoked the ashes in the large fireplace, searching for live embers to fuel his new fire. Reaching into his kindling bucket he pulled a handful of very thinly cut pieces of wood and laid them loosely over the cooling embers. He blew deep into the pile of wood chips through to the hot coals that smoked and glowed as ashes flew.

After a couple of well-directed puffs of air, the coals sparked and ignited the wood. As the flame grew stronger, William added slightly thicker pieces and nurtured the young fire until it was strong enough to burn unattended. The fire popped and cracked, spitting small embers onto the raised stone hearth. He placed a large fire screen in front of the fire and headed to the pantry.

From the top shelf, he pulled a large glass canister filled with unbleached flour, sealed with a rubber gasket. From the fridge, he pulled the milk, butter and yeast.

He poured a small amount of water into a medium-sized glass bowl and put it into the microwave for 20 seconds. Not too hot or it would kill the yeast. He added ½ teaspoon of sugar and the yeast to the lukewarm water, stirred it with a whisk and set it aside.

Pouring the milk into a small stainless pot, he placed it on the stove and watched as the hot milk slowly rose to the top of the pot. He quickly removed the pot from the heat and blew at it so the foam would settle back down. To this he added butter and salt until it melted together.

While waiting for the hot milk to cool and the yeast to become active, William made coffee and pulled down a large stoneware bowl from a shelf above his counter. This bowl was large enough to hold two gallons of water and had very thick sides. William wiped the dust out of the bowl, greased it with butter and set it on the warm hearth.

He pulled the lukewarm milk from the stove and added it to the bowl of his large electric mixer. He went to check on the progress of the yeast. William could forecast the weather by how the yeast performed. Today it was very thick and not as light as yesterday. This usually meant it was going to rain and also that he wouldn't be adding as much flour to his bread.

He poured the thick, bubbly yeast into the mixing bowl with the lukewarm milk, locked the dough hook into place and turned it on a low setting. To this liquid he added the carefully measured flour one cup at a time. The key to measuring flour for bread was not to pack it into the measuring cup. Not even to tap the measuring cup. Simply spoon the flour into the cup and scrape off the excess flour from the top of the cup with the flat side of a knife. Once all the flour was added, he allowed the mixer to work the dough until the dough become slightly sticky. If it was too dry, he would add a little water, or if it was too wet, he might add a little flour. The key was to find the perfect middle. Not too sticky, not too dry.

William turned off the mixer and pulled the dough off the dough hook. He removed the hook, pulled the dough from the bowl, formed it into a ball, placed it into the large, warm, buttered clay bowl and covered it with plastic wrap and a dish towel. He placed the bowl on the right side of the hearth where it was warm, but not too hot. The dough would rise for an hour before he would form it into loaves. William poured himself a generous cup of strong Colombian coffee and sat at his long kitchen counter where he started a list for the market.

This was a typical morning for William. Making bread was as much a part of his daily routine as brushing his teeth. Coffee came second and if he was working on a book, he would write after he dressed. It wasn't long before the phone rang, breaking the morning silence. It was early for calls, still not even 7 am. William picked up the phone.

"Hello?"

"Good morning Villiam, it's Gertrude. I haven't heard from you in months, thought you might have died, did you die?"

William smiled. "Yes Gertrude, I've died and gone to Heaven."

"Wow, Heaven? Well, how could I possibly pull you away from Heaven?"

"You can't."

"Oh, but dis time I'm really in a bind, Villiam, I need your help and no von else will do."

Gertrude was an old friend from the East Coast. She spoke with a thick German accent that lilted with humor and sometimes sarcasm. She and William had met in a deli in New York. Gertrude had nowhere to sit and seeing William alone, invited herself to his table. Gertrude was twenty years older than William and widowed. She and William shared many interests. Music, food, architecture and travel were the subjects of many a late evening's conversation. Gertrude eventually purchased a fantastic old house in West Virginia, which she refurbished and turned into a beautiful and successful bed and breakfast. Her connections in New York helped her attract many folks that were looking for a place to really get away, and her bed and breakfast fit the bill. It was called Whippoorwill Ridge Manor. Gertrude's German nature and high energy kept the place immaculate and the service unsurpassed. You had to book months in advance and even then, you might only get the maid's quarters, but even the maid's quarters were quite worthwhile.

It had been nearly a year since William had heard from Gertrude and he too was wondering if something had happened. "Hold on now, Gertrude. You know I'd do anything for you. What do you need?"

"Tank you Villiam, I knew I could count on you. I need you to come und work at my B&B and very soon, too. I'm having surgery and dey say I need time to rehabilitate. It is urgent dat you come, no von else can do it."

"Hang on Gertrude. How soon do you need me to come out and for how long?'

"I'm scheduled for surgery in 10 days, dey said I can't put it off any longer und I vill need at least tree veeks, maybe even a mont. Oh my Gott, Villiam, I don't know what I'd do mit out your help! Tank you schatzi!"

"Wait a minute, Gertrude, a whole month?"

"I know, Villiam, I am asking a lot, but I have some very important guests coming dat I can't afford to turn away. They booked a year in advance and dey are going to use all six of my rooms. It's a big deal for me und for da town. Dey're going to hold auditions here at my house for a summer Opera Program for college students und anyone is open to audition. They're going to use my teater Villiam. Remember da teater? You wouldn't believe vhat we have been doing here. So, you need to make your flight reservations today. Oh, I knew you would help me. Ah oh, I have anoder call coming in, it might be my neurologist. I need to go, tank you Villiam. My Gott, I don't know vhat I'd do without you. Tschuss William."

Stunned, William looked at the receiver and put it down. He warmed up his coffee with a fresh shot and returned to his seat.

"Wow, I didn't see that coming." Speaking to himself. It was nearly 10 am when he heard the front door open and close. It was Barbara. He knew by the jingle of her keys. "Good morning, William."

"Good morning, Barbara. Did you sleep well?"

"Like a rock. You?"

"Good as usual."

"You have that dream again?" Barbara climbed onto the stool next to William. "Yep, seems to be the status quo these days." William took a drink of his coffee. "Hmmm, I wonder what it means?"

"Probably means I'm eating too late. Must be all the food you've been bringing me that I can't seem to stay away from especially late at night."

Barbara laughed, "O.k., o.k., I'll stop the evening deliveries. You need your sleep, it's quite obvious."

With his right hand, William was doodling on his notepad while his left arm rested on the counter and held up his chin. "Barbara, I'm going to have to make a trip back East. I got a call from my friend Gertrude. Remember me telling you about her. She owns that B&B?"

"Oh yea, I remember her. The German lady, right?"

"That's right. Well, she needs me to watch her B&B for her while she goes in for surgery and I'll probably need to leave in about a week and be gone for nearly a month."

"A month! William, we made plans. How can you pick up and leave? Can't she get anyone else?"

"No, she insists on me; we've worked together before and I know how she likes things. I know we've made plans but I'm afraid she is desperate. She's having surgery and will need a month to recuperate. Believe me, I'm not thrilled either, but I really can't say no. It would be like saying no to you if you were desperate! I am sorry. But I'll be back before you know it."

Barbara, now very familiar with William's kitchen, poured herself a cup of coffee. She sat on the stool across from William and looked into her cup. "This is such a bummer. I was envisioning a grand Thanksgiving. You and I cooking and baking and having at least 20 people come over. I feel like the wind has been knocked out of me."

William too was looking forward to Thanksgiving. It would have been with members of his birth family and with many new friends. But William was a dedicated friend and didn't hesitate. He knew he could not let Gertrude down especially in her time of need. She had no family and didn't make friends easily. He started making mental plans as he listened to Barbara. It was then an idea came to him. He smiled, boy if this worked this could turn out to be a great trip for both him and Barbara.

"Barbara, have you ever been to West Virginia?"

"Why?"

"I just wondered if you would like to join me? It's a big place and my work ethic is not as strict as Gertrude's, she could work circles around me. I'd never be able to keep up alone and the B&B is really beautiful. Near a town that is full of really neat shops. They have antique stores, handmade gift shops and a bookstore that has a collection of rare books. Plus, and I can't say for sure, but I might be able to get you some experience cooking with a friend of mine who is the executive chef at the Stone Hill Hotel. It's about an hour's drive from the place but worth it. His skill level is remarkable and a more creative chef you'd be hard pressed to find. Let me call him and see if he is open to the idea."

Barbara's mouth was open as she stared wide-eyed at William. "Are you serious? I can't just pick up and leave. I've been making plans for a month now!"

"Yes, Barbara, I know but the plans just took a turn. I won't be here. I need to help my friend, Gertrude, and you need to help your brother who will drown in dishes and sheets if you don't come to help out."

"Is that supposed to lure me? The vision of dirty sheets and dishes?"

"No, but you wouldn't have to work all the time, the B&B is booked by one group for most of the trip, so you don't change sheets every day, just once a week, I need your help and Gertrude needs us both and well. Having a chance to work with Chef George is quite a carrot, don't you think?"

"Chef George? The Chef George who wrote my favorite cookbook, 'The Key to Hospitality'?"

William laughed, he knew that would get her. He hadn't told her he knew Chef George, he knew she would have insisted on an introduction and wasn't sure George would be open to meeting her. He was French through and through and sometimes a little brash. "Oh my gosh, you know Chef George? Why didn't you tell me? You're such a rat, you know I love that guy! I practically sleep with his book… probably shouldn't have told you that. He is such an amazing man! His cookbook is more than a cookbook. It's funny, and full of anecdotes about his life, his family…His family. Is he married?"

William had been looking up Chef George's number as Barbara ranted on.

"Okay, I'm sorry I didn't tell you I knew him. We were in culinary school together. I should have told you, but things have a way of working out, don't they? I'll call him and see if he is open to the idea of having an apprentice in the kitchen. No guarantees, you understand? He is very busy and under a lot of pressure. That hotel is a 5-star hotel and I'm not sure how fun it would be for you. However, he owes me one."

Barbara was fully alert as William dialed the number. She could hear the phone ring through the receiver and then a voice answer. In a heavy French accent she heard the word "Hello?" Barbara felt herself go hot and cold at the same time. Her heart raced as she listened to William speaking with Chef George. The conversation seemed more polite than friendly. As the conversation closed she heard William saying, "I understand, of course, I appreciate that and please call if you change your mind."

Barbara's heart sank…. "Change his mind? What?" She heard William say goodbye and thanks and then hang up the phone. He looked up at her.

"Well, I guess you heard most of that. He seems to be very busy right now and is not sure having an apprentice would work out. But, he did say if things slowed down he would call me. I'm sorry Barbara, I probably shouldn't have mentioned anything until I knew one way or the other."

Barbara sat at the counter with her head resting on her two hands. They pushed the flesh of her cheeks upward shaping her mouth into a grotesque shape. "He doesn't know what he is missing. I could be such a big help. No one chops faster than I do! Dang it! It's not fair!"

William felt very bad about what had just happened. He sat down beside her and put his arm around her. "I'm sorry, Barbara."

Allowing herself to be hugged by her brother, she leaned into him and let herself be pitied. She was hurt but not totally devastated. "O.k., o.k.," she said. "You've convinced me. I'll come with you and change those dirty sheets and help you wash those dirty dishes. But! Only if you will promise to introduce me to Chef George. Surely, he couldn't say no to that!"

William grinned, Barbara was so resilient. That was one of her best traits.

"Of course, Barbara, I'll do one better. I'll take you to dinner the day we arrive. The Stone Hill Hotel is close to the airport. How about that?"

"Just be sure he knows we're coming. I don't think I could handle another Chef George rejection."

"Don't worry Barbara. He'll be there. He is a workaholic and never leaves that place."

William's Daily Bread

2 packages of dry yeast
1 cup lukewarm water
1 teaspoon sugar
2 cups scalded milk (whole milk best)
1 tablespoon salt
1/3 cup sugar
2 eggs, beaten
9 ¼ cups all-purpose flour (unbleached) (1/2 cup more or less depending on weather)
1/4 cup butter (plus a little more for greasing the bowl)

- Add sugar to lukewarm water and mix well.

- Add yeast, mixing it in with a whisk.

- Allow to bloom for 10 minutes.

- Pour milk into a small pan and cook over medium heat.

- Watch as the milk comes up the sides of the pan and turn off heat just before it reaches the top. To the hot milk add salt, sugar and butter. Allow to cool to lukewarm.

- Butter the inside of a large thick clay bowl and place in a sink 1/3 filled with very warm water. This will warm the bowl and help the dough to rise. Be sure not to get water inside the bowl while it is in the sink.

- If the yeast is active, it will have expanded to twice its volume. If it hasn't, then your bread will not rise well or not at all.

- Pour the expanded yeast water into the bowl of an electric mixer and attach the dough hook. Turn on the mixer to low, add the beaten eggs and the cooled milk mixture.

Turn up speed and blend well.

- Turn down speed and slowly add the flour ½ cup at a time until all is incorporated. Dough should not be too sticky or too dry.

  NOTE: Don't add all the flour if the dough is becoming too dry. It should be in the middle, a little sticky, very stretchy. (Described most often as being smooth and elastic.) This will allow the dough to grow when the yeast gases expand during the rising period.

- Continue mixing using the dough hook until the dough forms into one large ball and pulls all of the residual bits of four off the sides of the mixing bowl. This can take as long as 5 minutes or more.

- Once the ball has formed, pull the dough from the bowl and place into the warm, buttered clay bowl, turning once to coat both sides. Cover top of bowl with plastic wrap or a scent-free dish towel. Place in your microwave to rise. Be sure not to turn it on. This is a good place to allow the dough to rise as it is draft free.

- Allow dough to rise for 1 ½ hours. Meanwhile, grease three bread pans with butter or olive oil.

- Divide dough into three equal portions. Form dough into a rectangle shape, tucking the edges underneath. Place into the loaf pans and allow to rise for one hour more until doubled in bulk.

- Preheat oven to 400 degrees and bake both loaves in middle of oven for 15 minutes. Reduce heat to 375 degrees and bake for 25 minutes longer. When the bread is done, the top crust will look well rounded and will have a golden brown color.

- Remove loaves from oven and pop them out of the pans.

Tap them with your fingers. If they are done, you will hear a hollow sound. Allow them to cool out of the pans on a rack. While cooling them, avoid a draft. Cooling them too soon can result in shriveling the crust and will become soft and hard to cut.

- Be sure bread is completely cooled before slicing using a serrated knife. Once cooled, place into a plastic bag and store in the refrigerator. No preservatives means it can mold quickly. Will hold in the refrigerator for several days.

Variation: You can make this into an herb bread by adding one teaspoon of Herbes de Provence to the warm milk mixture. This is great with roasted meats for sandwiches.

LE CHEF ARROGANT

It was 4:30 am. The night air was clean and cold. The damp fragrance of decaying oak leaves and wet pines floated on the soft autumn breeze. The clouds from the rains had cleared and the stars were bright. The oak leaves that remained on the skeletal tree branches rustled as only October leaves can. The only sounds were from a dog barking down the street and the sound of Cathy's car running in the driveway. Both Barbara and William approached pulling their luggage. Cathy's arms were loaded down with their carry-on bags.

William laughed surveying all the luggage. "I'm not sure this will all fit in your trunk, Cathy."

"Oh you'd be surprised how roomy my trunk is."

She hoisted William's large bag in first, followed by Barbara's, then proceeded to squeeze in the carry-on cases. "Tell you what, Cathy, I can hold this piece on my lap."

"Thanks Barbara." Cathy brought the trunk lid down with such force it echoed off of the houses down the street and set the dog to barking again.

"Well, I'm figuring everyone's up now."

William liked to tease Cathy, although at this hour, Cathy was not easily riled. She was one of the few true morning people. "Do you both have your tickets?"

"Yep."

"Yes."

"Did you pack coats, extra shoes and any special

35

medicines?"

"Yes, Cathy, thanks but you asked us all this yesterday remember?"

"I'm just trying to save you guys from forgetting anything. There's nothing worse than forgetting something important."

They all piled into the small car and headed down the dim-ly-lit street. Just as Cathy was about to exit onto the main road William said, "Wait, I forgot something!"

Cathy slammed on the breaks and brought the car to a stop.

"Ah-ha, I knew there would be something. Well at least we didn't get far."

She turned around and pulled into William's driveway. He jumped from the car and ran inside. Within minutes he returned carrying a small bag. "Oh my gosh, he nearly forgot his MP3 player, God forbid."

William got into the car and belted himself in and said, "O.k., now we can go."

"You're sure?" Cathy teased.

"I'm sure."

It was nearly 6 am when they arrived at the airport. Cathy got out and hugged them both. She, more than anyone was going to miss both William and Barbara. They were together almost every weekend. She pressed a brown, grease-stained bag into Barbara's hand and gave her and William a hug.

"Be sure to call me as soon as you land, o.k.?"

"Of course, Cathy, and you're going to be coming out to see us the last week we're there, right?"

"Yes, I've already have my tickets. I'll email you with my flight information. I'm gonna miss you two! Love you both. Have a safe trip."

Barbara put her arm around Cathy and walked her to her car door and said, "Thanks Cathy, we will call as soon as we land."

She watched as Cathy drove away and joined William who was standing at the outside check-in. There were very few people at the airport at this hour which made unloading and checking bags go very quickly. Flying to the East Coast always took an entire day with travel time to and from the airport and then waiting there and finally the flight which was nearly six hours.

Barbara and William were armed with plenty of reading material and music. William had already plugged into his MP3 player and was reading a newspaper someone had left on the seat. Barbara was munching on the almond croissant Cathy had given her. They shared a passion for this pastry that went way beyond the norm. William looked up from his paper, "Are you going to save any for me?"

Barbara reached into the grease-stained bag and handed him the other half, hesitating as she did.

"You said you didn't like almond."

"I said, I don't like almond extract. I love almond paste and besides, you're making me hungry with all that smacking," he smiled.

She glared back, licked her fingers making extra loud noises and wiped her hands on her napkin. Indeed, there was no doubt they were related by the way they teased each other.

Just as Barbara got up to dispose of her napkin, the flight attendant announced the plane was ready to board.

The flight was pretty uneventful. William slept most of the time with his earphones on and Barbara read her *Chef George Cookbook*. She studied it in detail staring long and hard at the photos of Chef George. Photos from his childhood, photos of his family. Photos of his first restaurant in France. If she had been given a quiz on Chef George trivia, she would have aced it. They were blessed with a light tailwind that took 20 minutes off their flight time. Stiffly they de-planed, got their luggage and headed to the curb outside to wait. The sky was grey and the air was heavy with moisture.

"Mmmmm, the air smells clean and fragrant, even here at the airport." Barbara looked over at William who hadn't even heard her. She tugged on his coat. William jerked as though being awakened, looked over at Barbara and pulled off his headphones. The sound of a beautiful tenor voice drifted from the loose earphones.

"You're going to lose your hearing using those earphones all the time."

"What?" he said as he smiled looking over at her.

"I hope she gets here soon, I just want to get there."

No sooner had she said that when an older-model Jaguar pulled alongside the curb. It was light silvery blue and buffed to an expensive shine.

The passenger window opened and a voice with a strong German accent called out, "Villiam!, Villiam! You're here!"

William shouted, "Gertrude is that you? When did you start driving a Jag?"

In the wink of an eye, Gertrude was out of the car and opening the trunk. She was shorter than Barbara by two inches and had short grey hair. She was dressed very smartly in pressed brown pants and a tailored jacket. Elegant yet very animated, she held the trunk open and signaled for them both to load up.

"Don't just stand dhere, I don't vant a ticket. Dat guy keeps telling me to move along. I've done more laps dan die Indie 500. Doesn't he see that I'm olt? I even tried to tell him I didn't understand English, but he just pulled out his ticket pad. Dere, look how he is looking at us."

She waved her hands at him as if to say look somewhere else. It was kind of a rude gesture. "Dhese guys don't have anyting else to do, I mean look around you do you see many cars? He vould never make it in New York, oh my Gott, no."

William had loaded everything and was opening the door

for Barbara who insisted on the backseat. Gertrude shut the trunk and got in the front and William too got in quickly, shutting the door loudly.

"Villiam, don't slam da door so hart, I just got dis car paid for, oh my Gott, you're going to break da hinge."

William looked over at Gertrude and started laughing and not just quietly, it was a loud laugh that filled the car and took the tension out of the air.

"Gertrude! You haven't changed a bit, not a bit, how do you do it?"

"It's da vater shutzie, I swear it's da vater. You should see some of da people in dhis town. They look so young und yet are so old, vell, not all of dhem of course, but most of my friends.

I bottle vater at the B&B und sell it you know. My old building is built on top of many underground springs. Dhat's why I can't keep the basement dry, Oh my Gott, da basement vould be a swimming pool if I didn't keep da sump pump running 24-7. It's da vater dhat keeps me young. And you, look at you! You look fat Villiam, not like you did in New York, und you look more manly, yes, manly. You'll do just fine at da B&B. Plenty of hard vork to vork off dat fat."

She poked his ribs and he laughed again. Barbara was not at all sure what to think of this brash woman. But William seemed very comfortable with her, even with her insults. "Barbara, this is Gertrude, as if you hadn't guessed by now. Gertrude, this is my sister Barbara."

Gertrude adjusted the mirror as she drove to look at Barbara.

"Oh my Gott, William, she looks like you, only prettier und tinner! How vonderful to meet you, William has told me so much! What a remarkable thing da vay you met. It was obviously no accident, no indeed. It was Gott's plan for sure. His mercy is boundless."

Barbara found herself stumbling for words, "William has told me a lot about you, too. Errrr, so you're German? Where in Germany are you from?"

Boy, that was a dumb thing to say, she thought to herself, but it didn't matter, Gertrude didn't seem to hear her. She started to prattle on about her surgery and her important guests. Already she was running through a list of duties William was to take. William interrupted Gertrude with the reminder that they were to stop at the Stone Hill for an early dinner.

"An early dinner? The Stone Hill? Why there, Villiam? You don't need dinner now, we vill eat later."

But William insisted and Gertrude acquiesced. It seemed that as loud as she was, she was not unbendable. William could probably get away with anything. Barbara, on the other hand, would not even attempt to oppose this formidable lady, even for Chef George. William was correct in his statement of the hotel being near the airport. Within fifteen minutes they were in the country and driving up a long and grand entrance to a beautifully restored plantation-style manor. The outside of the main building was river stone and white grout. Several large leaded glass windows were framed in black shutters. Two old hitching posts shaped like horse heads with iron rings coming out of their mouths stood shiny and black at the entrance to the sidewalk that lead to the main dining room. The door stoop was decorated with several large pumpkins, cornstalks and gigantic baskets of brown and golden mums. As they entered into the hotel's restaurant, the smell of well-oiled wood and freshly baked bread filled the air.

A long, well-polished, wooden bar with a brass rail stood to their right and just ahead, two French doors stood opened to the main dining room which gleamed with elegance.

Small tables covered with white linen cloths and sparkling wine glasses stood near the entrance to the room. Delicate crystal candle holders flickered and on each table, a delicate silver vase held a single rose. Toward the back of the dining room, large, bare-wood tables gleamed with reflections of tiny lights that laced bare tree branch arrangements at the two back corners of the room. Barbara gasped, not realizing that she had held her breath almost to this point. She felt dizzy and nervous. She was standing in Chef George's dining room and in a short time she would be eating food prepared by him and then, she would meet him. This man she had admired ever since she found his cookbook among William's vast collection.

She tried to calm herself. She rationalized, he is just a man like any other. He puts his pants on one leg at a time just like every man. Ahhh, his pants....his legs.... She sighed audibly.

"Well, what do you think, Barbara?" William had been watching her as had Gertrude.

"Vhat's wrong mit her?"

"Oh, she just has a little crush on Chef George."

At this, Barbara threw William a look that could have fried an egg. "I don't have a crush on Chef George."

Just then from behind the bar came the unmistakable voice of Chef George himself. "William, Gertrude!" I can't believe it! You actually came! How marvelous!"

He motioned for the hostess. "Seat them at the Mahogany Round."

The hostess stiffened, "Chef George, the round has been reserved for tonight. Can we offer them the Sycamore Table?"

She looked as though she was bracing herself for his answer when he replied. "Look Doris, you work it out, but put my guests at the Mahogany Round, o.k?"

It was clear she would not argue. She motioned to Gertrude to follow and led them to a beautifully-polished round claw foot table that was clearly the best seat in the house. It was situated so you could see the view of purple mountains silhouetted by the setting sun and a large meadow which stood in its shadows. The table was also positioned near a rustic riverstone fireplace graced with antique long-handled copper pots hanging from hooks. Its mantel was a thick, hand-hewn beam which gleamed with polish. Above the fireplace hung a painting of a woman wearing a deep blue brocade grown. She had pale skin and very dark eyes that looked out over the dining hall. A Victorian lavaliere hung from her long neck. It had a single jewel in the center and from the bottom a small teardrop pearl hung. Her mouth was open as though she was singing and her right arm was held forward and low with her hand out-stretched.

All three were held captive by the grace the painting exuded, but it was Gertrude who spoke first.

"Dhat's remarkable!"

William responded. "Yes, it is remarkable, She looks so familiar."

"Who does?"

"The woman in the painting."

"That painting?"

"Yes, that painting, I can't seem to take my eyes off her."

"Vell I'm glad to hear it because I have almost da identical painting at da B&B except she is vearing yellow und it's brighter. Can you make out da name of da artist?"

William got up to look for the artist's name but as he looked, he found himself caught up in the detail of the room that surrounded the lady in blue. It was a dark painting, but if you took the time, you could see a tapestry of a harvest scene on the wall behind her. There was a scrolled metal music stand with music on it and a very odd-looking piano. It was square and was held high on four legs like a piece of furniture.

William was up so long that Barbara joined him. "Any luck?"

William shook to attention, "I'm sorry, what did you say?"

"Were you able to find the name of the artist?"

"Well, I think I see a partial name in the bottom corner,

but it's so dark. Do you see? There are three letters; T, H and I think an A, but it could be part of an M, it's just too hard to make out."

Barbara looked up at the painting.

"She has such a presence, a lovely warm presence. I can almost hear her singing." She smiled at William. "Come on and sit down."

It wasn't long before a young lady in her early twenties came to the table with the wine list. She too had long dark hair and dark eyes. She introduced herself. "Hello, my name is Sarah, welcome to Stone Hill. Would you like to start off with some wine? We carry a large selection of both imported and local wines."

Before she could finish her description, Doris, the hostess, came with an already open bottle. "Compliments of Chef George."

She handed it to Sarah, who instead of pouring a sample which is customary, poured into each of the three glasses at the table. Just as she finished she looked at them and smiled.

"I think you will like this wine, it is our 'top of the line.' Oh, and we have some amazing specials this evening."

But once again she was interrupted, only this time, by Chef George who was carrying a large plate of beautiful appetizers. There were cheese puffs, made with blue cheese, and spinach puffs with cream cheese. A beautiful Pissaladière made with red onions and balsamic vinegar, anchovies and nicoise olives and on a small silver plate a tight bunch of crimson-red grapes the size of walnuts.

Chef George placed the plate in the center of the table and motioned to the girl. "Sarah, go get some small plates." As she left to retrieve the plates, a young man placed two linen runners on the table where their plates would soon be, then Sarah came with the smaller plates and they began their feast.

Barbara was so nervous she couldn't look up from her plate.

Chef George would come and go until the final course was served and the table was being cleaned off. He then pulled up a chair and sat down next to Gertrude.

"So William, you look good. Obviously, you are very happy and I can see why. She is lovely."

He held his glass up to Barbara, who was stunned.

William replied. "Yes, meeting Barbara has changed my life, but not the way you think it has."

Chef George raised an eyebrow. "You see, George, this is my newly found sister, Barbara. It's a story I'd love to share with you when you have time. Barbara Kinder, I'd like to introduce you to Chef George."

Chef George looked incredulously over to Barbara. "Your newly found sister? I'd like to hear that story sometime." He looked over at Barbara who had found her nerve. Chef George rose and extended his hand to shake hers. She extended her hand which was cold from being so nervous and just as their hands were about to meet he took her hand and turned it over with his other hand. She pulled her hand back. He looked up.

"You're the one William called about right? You have strong hands but do you have what it takes to make it in my kitchen? Hmmm, I wonder." He took a drink from his wine glass. "You know cooking at home is very different from cooking in a busy restaurant kitchen. It is exhausting and working with me is no cakewalk. Just ask anyone here. They will tell you."

He sat down again and turned to William. "So, how long are you going to be in the area?"

"About a month, give or take. We will be here through Thanksgiving and depending on Gertrude's recovery, will probably head back the first week of December."

"It must be nice to just pick up and go whenever you want."

At this Gertrude interrupted him. "I vould hardly say William is doing vhat he vants. He is helping me because he is a good friend, not because he is just doing what he vants."

"Point taken, yes it is admirable, but not surprising. William has helped me out of a pinch before, too." Chef George winked at William and emptied his glass. He looked over at Barbara whose eyes were hot with anger. "O.k. William, I'll tell you what, she can work here on Tuesdays and Thursdays. We'll see how she does."

Barbara was shaking with anger and wanted to throw her wine glass at him, "What a pig!" she thought to herself. He wasn't even addressing her at this point. He was negotiating her time with William and not even caring about what she wanted. She was just about to object when Chef George got up and spoke directly to her.

"Well, I'll see you on Tuesday then. Wear black pants and comfortable shoes. Oh, and tie back your hair. I'll provide you with a jacket and apron. Trim your nails and no perfume or jewelry, got it?"

He shook William's hand, held up his glass as if to toast them and went back to the kitchen. Barbara at this point was totally steamed. She looked over at William who knew exactly what she was thinking.

"Look Barbara, before you say anything, take a deep breath and count to 10. You got what you wanted, didn't you? A chance to work with a Chef George, thee Chef George. Surely you didn't think he would be a humble man, did you? I mean think about it."

Gertrude excused herself and headed for the restroom.

The only thing Barbara knew was that she wanted to get out of there and the sooner the better. She finished her wine and got up from her chair.

"I'll meet you outside." She found her way to the front entrance and out onto the front walk. It had gotten dark and the air was damp and filled with the sweet fragrance of decaying leaves and the heady fragrances from the baskets of mums that adorned the front stoop. She bent down to breathe them in, then stood up, exhaled and started to feel better.

Within moments, William and Gertrude joined her and they all headed for the car. Gertrude handed the keys to William and they drove for a while in silence, each in their own world. As the car glided down the road, Barbara looked up and saw a sky full of stars framed in the silhouette of the trees that lined the road. Exhaustion overcame her and she drifted off to sleep, then was awakened by Gertrude's voice.

"No Villiam, it's the next left, the entrance is hidden. There, see the sign? Just after the sign go left."

With the exception of the sign for the Bed and Breakfast, the driveway was dark and curved around to the front of a very long, two-story house with a front porch that was just as long. Gertrude quickly got out and stiffly scurried up the walk. She unlocked the front door and turned on several outside lights that lit up the front lawn and walkway.

The spicy fragrance of the boxwood hedge filled the air with a lovely, musty, herby scent. Here, like home, the wind gently rustled the dry oak leaves. Barbara remembered the early morning departure and marveled at how long ago it seemed, as she and William carried their luggage inside. Gertrude stopped them before they came inside. "There are two small rooms over the garage where you could stay, or you can stay in da main house until da guests arrive next veek."

William headed into the main house following Gertrude. The house was filled with beautiful period pieces making them feel as though they had stepped back in time. There was a large stone fireplace with a painted mantel and in front of it were two cloth-covered wingback chairs sitting on a braided rug. Above the fireplace was the painting Gertrude had spoken of earlier, and she was right, it was the same singing woman, just as she described. "Dere is a light switch over dere, Barbara, vould you turn it on?"

Barbara found the switch and flipped it. Several lamps came on at once that brightened the room but didn't help to illuminate the painting. Just in front of them was a grand stairway. The steps were two colors of wood, the step being darker and the riser a golden yellow. A shiny dark banister started at a round-carved wooden pillar and gracefully spiraled upwards.

"Da two rooms above the garage are more modern dan the vons upstairs. I had dem revired und each room has its own small heater if you get colt. If you stay in here tonight you may get cold, I haven't brought in da firewood yet, but dhere are lots of qvilts."

William looked at Barbara, "Well, would you like to stay here or above the garage?"

"I don't know, I'm too tired to think, let's just stay here."

William agreed and led her to the first room at the top of the stairs. The first thing Barbara noticed was the beautiful floors. Gertrude was behind her with a quilt in her arms.

"Aren't dey beautiful! Dere valnut." Lots of wax brings out a glow in them, but be careful, they can be slippery." She placed the quilt on the bed and showed Barbara the bathroom which was not in her room.

"Breakfast is at 8, vich is 5am your time. If you don't vake, you can heat it vhen you get up. I'll leave out coffee for you to make. I have an early morning appointment and von't be back til after lunch so make yourself at home, und check out da rooms over da garage. You'll like dhem too."

William had taken the room at the end of the hall and was already settling in. Barbara heard him unzip his luggage and then saw him with his shaving bag.

"Old houses creak, Barbara, so don't become too alarmed at the noises you hear."

"Don't worry about me, I grew up in an old house, remember?"

"Not as old as this one, it was built in 1765. It's on the state historic registry as one of top ten oldest surviving houses."

"Well, as long as it's not on the register for being one of the top ten haunted houses."

William laughed, "If there were ghosts here, Gertrude would have put them to work or scared them off ages ago."

Gertrude yelled from the bottom of the stairs, "I heard dhat! Now get to bed, morning is going to come early for da two of you and I have a lot to tell you!"

Spinach Gougères with Feta and Dill

Servings: 36

Full flavored, extreme comfort food. These little gougères are very nutritious. A perfectly balanced meal as they contain-veggies, herbs and lots of protein.

1 cup milk
1/2 cup butter, no substitutes
1 1/2 cups flour
1/2 teaspoon salt
4 large eggs
10 ounces frozen spinach, drained completely
   and chopped
1/2 cup fresh dill
3/4 cup feta cheese
1/2 tablespoon dried oregano
1 dash salt and pepper
1 pinch cayenne

- Preheat oven to 375 degrees.
- In a large saucepan bring milk and butter to a boil.
- Add all the flour at once and stir well to form a smooth batter.
- Allow to cool slightly and add the eggs one at a time mixing quickly so egg doesn't cook but blends in.
- Once all eggs are added mix in the spinach, dill, oregano, cayenne, salt, pepper and feta cheese mixing well. Dough

should be smooth and soft.

- Once dough is made, scoop slightly rounded tablespoons onto a Silpat˚ or parchment covered cookie sheet.

- Bake for 30 minutes and serve hot. When done, the gougères should be light and have lots of air pockets in them.

Gougères are best hot, but the dough can be made ahead and stored in fridge for a least one day. Also, can be made and frozen. Heat in 375 degree oven for 5 minutes, or until heated through before serving.

Serving Ideas: Serve with a Greek salad as a light lunch, or with stuffed grapes as a dessert.

Savory Blue Cheese Gougères

Servings: 24

Fabulous flavor and texture. You can substitute the blue cheese with feta or even a sharp cheddar.

Fantastic served hot. O.K. cold, but really special hot.

3/4 cup water
5 tablespoons butter, salted
1/8 teaspoon salt
1 cup unbleached flour
3 eggs
1/2 cup blue cheese, crumbled
1 pinch cayenne pepper
1 pinch black pepper
1/2 teaspoon dried marjoram

- Preheat oven to 375 degrees.

- In a medium saucepan over medium high heat, combine water, butter and salt. Bring to a boil and remove from heat.

- Add all of the flour, salt, marjoram and cayenne and stir vigorously with a wooden spoon until blended.

- Mix thoroughly until there are no lumps. Place pan back over heat and stir to dry out batter.

- Remove from heat and add the eggs one at a time stirring quickly so eggs don't cook. Dough should be soft and shiny.

- Once dough is made scoop slightly rounded tablespoons onto a Silpat or parchment-covered cookie sheet.

- Bake for 30 minutes and serve hot. When done, the gourgeres should be light and have lots of air pockets in them.

Serving Ideas: Serve along side fresh fruit like figs and balsamic vinegar.

Pissaladière

Servings: 8

Crunchy, chewy, robust flavor, wonderful! If it's cold where you live, you can raise dough in the oven with the oven light on. Don't turn oven on though, just the light. This creates enough heat and is a draft-free place.

Divide the dough and use the other half later for pizza or bread sticks. Will keep in refrigerator for up to two days.

You can use a deep clay baker so your Pissaladière will have sides, or you can use a flat pizza stone and create a little edge like a pizza.

If you are using unpitted olives, be sure to let your guests know. Nicoise olives are traditional for this recipe, but Calamata olives would work as well or better for this dish.

If you don't have a clay baker or pizza stone, use an insulated cookie sheet. If it is aluminum, be sure to coat with parchment or use Silpat.

TOPPING
3 large red onions, peeled and sliced thin
1/8 cup olive oil
1 teaspoon dried thyme
2 bay leaves
1 tablespoon balsamic vinegar, good quality
1 dash salt
3/4 cup nicoise olives, Calamata work well, too

1/2 cup salted anchovies, not in oil/ sliced longways in half

FOR CRUST
1 pinch sugar
1 1/4 cups warm water, tepid
1 tablespoon active dry yeast, not rounded
1/4 cup olive oil
1 teaspoon salt
5 1/2 cups unbleached flour

TO FINISH
1/2 cup feta cheese, crumbled

- You will need one 10" round with 2" rim clay baker or a pizza stone. Add a thin coating of olive oil to your stone baker.

- Add a pinch of sugar and the yeast to the tepid water and use a small wisk to incorporate. Allow to sit for 10 minutes until the yeast blooms.

- While waiting, add olive oil, onions, herbs and a dash of salt to a large iron skillet or stainless steel fry pan and cook over medium-high heat. Saute, stirring occasionally, for 10 minutes until onions are quite limp.

- Add the vinegar and continue to brown for five minutes. Turn off heat.

- Add the yeast with water, olive oil and salt to the bowl of an electric mixer. Using the dough hook attachment, start to mix on a low setting adding 1/2 cup of flour at a time until all of the flour has been used. If the dough appears to be very dry, add a little more water or a little more olive oil, until it becomes an elastic dough, not too wet, not too dry. Mix until all of the flour and bits have been pulled from the sides of the mixing bowl and a ball has formed. You may need to shut the mixer off a couple of times and pull dough from hook for this to happen.

- Grease a large clay bowl with butter or olive oil and place the ball of dough into the bowl. Turn dough over once to coat top of dough with oil.

- Place plastic wrap on top of bowl and put in a draft-free place to rise for 40 minutes to one hour.

- Preheat oven to 350 degrees. Once dough is ready, pull from bowl and split in half. Wrap one half and store in refrigerator until ready to use.

- Place the other ball of dough into the center of your baker and press to cover the entire bottom of baker and up the sides. Strive to make the dough even in thickness. If you are comfortable with pizza dough you can use your hands and fists to make a disk using gravity to strech the dough, tossing it around on your fists. When dough is near the right size place in the baker and press to the side walls.

- Place baker in oven and allow to bake for 10 to 15 minutes for a light crust.

- Remove the bay leaves from the onion mixture and discard.

- Pour the onions onto the crust and spread to coat evenly.

- Add the anchovies and the olives on top of the onions making a pretty pattern.

- Place the pissaladière into the oven and bake for 15 minutes or until crust is golden brown. If crust does not brown after 15 minutes, turn broiler on for 2 mintues and watch closely. You want a light brown crust.

- When done, pull from oven and allow to cool for 10 minutes before serving.
- Cut in half then in quarters then eighths.
- Sprinkle with feta cheese and serve.

I LIVED FOR MY ART

William always stayed in the same room when he visited Gertrude. It was, in a way, a very manly room with a chunky antique headboard and matching Chippendale dresser with marble top. He crawled into bed and slid under the fat down comforter, pulled it up under his chin, tucked in his arms and quickly fell asleep. Dreaming, William sat in a dimly lit theater full of people. Near him, someone whispered, "Her husband won't let her sing anywhere else, only here in this theater."

The room became quiet as a single note played on the piano, the same note repeated and hung in the air. Then, with a sweet, grand sentiment, a woman's familiar voice sang out the lament of *Vissi d'Arte*.

William knew too well what this piece was saying. It was one of his favorite arias from the Puccini's *Tosca*. He listened transfixed and translated as she sang in Italian.

"I lived for my art, I lived for love,

I never did harm to a living soul!

With a secret hand I relieved as many misfortunes as I knew of.

Always with true faith, my prayer rose to the holy tabernacle.

Always with true faith I gave flowers to the altar.

In the hour of grief why, why, o Lord,

why did you do this to me?

I gave jewels for the Madonna's mantle,

and I gave my song to the stars, to heaven,

which smiled with more beauty.

In the hour of grief why, why, o Lord,

ah, why did you do this to me?"

Now standing in front of him, he could see the outline of a young woman with long dark hair. Her features were obscured but her voice was so familiar. Clear and bell-like, full of life and emotion.

The scene faded and the dream brought William to a bedroom where he is standing next to her bed. The room is elegant, but the furnishings are of an earlier time.

He sees the back of the same woman who sang earlier, sitting in a rocking chair by a window. She is holding a baby and singing a French lullaby. Her voice is weak and sounds like she is crying. She doesn't seem to know William is there.

There is a knock at the door, it opens and a large-framed man walks in. He stands next to the woman and the baby and speaks. The woman says nothing. She gets up with the baby and walks from the window and away from the man who follows her persisting. William can't make out the words but knows the woman is very upset. The baby starts to cry, the man leaves slamming the door and the woman sobs, gentling rocking the baby.

The dream faded and William awoke, feeling the sadness of the dream. He rose and sat at the edge of his bed leaning his head into both of his hands. This was the first time he had heard her cry or seen her baby. He whispered into the darkness. "Who are you and why do you haunt my dreams?"

William couldn't sleep. He thought of her, and the recurring dreams. He loved her, this singing woman, but each dream ended with his being pulled away from her.

The sun was just rising when he fell back to sleep only to be awakened by the sound of Gertrude leaving an hour later.

Barbara was awakened by the rich aroma of fresh-brewed coffee and crispy West Virginia bacon. The combination of the two made her very hungry.

The sun beaming through the window drew Barbara to look out at trees decked in autumn reds, yellows and oranges next to a large field filled with tall golden grasses. The warm golden hues and beauty of the rural landscape called to Barbara; she promised herself a walk right after breakfast.

Downstairs and across the great room was a large wooden framed doorway which led to the kitchen.

Inside, William sat at a small, square table in front of one of two, almost floor to ceiling windows framed into a solid stone wall. A matching stone fireplace stood between the windows, endowed with a hand-hewn walnut mantel. You could tell the walls were thick by the depth of the windowsills, which were easily one foot deep.

A colorful collection of small blue and green bottles graced the middle ledge of the windows and from the tops of the window frame hung several bunches of herbs to dry.

A large wooden island stood in the center of the kitchen. It was higher than the counters and was of rustic design. Its wood gleamed with many years of polishing, and it had several small drawers with button knobs and a lower shelf where beautiful copper and stainless pots were stored.

The kitchen sink and cabinets were new and had a Williamsburg charm to them which kept with the feeling all through the house.

A large pewter chandelier with electric candles hung from the high ceiling in the center of the kitchen over the island, and hanging on the wall to the left of the fireplace was a large hand-carved mahogany Black Forest cuckoo clock which looked like a large provincial farmhouse with a thatched roof. Two tall carved pines framed the scene that was set in motion when the clock struck the hour. Two figures would dance and spin as the slightly out of tune chime would ring out. Then the whirling figures would return into the same door together. It was this very incident that brought William out of his morning trance and it was at the same moment Barbara walked in totally dressed and ready to go.

She wore jeans, a red-plaid flannel shirt, a black down vest and hiking boots.

"I have been called to breakfast by long and lovely strands of delicious fragrances. And now, I'm starving and in dire need of the coffee I've been smelling. Where is it?"

"It's next to the refrigerator." William's dream-filled night combined with jet lag had his head in a haze.

Barbara looked and found a thermal carafe and poured from it a large cup of rich smelling coffee. She always tasted her coffee before determining whether to doctor it up. As she suspected by its fragrance, it was perfect, well balanced, not bitter and just what she needed. She plucked a few strips of bacon from the paper towel where it had drained, placed them on a napkin and sat across from William.

As she munched the crispy bacon she looked around. The kitchen was so full of character, you could look around for an hour and not see all the unusual things Gertrude had on display or placed for storage.

Hand-carved, wooden springerle molds for shaping shortbread graced a small wall above a low wooden bookshelf. There were rabbit shapes, acorns, deer, Santa figures grouped together, all very European.

On the bookshelf below was a very old collection of German poetry books. It was all so beautiful to look at, but what made it so unusual was how polished it all was, there was no dust on anything. Even the old wooden floors, while worn, gleamed with attention. Barbara spoke, "We're really in for it you know. Look at this place, we'll be cleaning constantly to keep up with her standards. I mean it's spotless."

William got up to fill his cup then returned to the table without saying a word. "Look, it's a beautiful morning, I'm going to take a walk. Would you like to join me?"

Barbara didn't wait for his answer, she knew he hadn't really heard her. It would be another hour before he was human, and without a mission like bread to bake who knew how long it would take?

She headed out the front door and stood on the long front porch to determine which way to walk. She headed straight down the front walk, turned right along a gravel road and headed toward the field she saw from her window. In the distance she could hear a chainsaw whining. Then some hammering as though somewhere near someone was building something. The ground was covered with fallen yellow maple leaves that made it seem so bright.

The field she walked along was overgrown with tall Queen Anne's lace, fuzzy goldenrod stalks and empty milkweed shells that had gone to seed. All the grasses were in muted golden colors and bending from the weight of moisture.

There was an old rusted barbed wire fence that held the field grasses in and separated them from the road. She turned and saw the house disappear from sight as she rounded a bend and continued on heading slightly uphill. After about 10 minutes of fast walking she found the origin of the hammering. An old single-story farmhouse with a tin roof stood shrouded by wild rose bushes and Virginia creeper vines. In the front yard, two wooden sawhorses supported two large wooden beams.

Sitting under the beams was a beefy brown hound dog wagging its tail. Too lazy to get up and greet her, Barbara headed toward him and crouched down to pet him.

"Aren't you a pretty dog?" She scratched behind his long silky ears and his back foot started moving.

"Does that feel good?" The dog was thoroughly getting Barbara's attention, he licked her hands as she tried to see the name on his collar. "What's your name boy?"

"His name is Arthur."

Barbara, surprised, jumped up and hit her head on one of the beams on the sawhorse.

"Ouch!"

"I'm sorry, I didn't mean to startle you. Are you alright?"

Barbara's felt the knot forming on the top of her head and looked over at him with a grimace. "Yes, I'm fine. I probably shouldn't be trespassing anyway, so it's my fault."

"Nonsense, you're not trespassing. Why don't you sit down for a minute 'til you're sure you're alright. My name is Garrett, I work for Gertrude and I know who you are, you're one of the two chefs that will be watching over the place while Gertrude has her surgery. He had a very strong West Virginian accent that exuded warmth.

Barbara's eyes were watering from the bump. She allowed herself to be guided to the front steps of his porch and sat down.

The large hound dog came up to her in what seemed an apologetic manner and nudged her free hand with his large head.

"It's alright, boy."

"Arthur, give the lady some room."

Arthur laid down right on top of Barbara's feet and put his head between his paws.

Garrett got up, went inside, and came out holding a glass of cold water. "Here, have a drink of water, it will make you feel better."

Barbara took the small glass from him and took a sip, then another. "That's delicious water."

"Yea, the water here is famous for miles around. Folks will stop to fill their jugs from a pipe that sticks out at the road. They've been doing it for years. Gertrude sells it to her customers and folks in the next county have it delivered to their homes."

Barbara handed him the empty glass and got up. "Well, I can see why, it's really delicious." She watched him as he brought the glass back inside. He wore faded jeans and worn leather work boots. A suede vest hung open over his blue flannel shirt and a ring of keys hung from his back pant loop. His hair was wavy and dark with patches of grey and he was of a medium build.

She couldn't help but look inside his house as the door and screen stood open.

Propped against the entry hall were several canvases used for painting. She couldn't make out whether they were painted on as the hall was dimly lit and the canvases faced the wall.

She looked up from them and smiled. "Are those canvases?"

"Yea, I just made them up yesterday. They need to sit a few days before they get good and tight. Has everything to do with the humidity you know."

"No, I didn't know that. You are a painter then?"

"Well, that's a matter of opinion, but yes, I paint, mostly for pleasure. Although, I've sold a few now and again. I'll show you sometime if you like."

Barbara could see he was anxious to get back to his hammering.

"Well thanks for the water and sorry for the interruption."

"No need to be sorry, I'm sorry about your head. You should probably get ice on that bump when you get back to the house, and if you need anything, Gertrude has my phone number, you can always call."

Barbara headed back to the house. As she drew closer she saw Gertrude pull up in her Jaguar. She got out and popped the trunk. Seeing Barbara she signaled her to come closer. The trunk was filled with boxes of groceries. "I want to be sure you have everything you need for when the guests come." She loaded Barbara up and she too carried several bags with her strong hands. They headed into the kitchen where William still sat.

"William, you're not even dressed yet, oh my Gott! We need help unloading the car, I bought supplies and there are a lot of them."

William jumped to and headed outside in his robe and slippers to carry groceries.

"Is this how it's going to be when the guests arrive, you milling about in your robe till 10 am? That's not what I had in mind when I asked for your help, William."

William didn't respond. He carried in three large boxes stacked one on top of the other and sat them in the large pantry. Barbara kept her distance and listened to Gertrude as she continued badgering William. Finally after all the boxes had been brought in William seemed to finally be awake.

"What a beautiful day!"

"How would you know? You've been in the kitchen all morning."

He stood at the open front door and breathed in the clean air. "Now that's some fresh air. Hey Barbara, how was your walk?"

"Painful."

"Painful? What happened?"

"Let's just say, I met the handyman."

William gave her a half smile. "I see, and did he invite you in to see his etchings?"

Gertrude started to laugh at this and pulled down a large bowl and cutting board.

"What is that supposed to mean?"

"Nothing really, it's just that Garrett, it is still Garrett, isn't it, Gertrude?"

"Yes, it's still Garrett."

"Well, Garrett is a bit of a heart throb around here."

"Really, I hadn't noticed." Barbara plopped down on the stool next to the island and watched Gertrude. Gertrude smiling started to chop up celery at an amazing speed, then parsley. She pulled out some green pickled peppercorns and smashed them with the side of her large chef's knife.

"Garrett is a nice man, Barbara. Don't let Villiam put you off. Garrett has vorked for me since I bought dis place and lives in dhat little house just up da road. I don't know vhat I vould have done mithout him. He can fix anything und has da patience of a saint. He can't help it dhat he is so dam good looking. Oh my Gott, Villiam is just jealous!"

Gertrude added drained tuna into the large bowl and mixed it along with the parsley, chopped celery and peppercorns. Then she added ¼ cup of sour cream and 1 tablespoon of mayonnaise. She stirred it all up and added a dash of salt and pepper. From the toaster she pulled a slice of lightly toasted rye bread and spooned a dollop of tuna on top of it.

From the refrigerator she pulled a jar of pepperoncini peppers and laid them next to her sandwich, poured herself a cup of coffee and proceeded to the table where William had spent his morning in a haze. She carried a steno pad with pages of notes written on it, opened it up and perused her notes.

William headed upstairs to dress and Barbara went on a self-guided tour, stepping over a large wooden threshold into the main room of the house.

She couldn't help but notice the dark, wide-plank walnut floors that seemed to stretch the length of this very long room. Windows set deeply into the stone walls paralleled each other the length of the room, six total, and at the far end stood the large fireplace where the painting of the singing woman hung. The figure in the painting truly graced the room with her open-mouthed expression. You just knew she must have had a beautiful voice. Barbara drew closer and noticed similarities to the painting at the Stone Hill. The same strange square piano stood to the left of the lady in the painting and you could see the name of the music on the music stand. It was *Una Donna* from Mozart's *Cosi fan Tutte*. The singing lady was dressed in a pale yellow dress with lace around her shoulders. She had a chain of delicate flowers around the crown of her head and a beautiful color to her cheeks. Around her neck she wore a string of pearls and at her side on a pedestal was a vase that held several blooming branches of what looked to be apple blossoms.

Barbara reached up to touch the painting when she heard a nearby door shut. She looked around but saw no closed door. However she did see a hallway she hadn't noticed the evening before. It wasn't a long hallway and there was a door at the end of it with letters that read "Lilly's Theater".

She approached the door and pushed it open. Inside she found the small theater William had mentioned.

It was like stepping back in time. The room was not as large as the great room of the house, but easily 30 feet by 20 feet. The stage was small and canted at about a 15-degree angle. The back wall had a mural that looked like a tapestry of a woodland scene painted on it and there were three sets of panels on either sides of the stage that hid entrances at different levels onto the stage. Each panel was painted with a matching mural. A hidden window set behind the farthest back panel shed enough light to set the entire scene aglow. With the angles and the painted panels the stage was positively three-dimensional.

At the very front of the stage were two waist-high rails that shone with a high polish. There were gas sconces along the perimeter of the room and the stage looked to have little firepots for lighting. The room couldn't have held more than 45 people and the chairs were of black wood. At the back of the theater was another large fireplace with a mirror hanging from a long metal cable nailed to a thin band of molding at the ceiling and easily 10 feet high. It was a beautiful room and certainly the jewel of the house. As Barbara walked from the front of the theater to the back she marveled at the echo her footsteps made. Acoustically, this room was designed for projection. Barbara cleared her throat and sang a few notes, impressed at the resonance the small room added to her thin voice. She stepped onto the stage and walked to the very back which was only about 12 feet.

There was the window and a couple of stools hidden behind the left panel. She looked through the window and saw the road she had walked down earlier.

She smiled to herself as she remembered her encounter with Garrett.

"Barbara, you in here?" William had dressed and was standing with his head inside the door. Barbara jumped startled. "Yes, I'm here."

"I see you found the theater."

"Yes, it's so beautiful and unusual. I had forgotten about your telling me about it."

"Gertrude wanted to buy this place as soon as she saw it. She said she was going to bring culture to this one-horse town and from what she tells me, she's following through with her plan. The guests she has coming are from the Washington Opera, they are auditioning for next year's season. I guess Gertrude has been very supportive of their program and enticed them to make the trip, that and the fact that she has given them an extraordinary deal on their rooms and having the theater has helped, and her donation of $10,000.00 didn't hurt either."

"Oh my gosh, $10,000.00? Is she rich?"

"No, I wouldn't say she is rich, just really interested in promoting the arts. That, and she is trying to get them to start a summer music program here. You know kind of like a mini-Wolftrap festival, only on a smaller scale. It would bring people into the town and here to the B & B. She's a smart cookie, that Gertrude."

"That's extraordinary! Is there a lot of local talent here?"

"This state is full of musicians, poets, artists and philosophers. Plus, there are two universities within an hour of here that have pretty impressive music programs."

"Huh, I never would have guessed."

"Yea, I guess the banjo isn't the only instrument played here in the Blue Ridge Mountains." Gertrude has briefed me and is in the kitchen starting dinner. She is a marvelous cook and has promised us a feast."

"Is she strong enough to cook?"

"She doesn't feel sick, actually, and knowing her the way I do, you wouldn't notice it if she was. She doesn't know how to go easy."

Gertrude's Tuna Sandwich

Servings: 2

Lower in calories due to the use of sour cream. You can add boiled eggs, red peppers, onions, even relish to this salad. However, if you add the onions, you would want to consume all the same day as onions tend to take over flavors.

1 can tuna in water, small can, drained
1/4 cup chopped parsley, washed and dried
1/4 cup chopped celery, chopped fine
1/2 teaspoon green pickled peppercorns, crushed with side of knife
2 tablespoons sour cream, light is o.k.
1 teaspoon mayonnaise
1 dash salt and pepper, to taste
4 slices rye bread, toasted

•   In a medium sized bowl, mix all ingredients, except rye bread, till well blended. Spoon onto warm, toasted rye bread and serve with your favorite condiments.

THERE'S NO WINE LIKE GLÜHWEIN

Both Barbara and William headed through the house toward the kitchen. Gertrude was there working at the large wooden island. She had three small bowls to her left; one filled with thin wedges of dill pickles, one with onion wedges and one with short strips of raw bacon. To the right of her large cutting board were several pieces of butchers' twine cut into twelve 10-inch pieces and on her cutting board lay a large thinly sliced cut of beef. It was about 12" long and 6" wide and ¼ inch thick. Gertrude looked up at them. "Zo, you found da teater?"

"Yes, she found the theater. She was in there singing and pretending to be a big star."

"I was not!"

"Do you zing Barbara?"

"I wouldn't call it singing."

"Neither would I."

Barbara elbowed William in the ribs. "It really is amazing that a house this old and in this location would have a theater."

Gertrude ground black pepper onto the long strip of meat, then a sprinkle of salt. She cut the meat into three even sized pieces, then placed on each of those one onion, one piece of bacon and one pickle. She rolled the meat into a tight roll, grabbed a piece of twine and tied the meat into a neat little package and laid it aside on a plate. She worked through the next pieces and then seasoned an equal size piece of beef until she had nine bundles.

"What are you making?"

"Rouladen, beef roulades, the vay my mutter used to make dem."

Behind her on the gas range was a large, deep, stainless fry pan with melted butter bubbling slowly. She turned up the flame under the pan and added the beef rolls, leaving a couple of inches between each one so they would brown and not stew. She turned each roll after more than 5 minutes and sautéed them til they were evenly browned all the way around. Then she poured water into the pan and over the rolls until they were submerged by a good inch and one half of water. Turning down the heat, she covered the pan with a clear glass lid and pulled out a large bag of russet potatoes. "Here you go Villiam, make yourself useful."

William looked in distain, and chirped, "How about giving Barbara a knife, she peels very quickly."

"No Villiam, I have a job for Barbara."

Gertrude pulled out a large bag of green beans from the refrigerator and washed them in a colander. "Here Barbara, just take off da stems, not da tails, dhat's vhere the vitamins are. Also, cut them into two inch pieces."

The kitchen island was large enough for them all to work

together. Barbara pulled up a stool and sat down as she trimmed the beans.

"Who is Lilly?"

"Vhat?" Gertrude was coming from the pantry.

"Who is Lilly, the name painted on the theater door?"

"I'm not exactly sure. I've tried to do zome research, but dhere vas a fire at da courthouse und a lot of da old records vere lost."

"Have you tried asking any of the locals?"

"Actually, I have, but none of dhem seem to know who Lilly vas. I tink it sounds like da name of a Saloon…, you know, Lilly's Place."

"I do know dat dhis place vas an old tannery und a plantation. There vere slaves here und dhis home vas used during the civil var as headquarters for both da North und da South. It changed from da North und back to the South more dan fifty times during dat var."

Barbara marveled at what Gertrude had said. She had never been in a home so old. So many lives had passed through these rooms and the rooms probably didn't look much different than they did back then.

William came from the kitchen and found Barbara sitting in one of the two large wing-back chairs in front of the fireplace. She had pushed it back away from the hearth as William, true to form, had built an extremely hot fire.

"Hi Barbara, I brought you some Glühwein."

"What is Glühwein?"

He handed her a tall stoneware mug filled with a dark wine-colored drink. "It's a wonderful mulled wine that is made using Port wine, brandy and rum, plus spices like cinnamon, and star anise. It's served warm. Try it."

It sounded delicious to Barbara, she took the mug and tasted the warm spiced wine. It warmed her throat as she swallowed.

William pushed the other chair next to Barbara and sat down with his Glühwein. "Ahhhh… this is nice. No schedule, no phone calls."

Barbara laughed, "Yea, you're so busy."

"William," Barbara asked, "What kind of surgery is Gertrude having?

"She is having heart surgery, Barbara. She has a blockage and they need to put in a stent. They will also be running a number of other tests to be sure there is nothing more."

"I didn't realize the recovery time was so long for that."

"It's typically not, but with Gertrude's nature of being a 'workaholic', the doctor wanted her to make plans to try and heal for a solid month. She won't be back for two weeks after her surgery because her doctor is putting her in a rehabilitation center. Then once she is back, she will need to be kept fairly quiet."

Gertrude called them to a feast of German food. The roulades were so tender, the gravy perfect and the green beans cooked to perfection, seasoned with delicate marjoram, salt and butter. "Villiam I have made of list of da tings I need you to attend to vhile I'm away." Gertrude laid down a rather thick notebook in front of William. "Also, da guests vill be driving in next Tursday evening and vill be here till da following veekend, so nine days."

William opened the thick notebook and paged through the list, or rather lists. They were organized by day and even by time. Gertrude had included suggested menus as well as a list of the markets she wanted him to buy from. "Don't worry Gertrude, I'll follow your lists to the 'T' and Barbara will help me when she isn't off working with Chef George."

Barbara's stomach knotted when she heard William say that. She wasn't looking forward to her experience with Chef George, but didn't want to miss this opportunity, even if he was a jerk. Besides, she knew how to deal with jerks, just not good-looking, single, French jerks.

"Barbara, I vant you to drive me to da hospital tomorrow morning. I need to be dhere by 8am and I know Villiam will still be sleeping."

Barbara accepted the request and was looking forward to seeing this beautiful state. The countryside was picturesque. There was no trash alongside the roads, just beautiful trees decorated with autumn colors and little streams and rivers that weaved under the highways and into the valleys. A drive would be great!

Later that evening after Gertrude had gone to bed, Barbara and William once again sat in the soft wingback chairs in front of the stone fireplace. They were drinking the warm Gluhwein when William spoke. "I had that dream again."

Barbara was always interested in hearing about his dreams especially since they occurred so often. "Tell me about it."

"It started out like most of them in the darkened theater, with her singing but this time it didn't end with the song. I was in her bedroom."

"Really, and....?"

"No, its not like that, she was rocking her baby and crying and a man came in and caused her to cry even more."

"Why was she crying?"

"I don't know, but the aria she sang was *Visi D'arte* from *Tosca*. You know it?"

Barbara thought for a moment, half hummed the beginning, then spoke, "I lived for my art, why have you done this to me?"

William nodded his head, "Yes, that's the one."

"That's really interesting. Were you able to see her face this time?"

"No, only her shape. I swear I'd know her if I saw her even without seeing her face."

Barbara looked into the fire, "I wonder what it all means."

"I don't know, but if I don't get some sleep tonight, I won't be getting up till noon. I'm heading up."

William brought his glass to the kitchen then headed up to bed. Barbara stayed and sipped her wine. The house was quiet except the popping fire. After several minutes of being alone, Barbara smelled something. She put her glass on the table and sniffed the air. It smelled like linseed oil, or like oil paint. She got up and the smell got stronger. She walked around behind the chairs and the scent seemed to lessen. She approached the fireplace and looked up. The smell of paint was coming from the painting. Barbara squinted to see the painting, but the room was so dimly lit, she couldn't make out the woman's face.

"The heat from the fireplace must be heating up the painting. I better tell William to take it easy on the bonfires. I'd hate to see this painting destroyed."

The smell of the oil painting seemed to fade. Barbara sat her glass down and headed up. Tomorrow had the promise of adventure and she wanted to be well rested.

Beef Roulades

Serving Size: 4 Prep time 1 hour, cook time 1 hour

3 pounds beef flank – cut thin
2 dill pickles – quartered lengthwise 2 medium onion
– quartered
4 slices bacon 3 foot string (butcher's twine or cotton
thread)
2 tablespoons butter 2 tablespoons flour
1/2 cup milk
1/4 cup pickle juice

(You may end up with more than 4 rolls. Meat for roll
should be cut into approximately 4x5" rectangles and will
probably make more than 6 rolls.)

- Tenderize meat fillets with a mallet.

- Sprinkle with salt and pepper.

- Place 1/4 piece of bacon, the onion and a quarter pickle
  on beef fillet and roll up. Tie with string to secure.

- Melt butter in a deep stainless or non-stick skillet on medium high heat. Add beef rolls and brown for 20 minutes,
  turning to insure even browning.

- Once nice and brown, fill pan half full with filtered water.

- Add salt and pepper and the 1/4 cup pickle juice. Cook
  for 1 hour.

- Remove meat rolls from broth and let cool. Keep broth at
  a low simmer with a lid on.

- While meat is cooling, whisk flour with milk in a medium sized bowl until mixture is smooth. Set aside.

- Remove strings from the meat but DO NOT place back into the broth just yet.

- Bring the broth up from a low simmer to a rolling boil. Whisk the milk and flour mixture and add to the boiling broth.

- Take a flat-bottomed spatula and stir the broth and milk mixture, scraping the bottom to insure the flour doesn't stick to the bottom of the pan.

- Continue cooking and stirring until it resumes to a boil.

- Turn down the heat and allow to cook for 5 minutes stirring to insure a smooth gravy.

NOTE: If you were not successful in keeping lumps out of your gravy, pour the gravy through a sieve into another bowl. Take the strained gravy and place it back in the pan.

- Place the meat rolls back into the pan with the hot gravy and allow to cook for five minutes more.

Serving Ideas: Serve with seasoned green beans, mashed potatoes and if you have German guests, offer some delicious dill pickles with your meal. Traditional German side dishes also include spaetzle and red cabbage.

NOTE: You can ask the butcher to run the meat thru a tenderizer one time to save you from having to pound the meat.

Mulled Wine - Glühwein

Servings: 10

Full-bodied warm beverage for cold winter evenings. The wine can be a cheaper version as you are enhancing it with so many other ingredients. Cabernet, Port or a regular table red will do fine.

2 liters red wine, large bottle
4 cups port
3 sticks cinnamon
4 whole cloves
4 whole allspice
1 orange peel, from one orange
2 star anise
1/2 cup sugar, more if needed
1/2 cup dark rum

- Pour all ingredients into a non-reactive pot, such as stainless steel and place over a medium high heat until quite warm. Do not bring to a boil.

Beverage can be kept hot in a crock pot or in a coffee thermos, however, the coffee from this thermos will never be the same again.

5

WHO'S HUMMING ALONG?

The next morning Barbara rose early and drove Gertrude to the Winchester Medical Center where she was to have her surgery. It was a fifty-minute drive on winding, tree-lined roads through valleys and over mountains.

The fog had lifted and the sun lit the brightly colored trees that lined the mountainsides. The yellow foliage of the walnut and locust trees was set off by the crimson-colored dogwood trees and the deep reds from the old oaks. The lower-lying shrubs near the road were bright red sumac bushes and deep purple blackberry brambles. Indeed, Maine and Vermont had nothing on West Virginia when it came to fall colors. The hills were ablaze with color.

Gertrude was silent until Barbara opened up her door to help her out. "Barbara, tank you for coming to help Villiam. I don't know vhat comes over him when he visits me, he seems so preoccupied."

Barbara sensed it too, but thought it must be his way of coping with travel. "Don't worry about a thing, Gertrude. William and I will take very good care of your place and your guests."

Barbara walked Gertrude inside carrying her suitcase and checked her in.

"We will call you tonight to see how you are doing, o.k.?"

"Oh my Gott no, I don't need you to check on me, I'll be fine, dhey do dis procedure all da time. Don't vorry about me, please. Gott no, don't call either. I'll call you vhen I'm up to it."

A nurse escorted Gertrude to a wheelchair where Barbara watched Gertrude refuse to ride in it.

Barbara laughed to herself and thought, "Those nurses aren't gonna know what hit them."

William rose earlier than both Barbara and Gertrude would have guessed. He was motivated and excited at playing inn-keeper. He heated up a cup of the first brew of the day and sat down to study Gertrude's list. As he expected, every menu was preplanned with details of where canned and preserved foods were kept. Gertrude stored enough food in her cellar to feed her for two years, a vestige of having lived through World War II in Germany.

William headed downstairs to the cellar to examine her stock. The cellar was damp, but not wet; three very bright lights turned on at the switch at the top of the stairs. As he walked down the thick wood steps, William could see the beams that supported the entire house. He was amazed to find that they used entire trees as beams. The side that supported the wooden floors was flat, but the entire beam itself was the trunk of the tree, bark and all. Further down the steps, the musty fragrance of wet concrete and stone filled the room.

William had been down here before, but hadn't remem-bered how large the river stone was for the cellar walls - huge rocks locked together with ancient mortar. There were patches where recent repairs had been done, but not many. Luckily for Gertrude, the cellar was in amazingly good shape.

William stepped off the stairs and found the store of canned goods. Fruits, vegetables, olives, canned tomatoes, pastes, sauce, salad dressings, all in date and product order. On the back wall was an impressive shelf that housed many of Gertrude's home-canned goods. She made her own sauerkraut, jellies, pie fillings, brandied peaches, chutneys, olive tapenades, sweet pickles, dill pickles, and mustards. He marveled at the variety and was familiar with the quality of her products. She never spoke of her preserves because it was not legal for her to serve them without permits. But she would serve them to her loyal clients and there were many. They would come back for anniversaries, school reunions, or for the big Sunflower Festival in August. She would only accept reservations from her oldest customers as every hotel in town would fill up.

William scanned the shelves of homemade goodies looking for his most favorite. He knew she had made some, she had been bragging about it over the phone. Where was it?

He crouched down to the bottom shelf and pulled some of the jars out. Just as he suspected it was at the very back of the bottom shelf. Her precious Cherry Kirsch. A pint-sized wine bottle with a cork and a label that read. "Cherry Kirsch, for my dear friend William who loves it more than…."

William grinned and placed the bottle in his jacket pocket. As he returned the other jars to the shelf, he heard something fall behind. He got up and looked on top of the cabinet which came to his chin in height. Seeing nothing there, he crouched back down. Through the back of the shelf he could see what looked like papers curled and pressed into a small lump behind the cabinet.

"What the heck?" he said out loud. It was unlike Gertrude to leave a pile of anything laying around, even behind this old shelf in her cellar. He pulled the jars out again and reached blindly with his hand for the pile of papers. Thoughts of bugs and rats entered his mind and he pulled his empty hand out. Whatever it was, it wasn't worth a bite.

He put the canning jars back again and walked toward the

other shelf. He placed several cans in a small square box left there for just this purpose. Let's see, I need some tomato paste, some sauce and diced tomatoes. He checked off the paste and diced tomatoes, but couldn't find the sauce.

"Wait a minute, of course," William headed over to her canned-goods shelf and on the third shelf stood about 20 quarts of tomato sauce. "Bingo!" As he pulled two quarts off the shelf he heard the same sound of papers falling down the back of the shelf, only this time it sounded like something other than paper hit the floor. He tried to see past the canning jars, but couldn't make out what was there. He looked around for a flashlight and true to form, Gertrude had not only one, but two sitting at the edge of the large wooden stairs. William took the larger of the two lights and for the third time pulled out the many jars that were on the bottom shelf. He shone his light to see what had fallen behind. Reaching back, he was able to grab onto paper envelopes of a sort. He pulled one out and recognized it to be a record jacket, an extremely old record jacket. Reaching back again he brought out more jackets, all empty. He ducked his head under the shelf and shone his light lower. There on the floor were several old Victrola records lying in a pile. He crawled back through the shelf to get a better grasp and brought out every one he could find.

To his delight, they were opera and classical recordings by some of the greats: Caruso, Destinn, Melba, Rachmaninoff, Schumann-Heink and Giuseppe Ruscello. William felt as though he had unearthed a great treasure. He examined the recordings closely. Not too bad. Dirty, but they didn't seem to be scratched too badly. One was totally mildewed and would take a lot of t.l.c. but that didn't dissuade William. He stuffed them into the box with the other jars and went back up stairs. He washed the disks in a sink of warm water and dish detergent. Using a soft cotton rag, he washed the years of dirt off each disk and laid them to dry on a large linen towel.

Later, just as he was washing the vegetables for his sauce, the phone rang.

"Hello!"

"Oh my Gott, Villiam, you don't answer 'hello', you answer Vhippoorwill Ridge."

"Gertrude! How are you doing?"

"Not too good William, dhese nurses are driving me crazy. My procedure has been delayed for two hours. Da doctor has been called to an emergency. I'm just sitting here doing noting."

"I'm sorry to hear that Gertrude, but guess what I found in the cellar?"

"Found in da cellar, probably dust, I haven't been down there to clean in a couple of months."

"I found some old Victrola records!"

"Vhat!"

"Old Victrola records, behind your canning shelves."

"Dhat's unbelievable! I cleaned everything out of the cellar vhen I moved in, dhere vas noting left vhen I was finished."

"Well, lucky for me there was. Now I need to find a Victrola to play them on."

"Dere is a Victrola in da theater."

"What! Where? I don't remember seeing it."

"It's in the back of da theater. It's got a green cloth draped over it. It actually came with the place, but I never had any records to play on it and I don't know if it still vorks. Vow, dose records you found probably played on dhat Victrola. Dhat really is a vonderful find. I'm glad I called, now I have something nice to tink about to help me forget how bad the food is. Gott help me! Bye Villiam, I'll call tomorrow und you better answer da phone correctly."

William laid the phone down and headed toward the theater. Just as Gertrude had said at the back of the theater, covered in a green canvas-like material was a very large, very old

Victrola. "Wow! Look at you," William pulled the canvas off. The Victrola was housed in walnut wood with rosewood inlay. With the exception of a little mildew at the back, it looked pretty well preserved. It measured four feet high and two feet by two feet in width. William tried to lift it. "Offff, you are heavy!" He tried again and accidentally banged his foot on the base of the Victrola. "Ouch, what did I hit?"

Looking down, William saw a large caster wheel for rolling. "Wow, the first portable disk player." He chuckled to himself as he rolled the player down the hall across the great room and into the kitchen.

Opening the lid, he found the prop for the sound horn and snapped it into place. On the side was a crank which he turned a couple of times. "Well, I'll be damned, it still spins." Picking up the Victrola arm, he examined the large needle. It looked sharp enough and kind of resembled a thick, sharp, pencil lead. "Well, let's see if she'll play." He pulled one of the records from the stack. "Ah yes, this seems appropriate. He placed the large disk onto the turntable and gave the side handle a couple more turns, raised the heavy arm and placed it onto the record.

From the old tarnished horn came the voice of long-dead tenor, Giuseppe Ruscello singing *Che gelida manina* by Puccini from *La Boheme*! It poured into the kitchen and bounced off each stone surface, this tenor of so long ago. The signature scratchy noise and tinny fidelity gave a patina of the past to the room.

William was thrilled with his good fortune. He started chopping the vegetables for his favorite red sauce. Two green bell peppers, one onion and three cloves of garlic. Just as he finished, the record came to a scratchy end. William dried his hands and pulled from his pile of drying records. "How about a little Schumann?" He exchanged the first disk and placed the second onto the turntable, cranked the side handle and placed the large heavy needle onto the disk. To his surprise, a woman's voice lilted from the disk. "How wonderful! I wonder who she is?"

He went back to working on his sauce. William loved German Lieder music and was very familiar with Schumann. From the horn he heard the romantic *Du Ring an Meinen Finger.*

William started sautéing the vegetables in a large stainless sauce pan using olive oil. The voice from the recording cut though the loud sizzling noise of the vegetables and seemed to fill every corner of the room. William added the herbs to the vegetables and then the homemade tomato sauce, the paste and the diced tomatoes. He covered the sauce and turned the heat under the large sauce pot to medium.

Feeling the need for a pickup, William poured the last cup

of the morning's brew into his mug, heated it in the microwave, doctored it with cream and sugar and sat on the stool next to the island.

He propped both elbows onto the counter and held his cup to his mouth, closed his eyes and listened as the lied, *Widmung*, started to play.

For William, this was the greatest love song ever written.

Gertrude had translated it for William years ago after they had attended a concert filled with Schumann. This was Gertrude's translation:

Widmung by Robert Schumann
You are my soul, you are my heart.
You are my ecstasy, you are my pain.
You are my world in which I live.
You are my heaven in which I fly.
You are my grave in which I bury my soul.
You are the tranquility-you are the peace.
You have been given to me from heaven.
That you love me adds to my worth.
Your look has made me more beautiful.
You have lovingly lifted me above myself,
My good soul my better self.

William started to hear a humming as though someone were humming along with the music. It sounded like a woman's voice and lilted along with each phrase. William opened his eyes and the humming stopped. He looked around the room, but no one was there.

"I'm starting to hear things." He got up, pulled the lid from the simmering sauce and stirred it with a flat-bottomed spatula.

Just as he placed the lid back on the pot, the humming started again. William closed his eyes and listened as the humming became clearer and closer. He opened his eyes once more and once again, the humming stopped. "Boy, that's really weird."

"What's weird?"

William jumped about three inches off the ground, spun around and came face to face with Barbara who had just returned and was standing in the doorway of the kitchen

"Don't... do... that....! You nearly gave me a heart attack."

Barbara laughed, "Would it be better if I wore a bell? That way you could hear me coming. But, I'm not so sure you could hear anything over this music."

William walked over to the Victrola, picked up the arm and placed it to the side. He shut the lid and placed both his hands on the sides of the box as if to steady himself.

"Hey, you alright? I really am sorry I startled you."

William turned and smiled, "I'm fine, just a little weirded out."

"I'm sorry, I really had no idea I'd give you such a start."

"No, it's not being startled that really spooked me, it was the humming."

"What humming?"

"From the Victrola, I heard a humming as if someone, a woman, was singing along with the recording, but when I would open my eyes, the humming would stop."

Barbara smiled. "Humming, huh? Are you sure it isn't your brain buzzing from drinking really strong, really old coffee?

How can you drink that stuff?"

William started to laugh. "Yea, you're probably right. I've been cooped up in here all day. What's it like outside?"

"It's starting to rain, but beautiful no matter where you look."

"Yea, I guess that's why they call it 'Almost Heaven'."

"I really need to get out. Tell you what, I'll give you a tour of some of the buildings on the property. Did you know this used to be an old tannery? There are old vats where they used to store the solution to soften the skins. They still have stuff in them."

"Now that's just gross. Old vats containing old liquids that have softened old animal skins, yuck!"

"Don't be ridiculous, they haven't been used in 180 years, and we're not going to swim in them."

They headed outside to the west side of the house where a lichen-covered stone building was nestled into the hill in front of the house. From the front, it looked to be two stories tall, but from the back it seemed to only be one.

To the left of the building was a greenhouse of a more modern era and next to the greenhouse, a concrete patio. Below the patio was a dark and deep vat, visible only through a crack that was about six inches wide at the top. "Boy, that is kind of ominous isn't it? You can bet I won't be wandering here often."

William showed Barbara all around the property. There were three outbuildings and a modern garage. They walked just past the entrance to the property and into an overgrown portion where the base of the mountain met the flat land.

"Check this out, Barbara."

Barbara walked toward where William had stopped and looked at an old decrepit building. The roof had fallen in but the stone walls were still standing with a fireplace at the north side.

"Wow, I didn't even see this place."

"Yea, neither did Gertrude 'til I walked the property with her. I'd love to rummage around in that place. The realtor said no one's probably been in the place for more than 50 years. Said it's looked like this since she was a little girl, and she wasn't young."

"Rummage around, you must be crazy. How would you even get in?"

"Oh, I have my ways." William walked around the back of the building and called Barbara to join him. "Look there." He pointed to a door at the bottom of six large stone steps. "Oh my gosh, it's got a cellar."

"Yep, and I would bet lots of really neat stuff down there too."

"Yea and really neat creepy crawlers, too."

"Relax Barbara, there have already been a couple of frosts. Most of the crawlers are in hibernation by now." William walked down the steps which were heavily covered in leaves and sticks. The bottom step had standing water on it, indicating there was water in the cellar too.

"William, please don't go in there now, maybe we should call what's his name to help out!"

"What's his name! You mean Garrett? We don't need him here." He stepped onto a ledge, avoiding the water at the bottom step and pushed with both hands against the door. To his surprise, it gave and opened about ten inches.

Barbara didn't like this, she was not one for these kinds of adventures, especially in foreign places. "Please William, I would really feel better if we had one more person here. What if you cut yourself? I don't even know where the nearest hospital is and if it's in Winchester, then you better have a big bandage cause it's a 50-minute drive from here. And when did you last have a tetanus shot?"

William looked up at her. She was working herself into a frenzy. "O.k, o.k., we'll call Garrett and see if he will help us explore this old shed."

Relieved, Barbara smiled, "Thanks." She put out her hand to help him up the crumbling steps. "That will make me feel much better."

"I'm sure you'll be right brave when Garrett comes along."

At that, Barbara let go of William's hand causing him to slip slightly. "Ha, ha, very funny," she said as she started back to the house. William climbed out, caught up with her and put his arm around her laughing out loud and teased her all the way up to the front walk of the house.

William's Red Sauce with Cabernet and Bay

1/8 cup olive oil – extra virgin
3 cloves garlic – peeled and chopped fine
1 large onion – peeled and chopped
1 large green pepper – cut into 1/2 inch pieces
2 pounds tomato sauce – canned
6 ounces tomato paste
1 teaspoon sugar
1 teaspoon Greek oregano
1 teaspoon basil
1 bay leaf
1/2 teaspoon salt
1/4 cup black pepper – freshly ground
1/4 cup cabernet sauvignon wine

- Sauté the veggies in the olive oil for 8 to 10 minutes.

- Add the sauce and paste. Cover and cook over medium heat for 20 minutes.

- Add the herbs and cook for 20 more minutes. Add the wine, salt, and pepper.

- Process in a food mill or in a blender for a smooth sauce....no veggies visible.

Serve over pasta of your choice and top with freshly-grated parmesan cheese.

GARRETT COMES A-CALLING

The house was cold when they walked in. William set to building a fire while Barbara cleaned up William's cooking dishes. It was a nice arrangement they had made several months back. When she cooked, William would do the dishes, when he cooked she would.

As she dried the morning's cups, she opened random cupboards to find their home. There it was in the last cabinet she opened just above the coffee machine. "Of course," she thought to herself, "Gertrude is so efficient." Pulling the cabinet open wide she noticed a list of phone numbers taped to the door. It had the number for the local rescue squad, the local hospital, the pharmacy, and Garrett's phone number right at the bottom. She smiled as she closed the cabinet door.

"Well, at least I know there is a hospital close by and how to get hold of Garrett, should I need to." It was then she smiled again as a thought came into her mind.

She picked up the phone, which was right under the cabinet, next to the coffee pot, and called Garrett. He did not answer, but his machine did. She left a brief message and hung up.

The smell of newspaper and wood smoke hung from the ceiling of the great room as the newly lit fire crackled and popped. William was on one knee fiddling with the fire poker and a stubborn log that was trying to roll out.

"The sauce smells wonderful, William, what time is

dinner?"

"I used some of the home-canned tomato sauce that Gertrude makes. Wait until you try it, you'll never want my old sauce again."

"Sounds wonderful. You want me to make a salad?"

"Sounds good, if you're willing. I may run to town and get some wine. There is a shop in town that sells a lot of local wines called Anderson's Corner. It's a neat little shop that started out as a dealer for the original satellite dishes and rare coins. Then antique estate jewelry, fine jewelry then it branched out and became a gift shop with gourmet foods. No more t.v. dishes, just fine jewelry, handmade gifts, gourmet foods and an amazing selection of wines produced in the region. Wait till you taste their 'Ridge Runner Red'. "

Barbara was intrigued. Family-owned stores were becoming such a rare thing. Where she lived, all the stores except Marbella's carried essentially the same stuff, and most of it was made in China. This little shop sounded like a great place to escape to and find the perfect little something.

"Well, what time do you think we will eat?"

"It doesn't matter to me, when I return we can have a glass of wine, then eat."

William swept up the ash and bits of sawdust that had fallen from the fireplace and deposited them into the ash bucket which he carried outside. Returning, he grabbed the keys to the Gertrude's old Jag and his coat and headed to town.

Barbara walked into the kitchen and eyed the Victrola. "Humming, eh?" She looked through the pile of records and chose a Caruso recording. She marveled at what good condition the records were in. She looked on the counter and saw a pile of paper-record sleeves all laid flat with a heavy book on top. She smiled at William's handiwork.

Walking over to the Victrola, she lifted the lid and placed the disk on the turntable. She then found the crank, gave it several turns and flipped a switch. The record started spinning. She was impressed by the ingenuity of the machine as she lifted the arm onto the record.

Just as she was about to lightly place the needle onto the spinning disk, she heard a loud knock at the door. Startled, she dropped the Victrola needle onto the disk causing it to bounce and skitter across the top of the record. She quickly picked up the arm and placed it back into its cradle and closed the lid.

"Who would be knocking so loudly?"

She walked through the great room up to the front door and looked through the side windows of the old Victorian door frame. She quickly opened the door just as Garrett was about to start knocking again, causing him to step forward when she opened it and almost run into her."Whoa! Sorry about that!" Garrett caught himself on the door frame and started to laugh.

"That's quite a knock you have, Garrett. I thought I'd better open the door before you break it down."

Garrett grinned, "Sorry about that, it's just that when Gertrude is here, she never hears me knocking and I end up having to call her, right before I come, but today, I don't have my cell phone so I wanted to be sure to be heard."

"Ahhhh, well that's o.k. then, come on in."

"How is your head?"

"My head? Oh, my head, it's fine, no damage done, well, none from that little knot anyway."

Garrett stepped just inside the door and removed his jacket and folded it over his arm. "I see you have a good hot fire burning."

"I didn't build it, William did. He doesn't know the meaning of a 'small fire,' which actually is a good thing in a place like this, being as large as it is."

Barbara walked over to the fireplace, pulled the poker from the stand and pushed some of the larger logs further back onto the grate, then pulled another smaller log from the wood box and gently tossed it into the hot fire on top of the logs she had just moved.

"Did you get my message?"

"Yes, that's why I'm here. I'm afraid I have plans this evening and won't be able to join you, but I was wondering if you and William would like to join me tomorrow. I have a friend coming into town tomorrow. She is singing at the Coriander Café tomorrow evening. It's one of my favorite restaurants. They serve amazing meats there, anyway you like them; slow roasted, grilled, smoked, stewed, pulled, pickled, jerked, you name it. The father of the gal who owns it raises cattle just this side of the Potomac on a 1000-acre farm."

Barbara motioned for Garrett to follow her into the kitchen and up to a stool at the island. He sat down while she pulled vegetables from the refrigerator, washed them and placed them on a board. Garrett continued, "Anyway, they have a nice bar there too, no smoking, which is great. Matter of fact, they serve beer made with Whippoorwill Ridge water. It's on tap there. You should come just to sample the beer."

Barbara was pleased he'd come, and tried not to seem too interested in what he was saying. One thing her experience told her was, never stare at a good-looking man. "Well, that does sound like a lot of fun."

Barbara could feel Garrett's gaze on her while she sliced up a bright orange sweet pepper. He seemed to be studying every move she made. When Barbara looked up, her eyes met his and locked for a brief moment. She quickly looked away and went back to chopping, only this time a little more vigorously.

"I… I'm sure William would love to join you and me too."

At this point the peppers were being turned into mush. "What time does it start?"

Sensing her discomfort, Garrett got up from the stool and

fiddled with his coat.

"It starts at 7pm, let me know if you're coming and I'll save you a spot." He looked down at her cutting board and smiled. "Well, I should probably get going. I'll have my phone with me later on so if you need anything, just call."

Barbara stopped chopping and looked up. She grabbed a towel and followed him to the great room. "Ah…, Garrett, before you go, I was wondering if you might be available tomorrow in the morning, around 10am. William needs a little help with something, and I'm afraid I can't help him on this one. Could you come by around 10?"

Garrett agreed and let himself out.

Barbara went back to the kitchen and looked down at the mess on the chopping board. "Oh you are smooth Barbara, don't show your intimidation, just chop the peppers to mush. Oh my gosh, I am such an idiot."

Barbara cleaned up her mess, finished making her salad and set it on the small table in the kitchen. It was strange that William had not lit a fire in the kitchen fireplace. However, this was probably a good thing given his hot fire technique.

Within a few minutes William came in carrying a large cardboard box filled with twelve bottles of wine. He grinned, "They're cheaper by the dozen."

Barbara laughed and helped him unload the wines onto the counter. "This is quite a variety. Let's see what you bought. Of course, Elder Berry Zinfindel and a Blackberry Cabernet and there's the Ridge Runner Red. Well, if the wine is as good as the labels are pretty, then we're in for a treat."

William was already opening the Ridge Runner Red as she spoke. He poured just a little in a small wine glass and swirled it around. "Nice legs." He then put his nose into the glass and slowly inhaled the bouquet of the wine. "Lovely, fruity, with hints of cherry, and tobacco."

Critiquing and describing wines was William's latest passion, and any wines would do, he was not a snob. He took a drink and sucked air through his teeth, oxygenating the wine, then slowly swallowed. "Ah, this is delicious, just how I remember it. Are you going to give it a try?"

Barbara retrieved a glass and poured a small amount into it. She had learned a lot about wine from William. She swirled her glass and watched as a thin layer of wine clung to the sides of the glass and slid down.

"Good legs, indeed." She breathed it in, then like William, sucked it through her teeth to fill her whole mouth and sinuses with the flavor and fragrance of the wine. "O.k... I taste the cherry, but where you get tobacco from is beyond me. I'm tasting more of a Burgundian flavor."

William, laughed out loud, "Burgundian! What's burgundian supposed to mean?"

"Why, it's a perfect adjective to describe this wine, can't you taste the dark undertones and the bright overtones?"

"Barbara, this is wine you're critiquing, not a soprano."

William was in a light-hearted mood. He pulled a plate which held a clay bowl filled with a dark olive tapenade from the refrigerator. It was surrounded by slices of French bread coated with a thin layer of cream cheese. He took the bottle, his glass and the platter, placed them on a tray and headed into the great room toward the fireplace.

Returning to the kitchen, he pushed the Victrola into the great room, lifted the lid and saw the disk on the turntable. With a worried expression he called to Barbara. "Did you play this record?"

"Actually, no I didn't, I was about to, but turned it off when Garrett stopped by."

"I see, and how is Garrett doing today?"

Barbara could see William was ready to tease her, but before he could, she asked, "So William, tell me about this humming you heard."

Still standing at the Victrola, William thoughtfully turned the crank and lifted the arm gently onto the disk. Once again, like magic, the room was filled with the music of the past as *A'Vucchella* by Tosti played. Once again, the lighting in the room became colored by the music.

Sitting down in the wing-backed chair, William drank from his glass and looked into the fire.

"Wow, I've never seen you change moods so quickly. What's up with that?"

William looked over at her and smiled. He pulled a piece of bread from the plate and put a schmear of the olive tapenade over the cream cheese. Looking back at the fireplace, then up at the painting, he gazed at the beautiful lady in yellow, then spoke to Barbara.

"I don't know what I heard, but I heard something. At the time, it sounded like someone humming along with the recording, a woman's voice right here in the room with me. The first time I heard it, it startled me, but the second time, it intrigued me. I wanted to hear more but it stopped when I opened my eyes."

Looking over at William, Barbara knew he wasn't making this up. She herself had experienced unusual things before.

"William, last night, after you and Gertrude went to bed, I sat by the fireplace and was overwhelmed by the odor of linseed oil and oil paint. It was so strong that I found myself drawn to the painting to see if it was coming from there, but it wasn't. Even now as hot as the fireplace is, I don't smell it."

William pulled his eyes from the "Singing Woman" and listened thoughtfully to Barbara. "Well, this is a very old house. There are bound to be some spirits here, I mean, being as old as it is."

"Yes, I agree, but it seems to me that when a spirit tries to communicate, it needs something."

"Well, I guess we will have to wait and see how the plot unfolds." William grinned and finished his wine.

"I'm hungry, how about you?"

"Famished!"

"Good, let's eat!"

Greek Olive Tapenade

Makes 30 servings.

15 ½ ounces Black Pitted Olives
7 ½ ounces Greek Olives (calamata) pitted
1/2 small can Anchovies (drained)
2 teaspoons Capers
2 cloves garlic peeled and minced
1 teaspoon Dijon mustard
1 teaspoon fresh thyme or ½ teaspoon dried
The juice of ½ a lemon
8 ounces cream cheese
6 ounces goat cheese (optional)
One long loaf of French Bread

- First and foremost!!! Be sure all of the olives have had their pits removed. Double check by squeezing each olive. One missed pit can spoil this dish.

- Place all ingredients, except the cheese and the bread, into a food processor and blend. Tapenade should not be a puree, nor should it be too chunky. Strive for the in between!

- Allow cheeses to come to room temperature and blend the goat and cream cheese together.

- Slice the French bread, about 10 slices at a time. Spread the cheese mixture onto the bread and then spread the tapenade on top of that.

It looks a little like caviar.

THE TREAJURE TROVE

Both William and Barbara headed to bed very early. The time difference had finally caught up with them, causing them to go to bed almost right after the dishes were done.

Their sleep was deep and without Gertrude to wake them, or any immediate obligations, neither of the two stirred until the phone rang. Barbara sat up in bed when she heard William run from his room down the stairs. There were no phones in the bedrooms, only in the kitchen. She heard him run barefoot across the ancient wood floors and into the kitchen.

"Hello," he said breathlessly, "I mean, Whippoorwill Ridge Manor, can I help you?"

"What? Who? Oh, hi Garrett. What, in fifteen minutes? Gee, I'm not sure. You're asking for a miracle, you do realize that, don't you. No, she is still asleep. Yea, that'd be great, o.k., I'll make coffee. O.k., see you then."

Barbara had been listening from the top of the stairs. She ran into her bedroom and started to dress when William called from the bottom of the stairs.

"Wake up sleeping beauty, your handsome prince is an early riser and will be here in 15 minutes, better get a move on."

Before he could finish his warning, Barbara was running down the steps. Her hair was tied up into a twist and held with a silver clip. Wisps of hair framed her face giving her an almost Victorian look. She wore a cream colored, ribbed mock-turtleneck sweater and a blue-green denim overshirt, jeans and hiking boots. "Wow, that was fast!"

"What time is it?"

"It's nearly 8:30."

Barbara walked into the kitchen followed by William and looked at the clock on the wall to confirm what William had said.

"Why is he coming so early? I told him 10:00."

"Ah ha! So you invited him to come this morning. Are you going to be posing for him?"

Barbara played along with his joke. "As a matter of fact I am, he said he wanted to capture me in the early light of the morning. I just hope his studio isn't too cold."

"I have a feeling you wouldn't be cold."

Barbara spun around giving William a sisterly punch in the arm. Feigning pain, William held his arm, then changed his voice to sound like Garrett. "Hey there sugar, how's about I paint you 'a naturale." William took off running this time with Barbara right behind him. He ran across the great room and took the stairs three at a time. Barbara stopped at the bottom of the stairs and yelled to him. "You better not pull any of that stuff when he is here, do you hear me. I swear, I'll make your life miserable if you do. There will be no more Saturday morning crepes, no special orders from Marbella's. I'll make sure of it. Do you hear me?"

Just as Barbara was crossing back across the great room she heard knocking at the front door. She looked through the side windows and saw Garrett looking right at her. A flush of heat filled her cheeks as she pulled the door open. "I wasn't sure it was you there, the knocking so, well, civilized." Barbara held the door and beckoned him in.

"Well, if there is one thing we are here in the country, it's civilized."

"Would you like a cup of coffee?"

Garrett pulled off his vest and hung it off one of the chairs at the dining table.

"Coffee would be great, a little cream, no sugar. I'm sorry I'm so early but something has come up and I'll need to be gone by noon."

Barbara handed him a large mug and offered a seat at the small wooden table next to the window.

"No please don't worry, I actually was up, William just didn't realize it. And anyway, you are doing us, well me, a favor."

Garrett looked at her and smiled. "Well, what is it I can do for you?" He smiled again and then looked at his coffee, almost in a shy way.

"Well, not for me personally… it's me and William, well more William. Anyway, it would make me feel much better if you were there, and you don't even need to lift or carry anything, just be there in case."

As Barbara was stuttering on, William entered and poured himself a cup of coffee, then pulled a stool from the kitchen island, to the table. Looking at Garrett, he held out his hand for a shake and said, "Hey, Garrett, how've you been?"

"Hey, William, good to see you. Seems just like yesterday since you were here."

"Yea, to me too, only it's been nearly two years. Time flies, and look at all you've done to the place. Gertrude has been telling me. I hear you plan to put new glass into the greenhouse. That would be a really neat thing to have out here. And the floors in the great room are beautiful. Your restoration really brought them to life. I could go on and on, everywhere I look I see something that has either been fixed, polished or removed."

Barbara, relieved for the interruption, sipped her coffee.

Garrett, was smiling and again shyly looking into his coffee. "Well, you know that Gertrude, she keeps me busier than a one-legged man in a butt-kicking factory."

At this they all started laughing.

"I thought I was going to have a chance to do some painting while Gertrude was gone, but if you have something important that you want me to do than I'll get right to it."

William gave Garrett a funny look, "Something important to do?"

"Well, Barbara said you needed help with something."

William looked at Barbara with a mischievous and questioning expression, "What important job do we have for Garrett to do?"

Barbara glared back at William, "You know, that small house outside that you were going to risk breaking a leg or getting injured just to get into."

"Oh, that important job. You see Garrett, Barbara is paranoid that I'll get hurt and she won't be able to lift me to get me to the hospital in time. Morbid, huh?"

Barbara gave William a little kick under the table. "I never said that, but you're right, I probably couldn't lift you into a car if you were badly injured."

Garrett tried to keep a straight face, "Alright, alright, you have my curiosity, what house…. Oh, wait a minute, I know which house. You still want to get in there? Man you never give up do you?" Garrett, got up and refilled his coffee cup. "You know Gertrude is going to flip if she finds out you've been snooping in that old place. She's afraid it will come down on top of you, and I can't say I blame her."

"There! Hear that?" Barbara felt vindicated. "A sensible man. Hear that?" Feeling emboldened, she stood up. "And why do you want to get in there so badly?"

William looked at them both, and rolled his eyes, "What a couple of pansies, ah, no offense, Garrett."

Garrett, laughed, "None taken, but I too am curious. What draws you to that place?"

William, with a far-off look in his face answered, "I don't

know, but I do feel compelled to go there whenever I come here."

Within minutes they finished their coffee, grabbed their jackets and headed outside. It was cooler than the day before, crisp and bright with the early morning sun.

Garrett's dog Arthur joined them as they headed outside and down the driveway to the north side of the property. He loped over to Barbara and rubbed up against her, briefly stopping in front of her so she would stop and pet him. Then the massive hound walked over to William, gave him a dismissive sniff and ambled aheaddown the drive.

The collapsed building stood hidden just at the base of the mountain that shadowed the entire property, and was camouflaged by the fallen leaves and the trees themselves.

"Look at the size of those foundation stones. I'll bet they dug them right from this mountain."

"They probably did, lots of places around here were built from those stones and river stones."

They all ventured around the back of the house. The door at the bottom of the cellar steps was still ajar, but the sitting water from the day before seemed to have receded quite a bit.

As William headed down the leaf-filled cellar stairwell, he said, "Well, that's lucky, there's a lot less water." He had a flashlight with him and started to push the door further in. Garrett had a surprised look on his face. "I've never seen it so dry. I've come by here several times in the past and there was always at least 3 feet of standing water in there. I'm amazed to see it this dry."

Barbara bent down from the top of the steps to get a better look. "What if there are bears in there, William?"

"Well, that would be something considering they haven't seen a bear around here for some time."

"Yes, sadly there haven't been bear sightings in many years around here." Garrett smiled and dug his flashlight from his pocket.

Barbara was definitely not the adventurous type, at least not when it came to dangerous, risk-your-life kinds of adventures. She held her hands to her mouth as she watched William push open the door further until it stopped, nearly fully open. "See, that wasn't so bad was it?" Just as he shone his light into the cellar, there was a sudden sound of fluttering of wings that gave them all a fright. They ducked looking up to see a light gray barn owl fly from the fallen roof of the house to a nearby tree. "I think I almost wet my pants." said William with a big grin.

"Very funny William, keep laughing."

Barbara was in no mood for jokes. She had her arms folded at her chest and stood looking down at where William had been standing.

He had entered the cellar. Garrett went down the steps and shone his flashlight into the room.

"Wow, it doesn't look like anyone's been down here in years. There is so much sediment and water on the floor it's kind of hard to walk without sinking in. Lots of spider webs and salamanders and,.. wow! There's a ton of stuff in here. William's voice was quiet for a moment, but the sound of his boots being sucked out of the mud could be heard from the top of the stairs. "I see about ten crates stacked against a wall, and .... Oh... wow..., that's amazing."

Garrett started to go inside when Barbara gasped, "Please don't go in there, please wait out here with me."

Garrett obeyed, standing with one foot in the door shining his light to help William.

William held the flashlight in his mouth and reached for

the top box. It was wooden and covered with twigs, leaves and droppings. He handed it to Garrett, who lifted it to the ledge at the top of the wall of the steps, where Barbara was standing. William handed out another box, then another to Garrett, who stacked them again at the top of the wall. Barbara examined the boxes, still tense with worry. There was no way to determine how old they were, but they looked ancient, covered with years of dust and mildew.

Garrett watched as William crossed through the muck to the opposite wall. He reached for something that Garrett couldn't make out. William had gotten on top of a box and was reaching up for something. He was standing on his toes, reaching into the rafters of the cellar, when the box below him collapsed. "Whoa!"

William fell backwards into the water. At this, Barbara screamed and Garrett lunged into the cellar and picked William up. "You alright?"

"I'm fine, I'm fine, just a little scratch that's all, just a little scratch from some God-knows-how-old nails. Just a little scratch that is being invaded by ancient bacteria from brackish water that hasn't seen the sun since God knows when."

Garrett helped him up the stairs where Barbara was beside herself. "Are you hurt? Oh my gosh you're bleeding!"

"I'm fine Barbara. It's just a little scratch!"

"Well, darn you, why did you have to go in there, look what has happened! You're lucky to be alive."

At this William and Garrett both looked at Barbara and started to laugh. "Barbara, I'm fine, I just fell, and not far. There was no other danger, other than my own clumsiness."

"I think he'll be just fine Barbara, it doesn't look so bad." Garrett pointed to the tear in William's pants. It was pretty small and Barbara was relieved to not see any blood, well, not a lot of blood, coming from the scratch.

"Wow, look at all those boxes, man I can't wait to see what's in them. Hey Garrett, could you pick up what I dropped, I think it actually landed near the door."

Within a moment, Garrett was coming up the stairs with what looked like an old music stand made from metal. It was totally corroded, but its shape was unmistakable.

"That's remarkable!"

"Isn't it though!"

"It can't be, I mean that would really be something else!"

"I think it is!"

"What, what is so remarkable?"

Barbara stood over the metal music stand, then knelt down for a closer look. "Well, if it isn't then it's a close copy."

Garrett stood over Barbara and examined the stand. "Is it the stand you're talking about? 'Cause, I've seen a stand like this before."

Barbara looked up at Garrett, "Where, Garrett? Where have you seen a stand like this before?"

Garrett looked over at William, then Barbara.

"It's the stand from the paintings. The music stand from Lilly's painting. I'd know it anywhere."

Barbara and William were riveted by what Garrett had just said.

"Lilly, as in Lilly's theater?"

"The very same, but you must have known that. Gertrude must have told you."

William picked up the stand and headed toward the house. "No, she said she didn't know the name of the painting, or who painted it."

"Really, I thought she knew. I always thought she knew".

Garrett carried one of the large boxes up and laid it on the front porch.

"Well, you finally got your wish William, you got to see the inside of that old house."

"I think I got more than I bargained for." William leaned

the stand against the house. Are you going to be around later? I'd love to talk more about the painting."

"Well, I invited you and Barbara to join me this evening at the Coriander Café for dinner. I have a friend who'll be singing there tonight. You'll like it William, she's an upcoming opera singer and a real nice kid."

"That sounds great Garrett, thanks for your help, We'll see you later." William stepped into the house and up the stairs to shower and tend his wound. Barbara asked Garrett if he would like to come in, but he declined, saying that he would bring up the rest of the boxes and leave them around the back of the house in the mudroom.

As he was leaving, she heard him mumble to himself something about it being too cold for his model. Barbara went inside to find a rag to clean off the music stand and smiled, thinking, glad it's not me. I'd never pose in this weather.

FACE TO FACE
FOR THE FIRST TIME

William came downstairs and watched as Barbara finished wiping down the music stand. She placed it under the painting at the fireplace,

"That's quite a find, William."

He moved in front of the painting to compare the stand with the one in the painting. "Indeed, this has proved to be quite a day for clues."

"How about some coffee, William?"

"Sounds good. I'll make a fire."

Barbara headed into the kitchen, washed her hands and started the coffee. She pulled a house-shaped cookie canister from the counter and raised the roof-shaped lid. Inside she found little gingerbread cookies. She placed them on a plate, and the plate onto a tray. She pulled two Empire apples from the crisper drawer, washed, cored them and cut them into wedges placing them on a plate next to the gingerbread cookies.

Next to the coffee maker was a porcelain sugar bowl and creamer which she filled and placed onto the tray. Coffee ready, Barbara picked up the loaded tray and headed into the living room.

William had the fire burning brightly and was sweeping the sawdust off the hearth and throwing it onto the fire. He pulled a small colonial drop-leaf table over and placed it between the two wingback chairs.

"That smells wonderful, Barbara."

William poured cream and a little sugar into his coffee, and sat down. "Ahhh, this is the life."

Barbara smiled and joined him with her coffee in the other chair. "Indeed." She said, as she too sipped her coffee. They both sat quietly drinking their coffee and looked back and forth from the painting to the music stand. The warmth from the fireplace and the day's adventure had made Barbara a little sleepy. She placed her cup onto the table. Just as she closed her eyes and started to drift off, the phone rang.

William looked over at Barbara and seeing she was sleeping,rose quietly and answered the telephone.

"Whippoorwill Ridge Manor. This is William, may I help you?"

"Vow William, dat was beautiful! You zound so elegant und professional."

"Gertrude! How are you doing? Did you have the procedure yet?"

"Not yet, they have been running tests all day. Dey say tomorrow morning dough. I vanted to call to remind you to clean sie theater. Da guests are arriving tomorrow afternoon und dat is die entire reason dey are staying at my place is because of da theater, so I vant you to be sure it's clean. Now I know you may tink it's clean, but, it really needs a good dusting und da floors need to be dust mopped. Zingers don't like dust William. Also, in my betroom is an air purifier. Bring it down, put it in sie theater and turn it on. Da air vill be very clean in dere."

"Absolutely Gertrude, I'm on it. Gertrude, Barbara and I found out something very interesting about that painting above the mantel."

"You did? Vhat is it William?"

"Well, Garrett told us the lady in the painting's name is Lilly."

"Who told you that?"

"Garrett told us."

"Garrett told you the lady in the painting's name is Lilly? He never told me dat, I vonder how he knows her name? Dat's really interesting, so she must have lived in sie house und she must have zung on my stage, I mean her stage."

"Yes, I would imagine she did."

"Well, tings certainly get interestink vhen you are in town. Too bad it took a medical procedure to bring you in."

"Well, I'll get right to cleaning the theater. It will be so clean they won't want to leave."

"Thank you Villiam, I'll talk to you tomorrow evening. Good night."

"Good night, Gertrude."

William walked quietly toward the fireplace and looked over to see Barbara still asleep. He stoked the fire and put another log on, got up and walked back toward the kitchen to the closet where the cleaning supplies were. His leg started to hurt. It wasn't so much the scratch that hurt as the bruising around the back of his leg that throbbed. He started to limp a little. He found the large dust mop and dust rags and headed toward the theater, entered and flipped on the lights. As Gertrude had said, the place was dusty. He pushed a wide dust mop across the stage and looked back to see a clear path cut through a respectable layer of dust. Working like a seasoned professional, William pushed the mop quickly never lifting it. He swiveled it back and forth around the side entrances and back entrances til he came to the front of the stage. He pushed the dust off the stage and onto the floor of the theater itself. He continued with his dust mop through and around every row of chairs until he came to the back of the room.

He looked back to admire his work when the door creaked open and Barbara peeked her head in. "What'cha doing?"

"Oh, Gertrude called and was adamant about my sweeping up and dusting the theater before the guests arrive tomorrow."

Barbara stepped in and looked around.

"I was a little surprised at how dusty it was, kind of an unused room I suppose."

"Well, not this week. It's going into full use."

"Well, it looks great, but it's getting late and you need to get dressed."

"Get dressed for what? Oh, I forgot all about that! Say, would you mind if I didn't go, my leg is really starting to bug me."

"What! Oh come on William, I don't want to show up by myself."

"I'm sorry Barbara, I just don't feel up to it. Why don't you stay here and help me clean the theater?"

She looked at him incredulously, "Oh, sure, I'd love to stay and help you clean the theater....NOT! Fine! I'll go by myself, but I don't want to hear any sarcastic remarks from you tomorrow."

William smiled as he leaned against the dust mop. "No, I'll keep my comments to myself, but if you need anything, you know, a ride or a reason to leave, just call me."

"Not to worry William, matter of fact, you should probably be more concerned for Garrett!" She winked as she headed out of the theater. William heard the front door close and then the sound of the motor roar then fade as Barbara drove away. William continued his cleaning by wiping down each seat with a damp cloth. This was no small task as there were easily 45 oak chairs. Looking at the chairs he decided they needed to be oiled and walked to the utility closet in the kitchen.

As William started back down the hallway to the theater with oil and rags in hand, he heard a murmur of voices coming from the theater as though there was a crowd of people there.

He stopped cold and held his breath as the sound of an antique piano drifted from the room. William's heart was beating so fast he couldn't bring himself to move or speak. All he could do was listen, and as he did he heard a woman sing *Piangerò la sorte mia* from *Julius Caesar*.

William knew this piece well. What's more, he knew this voice. It was her voice, the one from his dreams. He closed his eyes to listen to her, like so many times before, only this time he was not dreaming.

Her song was so powerful, so beautiful, so incredibly filled with sorrow and fury that William fell to his knees and quietly sobbed and spoke her name for the first time, "Lilly, Lilly, Lilly."

He looked up from the floor and saw her looking down at him. Her eyes were so sad. She held out her hand toward William and spoke in a whisper that cut through the silence. "You must help her, William. Help her before he crushes her. She must sing or she will die, just as I died. You must help her, William."

William reached out his hand to touch hers but as he did, she faded away. The room started to spin, and then everything went black.

A LITTLE NIGHT MUSIC

The lights from the dash of the Jaguar glowed brightly as Barbara drove into town. The roads here were dark, narrow and full of turns, so even though the town was less than five miles away, it took nearly 15 minutes to get there.

Pulling into the heart of town, the glow of lights from the shops that lined the streets gave a feeling of warmth and welcome. "Let's see, he said to make a right at the light on High Street and a right again on Gravel Lane." She parked across the street from one of the oldest buildings in the county, maybe even West Virginia, and the home of the Coriander Café.

As she crossed the street, delicious fragrances of seared beef, garlic and spices filled the air. There were lights streaming from all of the hand-blown, paned glass windows and the muffled sound of music poured out from inside.

Barbara opened the front door and a gust of warm air greeted her. The hostess beckoned her to follow, and without any words exchanged, she did, and was taken right to Garrett's table, which was near the back of a large room filled with many tables and people. Garrett got up and pulled out a chair for her. As she sat, he pushed her chair in and ordered two Whippoorwill Ales from the hostess. Barbara placed her purse on the empty chair next to where she sat. "So, do I stand out that much?"

Garrett laughed, "Well, most folks around here have one leg shorter than the other, you know, from ridge running." He was grinning at her now. "I saw you pull up, I only just got here myself."

The hostess brought the two beers, placed them on the table, winked at Garrett and walked away. Garrett raised his glass, "To Lilly."

Barbara raised her glass, clinked Garrett's glass and said, "To Lilly." She took a long pull of the amber ale and put the glass down. She hadn't realized how thirsty she was. "Wow, that is delicious."

Garrett drank and sat down his glass. "Where is William?"

"He said his leg was bothering him, and decided to clean the theater instead."

"Ah, well that's too bad. He is gonna miss hearing my friend sing and I know he would have loved it."

Just then all the lights in the place dimmed, except at the front where there was a small performance area. A handsome young man with long brown hair and goatee spoke into an old-fashioned looking microphone. He wore an old tweed jacket with leather patch sleeves, white open-collar dress shirt, blue jeans and worn out penny loafers.

"Ladies and gentlemen, thank you for being here tonight. As many of you know this is an 'open mic,' that means that the musicians you hear tonight are not necessarily professional, but have a love of music that they are compelled to share, and we here at the Coriander Café are glad they come to share with us and with you.

"Tonight is a very special 'open mic' because not only do we have most of our regulars performing, tonight we have Miss Sarah, back to bring a little classical culture into our lives. That said, I'd like to open tonight's program with Miss Sarah singing a haunting aria from Puccini's *Madama Butterfly, Un Bel Di Vedremo.*"

"For those of you who don't know, this is the aria Butterfly sings as she stands on the hill and looks out onto the ocean's horizon. She waits faithfully for that plume of smoke from the ship that will bring back her love. She sings how she still has a secure faith in the fact that he will return to his dear little wife, his little orange blossom. For those of you who don't know, her waiting truly is in vain. Ladies and gentlemen, I give you Miss Sarah."

From the shadows a young girl stepped onto the stage, her hair long and pulled to one side. She kept her head down until a piano started with just one note to give her the first pitch. Then, out of thin air her first phrase streamed, pure and unfettered.

With her dark eyes, she looked out over the audience as though she really was looking out over the ocean from a hillside, making no eye contact with anyone. She appeared transcended as she sang her sad lament. As she rationalized her reasons of hope, she brought everyone, watching and listening, with her, through the doubt and pain, right up to the climax of the song.

When the aria finished, there was a moment of stunned silence and then a roar of applause.

Many of the people stood, applauding. Garrett stood, as did Barbara who was moved to tears. They applauded for a solid minute before people started to sit back down.

The young announcer returned to the platform, glowing with admiration of the audience's response. "One thing is for sure ladies and gentlemen. We here in Romney, West Virginia have a great appreciation for all kinds of music. Wasn't Miss Sarah just amazing?"

The audience applauded again as he pulled her back onto the stage and put his arm around her shoulders. The young lady smiled, but would not look up. "Now, Miss Sarah, please promise us you will stay and sing again later." She looked over at him and smiled, then pulled herself from his arm, stepped off the stage and exited through a near door. Within minutes the announcer brought on a couple who sang an original song accompanied by guitar and mandolin, lamenting the coming of winter.

As they sang, Barbara watched, and as she watched them, Garrett looked at her. She reached for her glass and looked over at Garrett, who did not look away. Barbara felt herself flush. "You were right, William would have loved hearing her sing. Who is she?"

Garrett pulled his chair closer toward Barbara so as not to speak too loud. "She's just a kid with a passion and a very artistic soul."

"Will she be joining us?"

"Probably not, she needs to get back home. She works in the morning and if she's late she really gets in trouble."

"Oh no, you mean she won't be singing again?"

"Nope, she only sings once, then leaves."

Garrett took a drink from his beer and looked up at the performers. He was sitting so close to Barbara that she could feel his warmth, which was nice because they were sitting with their backs to the window and there was a draft coming from above. She looked at him, his brown wavy hair, high cheekbones and strong chin. He smelled of clean cedar and exuded strength and confidence.

Turning to her he smiled and said: "You hungry?"

"I'm starved."

"Let's go eat."

124

GARRETT'S OBSESSION, WILLIAM'S QUEST

Garrett got up and headed back toward the hostess podium with Barbara following right behind. They were led to a table for two in a quiet corner of the restaurant.

Their waitress came up to the table and beamed at Garrett. "Hi Garrett," she shifted back and forth with an irrepressible smile. "You gonna have your usual tonight?"

"No, LaDonna, I think tonight I'll go with the cumin pork medallions in the wild mushroom sauce."

"That comes with special mashed potatoes, Garrett. They have fire-roasted Anaheim chilies, cilantro and garlic in them. They're delicious, everyone who's tried them loves them."

"Sounds good!" He looked over at Barbara who was studying the menu. "See anything you like?

"Yes, too many things... but what is Chicken of the Woods?"

Garrett and La Donna were smiling. "That's a local favorite Ma'am. It's a mushroom that grows in the woods here. It looks like a dinner plate that has sliced into a tree. It takes on the flavor of whatever you cook it with, but has the texture of chicken. If you cook it in chicken broth, it tastes like chicken too.

"Wow, that sounds intriguing and tempting but, I think I'll order the filet mignon with horseradish mashed potatoes."

"May I recommend the roasted root vegetables as a side

with that?"

"That sounds perfect, thank you."

The waitress gathered the menus and walked away.

The dining room had a Williamsburg feeling to it, which kept with the period of the house. Each oak table was surrounded by Windsor chairs and there was a handmade corner cabinet which displayed both pewter plates and salt pottery. Pewter-based electric lamps, made to look like old fashioned oil lamps, hung from wall fixtures. On each table was a "courting candle" named because the candle could be lowered or raised for a specific burning time, which was determined by the father or mother. Two turns down gave about half an hour visit, while four turns up gave a good hour. Once the candle burned down to the coil, the visit was over.

As Barbara looked around, she noticed very old portraits hanging together on one wall of the dining room. "Wow, those look so old and dark."

Garrett looked over, "Those are what we here call 'instant ancestors.' Folks pick up old paintings at auctions and put em up in their houses. Makes them look established, and respected. Of course there are some folks who have lived here for many generations, who have legitimate portraits hanging in their homes."

"Do many people have paintings of Lilly in their homes?"

William looked over at Barbara, "No, you won't find pictures of Miss Lilly at any auctions I can promise you that." Garrett seemed adamant and a little agitated.

"I must tell you Garrett, both William and I have been very curious about both paintings of Lilly. What can you tell me about them?"

Garrett looked up, "What other painting of Lilly have you seen?"

"We saw a very similar painting of Lilly at the Stone Hill Inn, near the airport. Have you seen that one?"

Garrett looked away as he spoke, "I haven't seen that one, but I have a friend who knows it very well. She says Lilly is wearing blue damask and the painting is very dark. It hangs over a large fireplace in the main dining room."

He was looking down at his hands now. "I've been meaning to go look at it, but just haven't." Garrett's voice got quieter and trailed off before he finished talking. Barbara felt his sensitivity, but was compelled to know more.

"Garrett, are there more paintings of Lilly?"

Garrett looked up at Barbara, smiled, and looked back down at this hands. "There were four painted, but one is missing. I've looked all over but had no luck finding it. I wanted to look in that old collapsed house, but there was always so much water down there, I figured whatever was in there would have been lost. This morning, after I brought up the boxes William pulled from the shed I went back down to take a look for myself."

"Oh Garrett, I wish you had told us, you could have been hurt."

"Not to worry, when I went back down, there was a good three feet of water in the cellar. I don't know how it got there so fast, but I've learned not to questions these things. I was not meant to go down there, William was. Just ask him about it. The last time he visited, it was all Gertrude could do to keep him away from that cellar."

Garrett took a sip from his ale. "I don't know how you feel about these things, but I really think William is connected to Whippoorwill Ridge. Haven't you noticed his behavior? Gertrude would say, 'something has come over him,' and I think she is right."

Barbara did not know how well Garrett knew William, but she could not deny that William was very preoccupied with the place and the paintings.

Music drifted from the other side of the restaurant. It was

a melancholy song sung by a strong female voice. She sang in an Appalachian style that cut through the entire restaurant. "Where have you gone my love, I look to see your face, to hear your voice, to hold your outstretched hand...."

Both Barbara and Garrett listened and were moved by the song's sadness.

Garrett looked over at Barbara whose eyes had filled with tears. He smiled, as she wiped her tears away with her hands. Barbara smiled back feeling a little silly. "I'm sorry about that Garrett. I'm a little mushy at times."

"No need to be sorry, it's nice to see a person with feelings."

Barbara was moved by his tenderness and had she been younger and more impetuous, might have kissed him right then and there. Resisting the urge, she looked into his eyes and tenderly said, "Thank you, Garrett."

He held her gaze with his eyes for a long time and as he did an invisible force held her captive. She did not want to look away. His gaze was warm and felt so safe, but to stay connected was to open up, and that was not something she was ready to do. She broke away, breathed deeply, exhaled and finished the last of the Whippoorwill Ale. Garrett did the same and as they both finished their drinks, the waitress arrived with their dinners. "Perfect timing, LaDonna!"

She smiled and winked at Garrett, "Well, we here at the Coriander Café strive for perfection Garrett, as you know."

"Indeed, LaDonna, indeed...."

The food was not only delicious but beautiful. The tenderloin was cooked to perfection, seared on the outside, and pink on the inside. Barbara cut into it and a beautiful puddle of beef juice surrounded the meat and ran toward the tangy horseradish-laced mashed potatoes. The accompanying roasted vegetables were caramelized from being slowly baked. This added a nice texture and balance of flavors to the meal with its salty and mellowed sweetness. There were beets, baby carrots, shallots, mushrooms and turnips.

Barbara was ecstatic! "Oh my gosh this is so good! The meat is so tender and flavorful."

Garrett's was slicing into his cumin-scented pork. It was surrounded by a mixture of mushrooms - crimini, oyster, chanterelle and little brown mushrooms, which were coated in a golden gravy made from the pork roast's drippings, wine, herbs and a little cream.

Just as La Donna had said, the potatoes were textured with bits of roasted Anaheim chilies that were flecked with bits of char from the grill. This added a wonderfully mellow smoked-chili flavor to the potatoes. That, along with the piquant flavors of the cilantro and garlic made for a mashed potato masterpiece.

Barbara looked over at Garrett's plate. "How is it?"

Garrett's mouth was full, but he smiled and brought his fingers to his lips and kissed them as if to say "Fantastic!"

After they finished their meals both Garrett and Barbara headed outside. He put his arm around her shoulder and walked her to her car. "Thank you for coming out tonight. I really enjoyed your company."

"I had a great time and loved hearing your friend sing. You know, this may sound strange but I think she looks a little like Lilly from the paintings."

Garrett did not say anything, he leaned against her car and looked toward the restaurant.

"Have you ever noticed that, Garrett?"

Garrett looked at Barbara, "You have a good eye, Barbara. Yes, I think she very closely resembles Lilly. As a matter of fact, sometimes I think she is Lilly." Garrett turned toward Barbara, "I know those paintings like I know my own name. I have spent hours staring into those dark eyes. As a child I would lie under my mother's piano and stare up at her. As my mother would play, I would fantasize about Lilly. I was going to grow up to be a great artist and paint nothing and no one else but Lilly."

Barbara was slightly taken aback, Garrett's voice had become very passionate and his words sent a chill through her.

Garrett rubbed his face with both hands then brought them through his hair grabbing it has he spoke. "I had forgotten all about wanting to paint Lilly until a couple of months ago. That was when I first saw Sarah and heard her sing."

"It was here at the Coriander Café. The vision of her standing there with her dark eyes and hair and that voice, it was as though Lilly was alive and standing right in front of me. I knew I had to paint her and asked her that very night."

Barbara listened intently as Garrett paced in front of her. He became quiet and stopped, his head down, his hands in his pockets.

"Well, did she say yes?"

Garrett was still looking down, "She said no."

It was nearly eleven when Barbara drove home. It had become a little windy and leaves were falling like snow as she pulled into the driveway.

Every downstairs light was on when she walked up the path to the house.

She opened the door and saw William sitting in front of the fire. Barbara took off her coat and hung it on the hall tree. "So, William, did you have a nice quiet evening?" William did not answer. Barbara walked over to his chair to see if he was sleeping. "Hey, did I wake you?"

William looked up at her, his eyes were glassy and unfocused and he had a glass of wine in his hands. Barbara laughed,

"It looks like you've been sampling the 'Ridge Runner Red.'"

Taking a sip from his glass he pulled himself from his slump. "Something happened after you left." His voice was quiet and pensive. "I was cleaning the theater and was going to oil the chairs so I went to the kitchen to get the furniture oil. When I walked back down the hall toward the theater, I heard voices, like the theater was full of people."

Barbara was riveted and sat in the chair next to William, who took another drink from his glass. "I heard a piano playing and then I heard her sing."

Barbara could not take her eyes off William. He looked as though the wind had been knocked out of him.

Again, he pulled himself up a little straighter in his chair and turned to look at Barbara. "It was the girl from my dreams, Barbara, the girl who has been singing to me my entire life. She appeared to me, right there in the hallway and she sang *Piangero* by Handel. Do you know what that song says? It says, 'when I die I will return to haunt him that caused tyranny and fill his heart with terror....'"

He looked toward the brightly-lit hallway that led to the theater. "And you know something Barbara, I knew before she appeared to me who she was." Tears rolled down both of his cheeks, "It's Lilly, Barbara. Lilly is the girl from my dreams."

Barbara's stomach was in knots as she listened to William. She walked over to him, knelt at his feet next to empty bottle of wine, and held him. "Did she frighten you?"

"No, how could she? I have loved her for so long and you know what? This time she spoke to me. She needs me."

Barbara's mind was racing. "What did she say, William?"

"She says we must help her."

"How, William, how can we help her?"

William stared up at the painting. "No, she doesn't want us to help her as in Lilly, she wants us to help her.... She says he's going to crush her, she said, she will die if she can't sing, just like Lilly died."

"Who, William? Who will die?"

William looked down at Barbara, "I don't know, Barbara."

Barbara got up and again sat in the wingback chair next to William. They stared up at the painting and said nothing for several minutes. Barbara kept thinking about what both Garrett and William had said. Somehow their stories were connected.

The cuckoo clock chimed from the kitchen. It was midnight and Barbara was mentally and physically exhausted.

"William, we need to get some rest. We can talk about this again in the morning. If we are to help her then we will need to get our rest."

She stretched out her hand to help him up. He sat his glass down and allowed himself to be pulled from his chair.

They turned off most of the lights and headed upstairs to bed. It was a breezy autumn night. The sounds of the trees outside the house scratching back and forth against the outside walls and the windows rattling their panes sent Barbara off into an uneasy and dreamless sleep.

Cumin Rubbed Pork Medallions with Wild Mushroom Gravy

3 to 3 ½ pounds pork tenderloin
2   tablespoons olive oil
3   teaspoons cumin
3   tablespoons butter
16 ounces oyster mushrooms
8   ounces white button mushrooms
2   large shallots-chopped
6   medium garlic cloves – chopped
1   large jalapeno – seeded and finely chopped
2   tablespoons cilantro – finely chopped
2   tablespoons fresh oregano – finely chopped
14 1/2 ounces low-sodium (with no msg.) chicken
    broth
2   tablespoons flour
1/4 cup dry sherry
Salt and Pepper

- Preheat oven to 375 degrees.

- Rinse pork and dry with paper towel. Place in a glass roasting pan.

- Rub pork with olive oil and lightly salt and pepper both sides. Rub 2 tsp. cumin over pork. Place in roasting pan.

- Roast pork until thermometer inserted into center registers 150 degrees, about 50 minutes.

- Meanwhile, melt 3 tbls. butter in large skillet over med-high heat.

- Add mushrooms, shallots, garlic and 1 tbls. jalapeno.

- Sauté until mushrooms are very tender and beginning to brown, about 15 minutes.

- Remove from heat. Add cilantro, oregano and remaining cumin. Season with salt and pepper and set aside.

- Transfer pork to platter and lightly cover with foil.

- Add broth to roasting pan; scrape up any browned bits.

- Transfer to heavy medium saucepan. Slowly whisk flour into sherry in medium bowl to blend.

- Whisk sherry mixture and 1 tbls. jalapeno into broth; bring to boil, whisking until smooth.

- Stir in mushroom mixture and any accumulated juices from pork on platter.

- Boil until mixture thickens to sauce consistency, stirring occasionally, about 5 minutes.

- Season with salt and pepper.

- Slice pork, garnish with cilantro sprigs. Serve pork and gravy.

Mexican Mashed Potatoes with Roasted Chilies and Cilantro

1   small can whole green chilies
5   pounds russet potatoes peeled and cut into
    evenly sized chunks.
4   medium garlic clove – chopped
1   cup whole milk – warmed
6   tablespoons butter – room temp.
1/4 cup fresh cilantro – washed/dried and chopped no
    stems

- Open can of chilies, drain and chop into 1/2 inch dice.
- Cook potatoes in large pot of boiling salted water until very tender, about 30 minutes. Drain.
- Pour potatoes into a bowl and mash using potato masher. Some lumps o.k.
- Add milk and butter.
- Stir in chilies, garlic and cilantro.
- Season with salt and pepper.

  Serving Ideas: Cumin Pork Roast with Wild Mushroom Sauce. If you want to lower the calories, use non-fat or 2% milk.

  NOTE: If you don't like to use cilantro, substitute parsley.

Horseradish Mashed Potatoes

Servings: 6

Preparation Time: 20 minutes

Tangy and wonderful with any beef dish! You can add more or less horseradish if desired.

4   pounds russet potatoes
1/2 teaspoon salt, for boiling water
2   quarts water
approximately 1 pint half and half or whole milk
1/4 cup butter or margarine
1 1/2 tablespoons horseradish, jarred variety
1/2 teaspoon salt
3   tablespoons chives

- Peel, quarter, and rinse potatoes.

- Place in medium stainless sauce pot filled half way with water. Water should just cover potatoes by 1/2 inch.

- Add 1/2 teaspoon salt to water. Cook potatoes uncovered for 10 to 15 minutes, or until a fork can penetrate through potato with no hesitation.

- Drain water from potatoes and return to pan. Allow potatoes to steam for a moment.

- Pour potatoes into a bowl and add the remaining ingredients except the herbs. Mash using a potato masher until desired texture is achieved.

- Taste for balance of salt and top with chopped chives.

THOMAſʼſ PROMIſE

It was after 9:00am when William came downstairs. This time it was he who had been lured by the delicious fragrances of Barbara's oatmeal cake and coffee. Once at the bottom of the stairs he stared into the shadowed hallway that lead to the theater. He felt a mixture of helplessness and fear, but at the same time he felt a sense of purpose.

The silence in the room was broken by the sound of a crowbar prying a lid off a long-nailed box. It was coming from the mudroom at the back of the house. William walked through the great room to the door that led out to the back porch.

Barbara was on her knees, crowbar in hand, and boards from the box lay on the floor with rusted old nails sticking out.

William cleared his throat, "When did you last have a tetanus shot?"

Barbara had a look of determination on her face, "Not to worry, all my shots are up to date." She placed the crowbar under the next board and pressed down. A loud squeaking noise sounded as the old rusted nails slowly pulled from the long-petrified wood. "I think this must have been the box from the top of the stack. It had the most crap on the top of it. One more board and we'll be able to see what's in here." Again, she plunged down pulling another plank from the box. William was standing right behind her now looking down into the wooden box. "Look at all that mildew."

Barbara started pulling what looked to be large pieces of parchment from the box. Most of it was totally mildewed and unsalvageable. She set it on the floor and dug lower. "Boy, it's all so badly mildewed. I don't think anything could survive the moisture in that cellar."

William seeing her progress, went to the kitchen for coffee. When he returned he found Barbara with a cloth bundle, tied with a water-stained satin ribbon. She got up and set it onto the patio table. It was black around the edges with mildew, but all in all, not as bad as the rest. The ribbon disintegrated as she pulled it. She unfolded the canvas-like fabric. It was wrapped around something many times. She turned and pulled, and turned and pulled until she came to a small leather-covered box. She looked up at William, "Would you like to do the honors?"

William set down his coffee and took the box from Barbara, "There, are initials on the box. 'T' 'H' 'M.' " He sat the box back on the table and opened the lid. Inside was another cloth-wrapped bundle only this time the cloth was not so badly damaged. Unwrapping it, he found a small-leather bound book. Inside the cover was a quill-written inscription which William read aloud.

"Christmas, 1870. For my friend and painter, Thomas Moore. Promise you'll put into words the memories your paintings cannot tell. -Lilly."

William looked up at Barbara whose mouth had dropped open. "We should call Garrett."

"Why should we do that?" William asked as he started to open the book.

"I really think we should call him before we go any further, William. I think he is as much a part of this as you are. He as much as told me so last night, only I don't think he knows why or even what he is a part of. That's why he needs to be here."

Barbara beckoned William to follow her into the kitchen. She washed her hands and poured herself a fresh cup of coffee, then served both William and herself a large piece of oatmeal cake. This was a simple cake, spiced with cinnamon and a hint of Chinese five-spice. The oatmeal in it gave enough nutrition to erase the guilt of eating cake for breakfast. They sat at the table next to the window with the diary between them. William ate as Barbara told him about her experience with Garrett the evening before. How he seemed to be obsessed with painting this Sarah because of how much she resembled Lilly. How he had grown up with a painting of Lilly in his house and how he had spent the last several years trying to locate the lost painting.

William listened quietly, trying to make sense of it but at the same time he was feeling pangs of jealousy. After all, Lilly was the girl from his dreams, it was his quest, and he would be the one to help her. Barbara went on to tell William how mesmerizing Sarah's performance was. The entire house was held captive by her voice. "I must say William, I felt as though I was actually hearing Lilly sing."

William looked out the window, then got up from his chair and headed toward the front door. "Well, looks like you will get your chance to show him."

Before Garrett could knock, William opened the door. Garrett looked as though he hadn't slept and asked if he could speak to Barbara.

William showed him into the kitchen where Barbara was pouring him coffee. "Garrett, are you alright?"

Garrett looked over at William and back to Barbara. "Can we talk in private?" Barbara looked over at William who was not about to move. "Garrett, before we do, we, both William and I need to talk to you about something."

"Listen Barbara, about last night, I would rather keep that between us."

William sat down at the table, "It's too late for that Garrett, she's told me everything."

Garrett gave Barbara a pained look and walked over to William, "Look William, I don't know what she told you, but all I can say is I was very tired and haven't been myself lately."

"Save your breath Garrett, sit down and have your coffee."

Garrett did not sit, he looked over at Barbara who gestured for him to sit down.

"I'm afraid, I really need to go." Garrett headed toward the door, but before he opened it, William yelled from the kitchen, "I saw Lilly last night."

Garrett, stopped, his hands still on the door latch. Barbara had followed him "Please Garrett, we really need to talk to you, for your sake and for William's and for Lilly's."

With one arm around his waist Barbara lead Garrett back to the kitchen and motioned for him to sit down across from William. There seemed to be a tension between them that was not there before. Suddenly, they were like opposite magnets.

Barbara pulled up the stool and told Garrett about what William had experienced last night. She told Garrett of William's dreams of the singing woman and how last night for the first time, he knew who she was. He had seen her face.

She looked over at William, "Tell Garrett what she said to you."

Garrett looked at William. "She really spoke to you?"

This time it was Garrett who was feeling tinges of jealousy. He looked over at William who was looking at the diary in the center of the table. Garrett now looked too. "It was Lilly. She told me we had to help her, and yet, she didn't mean herself, but someone else, she said he would crush her, and that if she didn't sing, she would die like Lilly died."

Barbara picked up the diary and laid it down in front of where she sat. "I don't know why, but one thing is for certain, you are both a part of what is going on here and for that matter, so am I."

Barbara carefully opened the book to the inscription on the first page. She gently slid it in front of Garrett.

Excitedly, he said, "Thomas Moore was my great, great-grandfather. He is the artist who painted Lilly."

"That's a pretty big connection Garrett, do you know anything about their relationship to each other?"

Garrett stared at the inscription. He rubbed his fingers over the writing and looked over to Barbara. "I don't, but I would bet he was in love with her. You don't paint someone over and over again without feeling something."

He turned the page to find the first entry.

December 28th 1870

Today I had the privilege of starting the second painting of Mrs. Lilly LeClaire. We have been blessed with a bright sunny day that reflects off a new snow. This bright reflection has sent a brilliant light into the windows of the Great Room.

Lilly looks like an angel in this light. Her skin glows like pearls and her eyes like two black pools. Her black hair is down and she has pulled it to one side leaving one shoulder bare.

She has chosen a beautiful dark red gown with a brocade bodice and has pulled the blouse underneath off her shoulders. She tells me this is her Carmen dress and shares with me a story written by an author from Spain named Prosper Mérimée. The story was of a Gypsy girl who had been killed by her jealous lover. She says it would make a great opera. She is so intelligent, so full of life.

I cherish these hours, these stolen moments. So happy to be a painter so that I may look upon her and know her like no one else can. TM

Garrett looked up from the diary and took a sip of his coffee. "I think we can say with some confidence that he was in love with her, wouldn't you?"

Barbara smiled and shook her head. William got up and walked into the great room and over to the painting of Lilly above the fireplace.

The painting seemed more vivid than ever.

Barbara got up and cleared the dishes from the table. "I think we should get together this evening and read further into his journal. You should come for dinner, Garrett." She walked into the great room next to William. "What do you think William?"

He turned, "Yes, I think it would be good for all three of us to take this journey."

Garrett, hearing William, entered the room and walked up to the painting. "It is amazing to me that her spirit has so much passion and love that it has punched a hole through time and space and entered into our hearts. I love her as I have loved no woman, I would defend her to the death and I would bet William feels the same way."

William looked over to Garrett and Barbara then back to the painting, "Tonight then, at 8pm."

Garrett agreed and headed for the door. Barbara followed him and opened it. Once he was outside, he turned and placed his hand on Barbara's which was holding the door. "I enjoyed your company last night."

Barbara smiled and stepped outside closing the door behind her. "I enjoyed yours, too."

Garrett drew closer and put his arms around her and held her, "I'm very glad you are here. I have been alone in all of this for so long." He held her so close that Barbara could hear the beating of his heart, which was racing. She embraced him back and they stayed that way until the sound of a ringing phone brought them to.

Letting go, Garrett started down the front walk, walking backwards, "I'll see you later."

Barbara watched him as he turned and continued up the road to his house. Walking inside, she closed the door, pressing her back against it. She took a deep breath and headed toward the kitchen where William was chopping up celery and carrots on a large cutting board at the center island. "Who called?" Barbara climbed onto one of the stools beside the island and watched as William professionally chopped everything to perfection.

Looking up he answered, "Gertude."

"How is she doing?"

William started finely chopping up the onion, "She's alright." Smiling at her he asked, "Is Garrett going to be alright?"

Barbara blushed, "I'm sure he will be just fine."

Scraping the vegetables into a sizzling pan of olive oil, William turned back to her smiling and said, "I'm sure he will be. Yes, indeed."

Oatmeal Cake

Servings: 10
Preparation time: 45 minutes

CAKE
1 cup quick-cooking oats
1 1/2 cups boiling water
1/2 cup shortening, margarine o.k.
1/2 cup brown sugar
1/2 cup white sugar
2 eggs
1 1/2 cups flour
1 teaspoon baking powder
1 teaspoon baking soda
1 teaspoon cinnamon
1 teaspoon salt
1 pinch Chinese five spice

TOPPING
3/4 cup butter
1/2 cup brown sugar
2 teaspoons evaporated milk
1/2 cup chopped pecans

- Grease and flour a 9 x 13 cake pan.

- Preheat oven to 350 degrees

- Combine oatmeal and boiling water, let stand ten minutes.

- Cream shortening with brown and white sugars.

- Add the eggs to the creamed sugar mixture.

- Sift together flour, baking powder, baking soda, cinnamon and salt.

- Mix flour together with creamed sugar mixture. Last mix in the oatmeal.

- Pour mixture into cake pan. Place in the oven on center rack and bake for 25 minutes to 30 minutes. Test for doneness by poking center with a butter knife. If it comes out clean, cake is done.

TOPPING: (optional)

- Mix ingredients together in a small pot on stove and mix until sugar is dissolved and bubbling.

- Spread on top of cake and broil until lightly brown, one to two minutes. Watch during broiling so as not to burn.

WE'RE IN THIS TOGETHER

Barbara made herself useful while William cooked, by dusting and dry mopping the beautiful walnut floors in the great room. The guests were due to arrive by 4pm giving her most of the morning free. She went upstairs, packed up her things and changed the sheets. Every bed was needed and she and William would have to head to the rooms over the garage.

Once finished, she checked each room to be sure there were extra blankets and towels. The rooms were joined by a long hallway. The center room was the largest and had the stairway to the attic in it.

Barbara walked over to the door to the attic steps and out of curiosity, opened it. The stairwell was so dark, she could not see past the fifth step.

The smell of old wood and dust wafted down from the attic on a cold wave of air, and with it, a great feeling of sadness. Barbara felt queasy and weak. She quickly closed the door to the attic and walked from the room to the hall. Tears streamed down her face as she gathered her things from her room and walked downstairs.

William was building a fire when she came down but turned to look when she reached the bottom.

"Hey, are you alright?" William quickly got up and walked up to Barbara. "What's the matter?"

Barbara dropped her bags and let him hold her. "I'm not sure what just happened, but I think I just got a sample of just

147

how very sad your Lilly is." She was trembling when she spoke and after speaking, she started to bawl and cry.

William held her for more than five minutes until her crying eased. He walked her to the chair in front of the fire and brought her a cup of tea. "Maybe bringing you here wasn't such a good idea."

She looked up at him, "Well, it's too late, I'm here."

William looked at her with a worried expression. "Well, maybe you should go home."

Barbara stared into the fire, part of her wanted to go home, but she knew she was a part of this too. "Look William, I don't know how to explain it, but I feel as though a woman's touch is needed in this. You and Garrett are so in love with Lilly that you can't see things clearly."

"Oh, and you can see clearly! Forgive me Barbara, but I have never seen you cry like that, so don't tell me you're not emotionally a little confused yourself." William was perturbed.

Barbara got up, "You're right William, I'm not immune to what's happening here and maybe 'seeing things clearly,' was not the right thing to say. Maybe I should have said, 'feel things more clearly.'"

Walking over to the door Barbara put on her coat and picked up her luggage. "Where are you going?" William followed her to the door.

"We're supposed to move over the garage, William. Do you have a key?"

William looked relieved and went to the kitchen to retrieve the keys. He then returned carrying a large ring with many keys. "I'll go with you."

Later that afternoon three cars pulled up to Whippoorwill Ridge Manor and six people checked in.

William showed them their rooms and said, "If any of you want a fire tonight in your rooms, just let me know. However, once I get it started you will be responsible for keeping it going. Each room has enough wood to keep a fire going for a good three hours. I will be turning the heat on, as it is predicted to freeze tonight, so you won't need to rely on your fireplaces for heat. Also, I'll be serving coffee, tea and perhaps a little something extra at 5pm You are welcome to join me and my sister in the great room."

Needless to say, William more than enjoyed playing innkeeper and had a beautiful spread of cookies and cakes, cheeses and meats laid out for the guests.

While they were not a licensed restaurant, he was permitted to offer purchased items to his guests, who did not hold back in their consumption.

After a tour of the house and grounds, William was able to break free and head back to the house where Barbara was setting the table for dinner. "You are quite the host, William."

William pulled the caramelized Chicken Pecant from the oven and using tongs, turned each piece over, coating the top with the reduced caramel-colored sauce.

No sooner had the cuckoo sounded eight times then there came a knock at the back door to the kitchen. Barbara walked over and seeing Garrett, let him in.

"Hi, Barbara."

He had showered and was clean-shaven.

Garrett removed his coat and hung it on a hook on the wall in the pantry. "It's supposed to freeze tonight." Looking over at William he asked, "Did Gertrude show you how to turn the heat on?"

William nodded yes, as he ladled hot Gluwein into three cobalt blue and cream-colored German punch mugs. He put a stick of cinnamon in each one and placed them on a tray. "Shall we have the first course in the great room?"

They sat around the hot fire and sipped the warming mulled wine. It had been laced with brandy and spices and gave a feeling of well-being almost immediately. Garrett looked over at Barbara who had pulled up a chair nearer to William. From his shirt pocket he pulled a photograph, which he handed to Barbara. "You had asked about another painting of Lilly. This is the one I grew up with, it still hangs in my mother's home in Winchester."

Barbara and William both looked at the photograph. In it, Lilly was wearing the red gown that was described in the first entry from Thomas Moore's diary. "It's so vibrant, and she looks so beautiful, so happy." Barbara handed the photo to William who pulled his glasses from his pocket to get a closer look. He got up and held the picture under a lamp, studying it for several moments. "This is the painting we read about in the diary remember? She said she was wearing her Carmen Dress."

William went into the kitchen and came back with a magnifying glass and continued to study the picture. "Did you notice the music on the stand in the background? It is *Granados*. I have heard her sing *Granados* many times." He returned to his seat and handed the photo back to Garrett. "That painting is in perfect condition, you must have had it restored."

This time Garrett got up. That is not the original, it is a copy, one of many that I have painted throughout my life."

Barbara asked to see the photo again and this time she examined it with a magnifying glass. "I want to see this painting, Garrett, do you have it?"

"No, it was destroyed, I only have the photo because my sister took it before it happened."

Garrett sat back down and finished his Glühwein.

"How was it destroyed?" Barbara and William were both looking at him now.

"I destroyed it. I had to. Lilly was taking over my life. But the original still hangs in my sister's house." Garrett had put his glass down and was running both his hands through his hair, grabbing it as he spoke. "I thought I had gotten past this, past her. But now it's all I can do to not think of her. Every day something new makes her more vivid, more real."

William got up and went into the kitchen to check on dinner and refill his mug. Barbara and Garrett sat staring into the fire, sipping and thinking. Barbara looked over at Garrett, then into the fire. "Don't worry Garrett, we will figure this out together. We will help Lilly and in helping her, we will help ourselves."

Garrett reached out his hand to Barbara who pulled her chair next to where Garrett was sitting. He took her hand and held it within both of his hands. He looked up at her and she back at him.

The room was quiet except for the crackling fire and William clanking around in the kitchen.

William called them to dinner which was good because the Gluhwein was getting the best of Barbara who was thinking, "One more sip and I won't be held responsible for what I do." She smiled to herself as she washed her hands, at least dinner would help to satisfy one need.

Chicken Pecant

Servings: 4

Preparation time: 1 hour

Be sure to turn chicken so it will fully absorb sauce. Do not overbake. Chicken should be moist however, sauce should have boiled down to a thick substance. If the sauce has evaporated, remove dish from oven and cover with foil until ready to serve.

Dark meat is much better with this recipe.

2 pounds chicken drumsticks and thighs
1 pound chicken wings
1/8 cup brown sugar
1/2 cup soy sauce
1 teaspoon oregano
1/2 teaspoon rubbed sage
4 cloves garlic, cut in half
1/2 teaspoon ground ginger

- Preheat oven to 330 degrees.
- Wash chicken and pat dry with paper towel.
- Place chicken in a large glass baking dish.
- Mix the brown sugar, oregano, rubbed sage, and ginger together in a bowl.

- Pour the soy sauce over the chicken pieces, then sprinkle with the dry herb mix, coating the top of each piece of chicken.

- Place the chopped garlic around the pieces of chicken and place uncovered in oven on center rack for 45 minutes.

- Turn chicken pieces and continue baking for 1/2 hour. The chicken should be tender and you should have some sauce at the bottom of the pan. You want the sauce to reduce and carmelize and become thick. It is not a gravy but a wonderful coating.

Serving Ideas: Serve with mashed potatoes or rice.

Excellent for picnics.

THERE YOU HAVE IT

By the time they had finished their meal it was after 9 pm. They cleared the table, washed the dishes and headed into the great room with Barbara carrying a tray with cups and a full pot of tea.

The guests had returned and had retired to their rooms upstairs. William stoked the fire and added two large logs. Sparks flew up the chimney as he stoked and prodded 'til the logs were secure. The large fire put off a flickering glow that reflected through the entire room.

Garrett, per William's request, wound up the Victrola and placed the needle on the ancient Giuseppe Ruscello recording. They sat and listened as his haunting voice sang Donizetti's *Una Furtiva Lagrima*. When it was over the needle sounded as it reached the edge of the recording and rode back and forth across the blank surface. Barbara walked over to the Victrola, picked up the needle and set it to rest on the base. She then headed to the kitchen where she retrieved the Thomas Moore diary. She handed it to William along with a small penlight. Barbara sat next to Garrett who along with Barbara sat quietly as William read the second installment from the diary.

January 28th, 1871

Today, I started the third of my Lilly paintings. We have agreed that the theater was the appropriate place for it, as it was the setting for a very successful concert last evening.

There were visiting dignitaries from near Washington and representatives from the Washington Opera, who found Mrs. Lilly's voice to be quite exceptional. So exceptional, that they have asked her to sing in a concert there in late April. The concert will be held in celebration of President Ulysses Grant's birthday. This comes as no surprise to me as I have always known that Lilly's voice was a special gift.

Mrs. Lilly was so excited she seemed to float inches off the ground. However, today, she is somewhat sullen and won't tell me why. While I am privileged to paint her, I dare not try and reproduce the color of her spirit as the palette would be several shades of grey to black. So, I will only sketch her in and hope for a change tomorrow. TM

William closed the diary and looked into the fire. "I saw Lilly in her room in a dream just three days ago. She was very upset. She sat rocking her baby and weeping when a man came in. I'm pretty sure it was her husband. He spoke to Lilly, but she would not listen. He stormed out leaving her to cry. I can't help but think this may have been the same day she was so sad for Thomas." He got up and looked over at Garrett and Barbara, "But it still does not tell us what had her so upset."

Just then one of the guests ventured downstairs.

He wore a thick flannel robe and fleece-lined slippers. "This looks cozy. Nice fire. Say, would you mind if I went into the theater to play the piano? I can't sleep. I've got a million melodies running through my head and if I don't play them out, I'll go crazy."

Barbara and Garrett looked up at William. "It's o.k. with me, but you might disturb the person in the room at the top of the stairs."

The man smiled, "Well, that's my room."

William walked the man down the hall to the theater and turned on the lights. The man walked over to the piano and uncovered it. It was an old baby grand. "Man, it's freezing in here."

William noticed it too. It was colder than the rest of the house.

William walked over to feel the radiators. They were warm, quite warm, even that side of the theater was warm, but the area around the piano was freezing. "I'll be sure to have some space heaters in here tomorrow when you are working."

The man started to play the piano. The brooding melody from *Im Treibhaus* by Richard Wagner floated across the theater. When the song was over, the pianist rubbed his hands together in an effort to warm them. He looked over at William who stood at the door. "You know, this is no ordinary cold."

The man stood up and closed the piano. He pulled the cover back over the top and walked up to William, who opened the door.

Bringing his collar up around his neck the man shuddered, "I haven't felt a 'cold' like that since I was a little boy. I sure hope it's gone by tomorrow."

He walked over to the fireplace and extended his hands

toward the flames and as he did, he looked up and stared at the painting of Lilly. "Is this Lilly?"

Barbara, Garrett and William were astounded at such an assumption, why was it so clear to him and not to them. William was the first to speak. "Yes, that is Lilly."

The man looked at each of them and back at the painting. "Ah, well there you have it. Well, good night." And just like that, as if he had summed it all up he returned back upstairs to his room.

They all listened as he closed his door. The cuckoo sounded in the kitchen. It was 11pm and the fire was starting to die down.

Garrett rose and looked at Barbara who stood up. "It's late, and I'm tired. I have to say, finding that diary has cleared up a lot for me. I hope we can meet again tomorrow, so we can get to the bottom of this."

Barbara looked over at William who had settled back down in his chair. He looked up and nodded, "Why don't you plan on coming for lunch, we can go through the rest of the crates."

Barbara walked Garrett back through the kitchen to the back door where he had hung his coat. She walked outside with him and stood on the landing. It was a quiet night, with bright stars. Garrett stood next to Barbara and they both looked up. "Are the skies this full of stars where you live?"

She turned to him. "I don't remember noticing before, actually."

Garrett continued to look up, "No one back there to enjoy them with?"

Barbara couldn't help but smile at the nature of his question. "Oh, I wouldn't say that. I have my brother and friends."

This time Garrett looked over at her, "You know that's not what I meant."

Barbara was looking at the stars now, and smiling. "No,

there is no one back home to enjoy the stars with."

Garrett stepped down from the stoop and turned to face her. His hands in his jean pockets he said, "Well, I know a lot about the skies here, perhaps you will allow me to tell you about them sometime."

Barbara moved closer to him. Standing on the stoop, her eyes were level with his. She too had her hands in her pant spockets. "I'd like that."

Once again she watched as Garrett walked backwards down the sidewalk. He stopped and looked up at her, "I'll see you tomorrow. Goodnight."

"Goodnight."

When, Barbara came back inside, William was at the sink washing out cups. Barbara picked up a towel, dried and put them away. Just as he was washing the last saucer the phone rang.

"Who could be calling this late?" Barbara picked up the phone. "Whippoorwill Ridge Manor."

From the receiver came a loud voice with a heavy French accent. "Aello, Barbara?"

Barbara's heart started racing and her palms got quite cold. "Yes, this is Barbara."

William wiped his hands on a towel. Leaning against the sink he watched Barbara and listened to her conversation.

"Barbara, this is Chef George. I need you to come in tomorrow. Can you be here by 10:00am?"

Barbara turned from William as she spoke to Chef George, "Tomorrow, oh, I don't know, I thought you only needed me on Thursdays."

"Ah well, tomorrow is Thursday, Barbara, and I am in need of another person. I hope you can come, and besides, you said you wanted to work in my kitchen, didn't you? Well, here is your chance. I'll see you at 10:00am and don't forget, wear black pants and a white blouse. I'll provide you with an apron.

Good night, Cherie."

Just like that, the line went dead. Barbara looked at the receiver in disbelief and looked over at William who was smiling to himself and looking down. "Do you believe that guy? Man he is so, so…."

William finished her sentence, "Chef George?"

Barbara shot a sharp look over at William and finished drying and putting way the dishes. "I really don't want to go. That guy infuriates me."

William pulled up a chair at the center island and looked over at Barbara. "Look Barbara, the guy is a jerk, but what difference does it make? Spend some time in his kitchen. He is a very talented chef with lots to share."

Barbara knew William was right. It would be a missed opportunity to not go.

William smiled up at her, "Besides, you need to take a break from Garrett. You get any hotter and we'll have to give you an ice bath."

At this, she threw the wet towel right at his face. He caught it, and threw it right back saying, "I'll drive you tomorrow. I need to get away myself."

"Who will mind the 'store' if you leave?"

He started shutting off lights and headed out toward the apartments over the garage with Barbara in tow, "Oh, I figure Lilly can handle it."

DAMSELS AND DONUTS

It was 9am when William and Barbara pulled onto Route 50 heading west toward Bickersburg. That was where the airport was and the Stone Hill Hotel and restaurant. It would take all of 45 minutes to an hour before they got there, and Barbara was not in a good mood. She tossed and turned the entire night and could not shake the anxiety of working with Chef George.

The sky was a brilliant blue and distant mountains glowed with hues of gold and orange. The surrounding fields were studded with giant rolls of hay which cast beautiful dark shadows giving depth to the wide stretching landscape. Barbara turned on the radio and searched for a clear channel. Finally she dialed in a classical station and listened to Vivaldi's *Four Seasons Concerto*. At the end of the piece an announcer came on and advertised an open audition for all students of classical voice. It went like this: "Saturday, November 15th, there will be an open vocal audition held at the Whippoorwill Ridge Theater in Romney, West Virginia. These auditions are open to anyone between the ages of 18 and 25 who is proficient in singing classically, as in operatically. Those who pass the audition will have an opportunity to participate, via scholarship, in a summer opera program being offered in Alexandria, Virginia. The goal of the program is to offer young people a chance to sing in an opera and to be exposed to professional opera performers and directors. This is an excellent and a once-in-a-lifetime opportunity for those who are lucky enough to win the audition.

Anyone interested in participating go to www.operaaudition-wva.bok for more details or call me here at the station at 304-c.l.a.s.s.i.c."

Barbara sat up in her seat and looked over at William, "Wow, this sounds big. Are we ready for this? I mean, shouldn't we be getting the place ready?"

"Well for one thing the place is ready and I don't think there will be all that many singers auditioning. Maybe 50, if that." They drove in silence for about ten minutes, when a thought came to Barbara. "I wonder if Sarah will be there."

William looked over, "Sarah?"

"You know, the girl I heard sing with Garrett. She was so gifted and so young. Surely, she'll be there."

It was nearly 10 am when William pulled into the driveway for the Stone Hill. Barbara got out of the car, turned around and looked back at William. "Well, here goes nothing."

William laughed, "You're all worked up for nothing. Just remember, he's a jerk, accept that and any good behavior that comes from him will be an unexpected surprise."

Barbara took a deep breath, "I know, you're right of course. I'll be fine. Pick me up at 3 pm"

Barbara watched as William pulled away and proceeded up the walk to the entrance to the restaurant. As she entered, she heard a vacuum whining in the distance. The chairs were all turned up and there was a smell of cleaning solution in the air. She walked into the main dining room and looked for the entrance to the kitchen. Walking to the back of the large dining room where the windows looked over the meadow and the mountains, she noticed a parking lot, and there in the lot she saw Chef George. He was on his cell phone beside his car. It was clear he was pretty upset as his hands were flying and he was pacing back and forth. Barbara stepped back from the window so as not to be seen and watched Chef George continue his rant. She was so engrossed in watching him that she didn't hear Doris, the hostess, come up and stand next to her. "Oh, he is in a mood today."

Startled, Barbara looked over at Doris, who continued to watch from the window. Doris looked back over at Barbara and extended her hand. "Hi, I'm Doris, and you must be Barbara, William's sister."

Barbara shook her hand. "Hi Doris. Maybe this isn't a good time for me to be here."

Doris laughed, "Nonsense, Barbara. There will never be a good time with Chef George. Everyday there is a new drama. That's the best part about working with him, but it is key that you don't take anything personally."

Doris headed away and beckoned Barbara to follow. They wound around the back of the dining room until they came to two double doors. "Always enter through the door on the right when entering or exiting the kitchen."

Once inside, Doris handed Barbara a long white apron that she tied at her waist. She then guided her to a dry-erase board where several names were written. Barbara's name was at the bottom, and next to her name were three words. Onions, garlic and shallots.

"Oh, you are a lucky girl." Doris smiled and guided Barbara to a large stainless steel prep table which stood under a large exhaust fan. Underneath the table, stacked vertically, were several white cutting boards. To the right of the table was the door to a cooler. Doris lead Barbara into the produce cooler where she pointed out the onions, shallots and garlic. Barbara picked out some onions, but Doris stopped her. "Don't start anything until Chef George shows you how. He is very particular as I'm sure you have guessed by now." They exited the cooler. "You can put your things in a locker near the restrooms, and I recommend you use the restroom before you start. If you have any questions, don't ask Chef George, ask Sous Chef Lawrence. If he is busy, ask the saucier, Chef Carlos."

Barbara could feel herself tense up. "Why am I doing this," she thought.

She did as Doris had said and put her things in a locker and used the restroom. As she washed her hands she heard Chef George outside the door. Barbara looked at herself in the mirror and said, "I am not going to let this guy bully me, I am strong, intelligent, and a damn good chef." She turned and headed back out to the prep table. From behind her she heard Chef George.

"Ah, there you are Barbara. Did Doris speak with you?"

Barbara turned and put on a confident face. "Yes, I spoke with Doris."

Chef George headed toward the prep table ahead of Barbara. "Good, I will need you to peel and slice 40 large onions, 50 shallots and 30 heads of garlic. There are bins under the table, use them to pull the produce from the cooler. Start with the onions. Please be sure to turn on the exhaust fans when you work."

Chef George pulled a cutting board from the shelf below and a large chef knife from a magnetic strip against the back wall. He went into the cooler and brought out two onions. He peeled and sliced one onion in half. He sliced it horizontally, then vertically several times. Then, like a surgeon he quickly and thinly sliced the entire onion. Once done, he rocked his knife over the chopped onions chopping them even finer. One of the sous chefs brought a large bowl in anticipation of Chef George's needs. Using the side of his large knife, Chef George scraped the chopped onions into the bowl in one graceful movement. He then stepped aside and indicated to Barbara to do the same.

Barbara did not hesitate; she knew a thing or two about onions and she was a quick study. She mimicked every move Chef George had made right down to the rocking of the blade across the chopped onions mincing them to a fine chop and scraped them into the large bowl.

Chef George pulled his cell phone from his pocket checking it for messages. "I want the shallots and the garlic done the same way and I will need them all to be completed by noon. O.k.? Oh, and be sure not to mash the garlic to remove the peel, the more you mash it the stronger it gets, so chop only, got it?"

Barbara nodded and proceeded into the cooler with a large bin. She started loading up the onions counting out 20. The produce was extremely fresh and the onions as firm as stones, making them crunchy to slice into and not so strong in odor.

She didn't mind that she had been given the smelliest job, she figured it was a test and for her, an easy one. She got right to work and for the next two hours immersed herself in an onion, shallot and garlic dicing frenzy.

William drove into downtown Bickersburg and parked in front of a large old-fashioned looking grocery store. Before going in, he headed across the street to the local bakery and coffee shop. The sign outside touted organic, fair-trade beans and pesticide-free flours used in their pastry.

Once inside, he couldn't help but notice how many young people were there and how many laptop computers were being used. In fact, most of the people there were sitting behind computers sipping their java and typing away. He walked up to the counter, ordered a double latte and perused the selection of baked goods.

There was a beautiful hazelnut espresso cheesecake sliced into single servings. He purchased two slices and two forks. Barbara would surely need a reward after today's experience.

He crossed the street back to the Jaguar and put the cheesecake in the trunk. The sidewalk had filled with people as it was nearing lunch time.

William entered the stream of people and walked through the downtown. He could see two young girls carrying what looked to be a box of costumes, ahead in the crowd.

They were talking and laughing and didn't notice when a pair of blue satin gloves fell from their box. William watched to see if anyone would pick them up, but no one did.

As he walked past them, he picked them up. They were opera gloves, beautifully made with pleats on the top part and a scalloped edge at the wrist. He looked up to locate the two young girls, but couldn't see them. He started a slow jog, moving through the milling people. After about two blocks he saw them. They were stopped at a light waiting to cross. Breathlessly, William approached them.

One girl balanced the box on a nearby park bench while the other pressed the button to cross.

"I believe you dropped these." William held the gloves out for them to see. The girls both giggled and thanked William. As he placed the gloves back into the box he asked, "Are these costumes from a local production?"

The girl with the short blond hair and rose tattoo piped up. "Those gloves were just used in an opera program here in town."

"Really? What was the program called?"

This time the dark-haired girl spoke up. "It was called, '*Divas, Damsels, and Donuts*'."

This time it was William who laughed, "Wow, that sounds like a wonderful program."

The dark-haired girl smiled, "Why, do you like donuts?"

"Indeed I do," William said without missing a beat. He looked into her eyes which were nearly black. "Did you sing in the program?"

The stoplight had changed and the walk sign had come on. The short-haired girl with the tattoo picked up the box and started to cross the street. William and the dark-haired girl did as well. She turned to him, "Well, thanks for returning the gloves."

Once across William stopped, but the two girls kept walking. "Wait, you didn't answer my question. Did you sing in the program?"

At this the short-haired girl turned around and shouted with an imposed British accent, "Dear Sir,... Sarah was the program!" She and the dark-haired Sarah laughed and ran up the street, around the corner and out of sight. William watched the two young girls disappear and thought out loud to himself, "Sarah?"

15

JHE FOUND HER VOICE

William waited at the bar inside the Stone Hill for Barbara to get off work. He sat there drinking a Whippoorwill Ale when Doris walked up. William looked over at her smiling, "Hey Doris, how have you been?"

"Hello William. I've been good. You here to pick up Barbara?"

William looked around to see if Barbara was there, "Yea, I am. So, how did she do?"

Doris sipped a glass of water, "She was fine, very efficient."

William looked around again and whispered this time, "How did she and Chef George get along?"

Before Doris could answer, Barbara walked up from behind William, "We got along great, he told me what do, I did it and then he disappeared."

Barbara sat at the bar and ordered an ale for herself. She poured the amber liquid into a tall tapered beer glass and filled it to the very top with an inch-thick head of foam, til a little ran down the side. "Isn't that pretty." She picked up her glass and held it up for a toast, "To Chef George, may he never run out of onions."

They each lifted their glasses and chimed in with a "Hear, Hear!"

Barbara took a long drink, then looked up and smiled, "Finally I got the taste of onions out of my mouth."

William put his glass down and turned to Doris, "So, where

is Chef George?"

This time it was Doris who looked around, "He is having some family problems, and probably won't be in until 4 pm."

William leaned toward Doris, "Family?

"His daughter."

"Oh, nothing bad I hope."

Doris looked over and grinned at William, "No, nothing bad, she is just finally standing up for herself and Chef George isn't taking it too well."

William smiled, "Yea, I'll bet not. Teenagers can be tough."

"Oh, she's no teenager, she's nearly 23. You met her last week; she waited on you, remember?"

Barbara looked over, "I remember her, dark hair, kind of quiet."

Doris, nodded, "That's her, only she found her voice two nights ago when she went storming out of here. You should have heard her. It was quite marvelous actually listening to her yell and scream at her father. She hasn't been back since and it has George going crazy. That's part of the reason you're here. We're short two people."

Barbara put down her glass, "Two people?"

Doris nodded, "There was another girl that worked prep, but when his daughter left, Nicky went with her."

Barbara's interest was piqued, "What was she screaming about?"

Again, Doris looked around, "I really don't like to gossip, but you will probably hear it from someone else anyway. Chef George wants her to go to culinary school in New York. He has already enrolled her and she has totally refused to go. I'm not surprised actually, he never asked her if she wanted to go, he just told her she was going."

Barbara looked over at William and rolled her eyes. "How has he gotten away with this kind of behavior for so long? You would think he would realize bullying people doesn't get you anywhere."

Just as Barbara finished this statement, Chef George walked in the front door into the bar. Doris casually took a drink from her glass of water and looked at him as did William and Barbara. He looked wired and pale, his eyes were bloodshot and his brow had beads of sweat.

William held up his glass, "Hey, Chef."

Chef George did not respond. He looked over at Doris who shook her head no indicating his daughter had not come in. He looked over at Barbara. "Did you get everything done?"

Barbara nodded, "Yes, Chef, as you requested."

Chef George then looked over at William. "Hey William, thanks for loaning me your sister."

He walked over to Barbara and picked up her hands. Barbara's first instinct was to pull away, but seeing Chef George up close she realized now was not the time to be coy. He brought her hands up to his nose and took a deep breath. "Ah, now that's a beautiful perfume."

Barbara blushed. She reeked of garlic and was a little embarrassed at his intimate contact. He put her hands down and headed toward the kitchen. "So, I'll see you here tomorrow at the same time, yes?"

Barbara answered as he walked away, "Yes, Chef."

Doris looked at Barbara and William, "Kind of makes you feel sorry for the jerk, doesn't it."

Indeed, Chef George looked as though the wind was knocked out of him. Doris got up from her seat, "Well, I better go before he regains his strength." Doris smiled and walked into the main dining room.

It was after 4pm before they got back to the bed and breakfast. Barbara helped William unload several bags of produce that he had purchased in Bickersburg. She walked into the kitchen and placed the bags onto the center island.

A note on yellow paper was taped to the coffee pot. It was from Garrett and read, "Where are you guys? I waited for an hour. I opened another crate in the sunroom, but found most of the stuff too moldy to recognize. Going back home to eat lunch. Call me when you get back. Hope all is well. –Garrett"

"Oh my gosh, I forgot to tell Garrett I had to work." Barbara grabbed the phone and opened the cupboard to find his number. She dialed and the phone rang until his answering machine picked up. "Garrett, it's Barbara, I'm sorry we missed you. Call me when you get in."

William was bringing in the last of the bags when he overheard Barbara leaving a message. "You call Garrett?"

Barbara started unpacking the vegetables and placing them on the island. "Yea, I totally forgot to tell him we wouldn't be here for lunch. I'm going to invite him for dinner when he calls back."

William quickly sorted the vegetables into baskets and placed many of them in the cool pantry. On the table sat a braid of garlic, several large red, white and, yellow onions and shallots. Barbara looked over at William, "What kind of sick joke is this?"

William grinned, "Didn't I tell you? Tonight I'm making Onion Focaccia, with creamy garlic bisque for the guests, they asked for a light meal and didn't want to go into town."

Looking green around the gills Barbara replied, "Well, I'm sorry to say you're on your own with that menu."

She headed out toward the apartment over the garage to lie down. It was getting dark and colder and it felt like it might rain, which, if it continued through the night, would make going to work in the morning no fun at all. "Maybe I'll call in sick." Barbara smiled to herself as she climbed the stairs to her room.

She showered, lay down on the four-poster bed and passed out.

CRYPTIC MESSAGE

When Barbara opened her eyes, her room was completely dark. She turned to look at the clock on the nightstand. It was 7pm. She got up, braided her hair and pinned it into a bun. She then dressed and headed outside and downstairs to the house. It was starting to sprinkle and very cold. There were no stars out this evening, but the air was perfumed with the smell of damp earth and wood smoke.

When she reached the bottom stairs she could hear laughter coming from the house. The front lawn was lit up with light streaming from the windows of the great room. Barbara looked in and saw eight people gathered around the great room's dining table. Not wanting to intrude, she headed around to the kitchen door. She tried to open it, but it was locked. Peering in the window she saw William and knocked lightly.

William opened the door. "Hey sleeping beauty, you hungry?"

The smell of garlic bisque and onions wafted through the open door and hit Barbara square in the face. "Wow, there will be no vampires around here tonight."

William laughed, "That's true, but just in case, you better eat some or you will be the only victim ."

There was a bright fire going in the kitchen fireplace and over it hung a medium-sized kettle filled with a steamy amber liquid. Barbara walked over to the fire to warm up, bent over and took a whiff from the steaming kettle. "Hot apple cider, yum." She reached for a ladle that was hanging from a hook on the right side of the fireplace, grabbed a cup from the mantel and ladled out a generous portion. "Oh this will definitely hit the spot."

She held the cup close to her mouth and nose, breathed in the fragrance and took a sip. Cup in hand, Barbara walked to a corner of the kitchen where she could peek into the great room at the crowd. They were happily enjoying William's feast.

The table was beautifully set with Royal Sultan china and hand-blown wine glasses. Two pewter three-candle candelabras lit each end of the table and several smaller crystal tea light holders flickered at the center. "The table looks beautiful, William. When did you find the time to do it all?"

William was busy putting out cheese and fruit on a narrow silver platter. "You were asleep a long time, and they helped me set the table. They're a very casual crowd."

Just as William was about to speak, the same man that had played the piano last evening came into the kitchen. "Ah, I thought it was you peering in the window." Barbara blushed and looked over at William.

She extended her now warm hand to the man.

"Hello."

"Hello, my name is Parker." He shook her hand as he spoke.

"I'm Barbara and you have met William."

He turned to look at William, "The meal was perfect, William. Absolutely delicious!"

William smiled and headed toward the dining room carrying the platter of fruit and cheese. "This certainly is a lovely inn. Do you work here too?"

"No, I'm just here to help William. He is the true hired hand here."

"Ah, well, he will be happy to know the theater was quite back to normal today. No cold spots. No, it was relatively serene in there."

Parker stood holding his wine glass. "Did you know we will be holding auditions here this weekend?"

Barbara walked to the nearby table and sat down. "Yes, we heard the advertisement for it on the radio today. Sounds like a big deal."

"It is a big deal for the few lucky people who get picked. They will be part of a life-changing experience." Parker walked over to the fireplace and stared into the flickering light for several minutes. "I'm going to make a big assumption here. I'm going to assume that you and William know this place is haunted."

Barbara looked over at Parker who was leaning toward the fire with one hand braced on the mantel. William walked into the room, looked over at Barbara who gave him a strange look. He then looked over at Parker who turned toward William. "William, I was just saying to Barbara that the theater did not have the same chill as it did last night. It seems your ghost was rather happy with our use of the theater today."

Once again, William looked over at Barbara who remained quiet. William got his wine glass from the center island and sat down in front of Barbara. "I'm not surprised, Parker. Lilly was quite a good opera singer."

Barbara's mouth dropped open. She did not think sharing information about Lilly was a good thing, especially with a stranger.

"An Opera Singing Ghost, well that is very special. Do you think she can be persuaded to sing for us?"

William remained remarkably unfazed by this man's calm demeanor. "I'm not sure Parker, but I would be respectful when in the theater. She has been communicating with us lately and seems to be bent on getting our help. So, I think respect and understanding of this lovely soul would be the best approach." Parker nodded and held his glass up, "To Lilly."

William held his glass up and replied, "To Lilly."

They both looked over at Barbara who held her mug up to toast as well. "Well," Parker said as he put his now empty glass on the kitchen island, "All that fine food and wine and this warm fire has made me incredibly tired. I'm off to bed."

He walked back into the dining room and bid his friends good night. Within minutes, they all got up from the table. Some moved to sit at the fireplace and some to the theater.

Barbara started clearing the table when out of the corner of her eye she saw Garrett peering through the dining room window. She smiled and motioned for him to come in. She watched as he passed by the windows toward the kitchen. She heard the kitchen door open and William greeted Garrett. Within a flash he was next to her pulling wine glasses from the table. "Hi Garrett, I'm so sorry I forgot to call you to cancel lunch today." She headed to the kitchen with him in tow. "I had to go to work today and will need to go again tomorrow."

Garrett put down his load and helped Barbara with hers. "Work? Where are you working?"

"I am working part-time in Bickersburg at the Stone Hill Inn. There is a famous chef who runs the kitchen there and I'm working under him with the hopes of learning more about French cuisine."

Garrett got very quiet and went back to the table for another load of dishes as did Barbara.

"I'll be working again tomorrow and Saturday, but probably not Sunday and only in the mornings."

Garrett seemed to be in thought and did not reply.

"Garrett, did you hear me?"

He put down his dishes and walked over to the kitchen fireplace. Noticing the cider and mugs, he poured himself some and walked over to Barbara.

"I have never seen the painting of Lilly that hangs in the Stone Hill, but I have always wanted to."

William overhearing this joined them. "Well that's perfect then."

"What's perfect William?"

"Well, you need a ride tomorrow morning and Garrett has never seen that painting of Lilly."

"William, Garrett's not going to hang around all day waiting for me to get off work."

At this Garrett moved to the island behind William who was doing dishes, "Actually, I have a few things I need in Bickersburg. There is an artist supply store there that I go to every now and again, and I'm in need of some paints for a portrait I'm working on."

William turned around drying his hands on a dish towel. "It's settled then, she needs to be at work by 10am."

Garrett smiled looking over at Barbara, "Is that o.k. with you Barbara?"

"It's o.k. with me, but I don't think you're gonna spend five hours in an artist supply store."

Garrett laughed, "Oh you'd be surprised at how much time I can spend in one of those places. Besides, I really do want to see that painting."

Barbara was secretly thrilled to have a chance to spend time alone with Garrett. She wanted to get to know him better and driving together would be a perfect opportunity.

Garrett got up and looked at his watch, "Can I use your phone? Mine is charging right now."

William motioned toward the kitchen phone and Garrett proceeded to dial. "Hello, Martha? This is Garrett, listen I need to reschedule tomorrow's sitting, can I come by later, say around 4:30?"

Barbara and William could hear an older woman's voice coming over the receiver. "Don't worry Martha, I won't forget. What? The lighting? No, it will be just fine, remember I always bring my own lights. Uh huh, that's right. Alright, I'll see you tomorrow afternoon and I'll call to remind you."

Garrett hung up the phone and looked up to see both William and Barbara had been listening. "Oh, that was Martha. I'm painting her portrait. Her family commissioned me this past month and I couldn't refuse. Martha is one of our oldest citizens here in Romney. She'll be 101 next month."

Barbara was touched by Garrett's enthusiasm.

He walked over to Barbara, "Maybe you could come with me tomorrow after work, if you're not too tired. Martha is a wonderful historian. She can tell you the history on any building in town.

Barbara was charmed by his description of Martha and loved listening to older people talk about their past. She looked up at Garrett, "I'd love to meet her."

"That will be great! She loves meeting new people too."

The cuckoo chirped nine times and the people sitting in the great room in front of the fireplace headed upstairs to their rooms. Barbara went out to the table in the great room and using a curved metal krummer, removed all the crumbs from the tablecloth. She pulled the cloth taught and pushed in the chairs but before she pushed the last one in, William came out of the kitchen holding a small casserole dish filled with a hot steaming bread pudding. Garrett followed in with three plates, three forks and a small pitcher filled with a hot, sweet-whiskey sauce. It was then Barbara realized how hungry she was. She hadn't eaten any of the garlic bisque which in retrospect was a good thing. "After all," she thought, "one never knows when one might have a close encounter."

Garrett pulled out a chair for Barbara who smiled and thanked him. "What kind of bread pudding is it?"

Garrett and William had both sat down and William started to serve. "It's Brandied Pear Pudding, and be careful, ouch! It's hot!"

The pudding steamed as William pulled three healthy-sized

servings from the deep casserole dish. He pushed a plate toward Garrett who pushed it toward Barbara who thanked him and reached for the pitcher of whiskey sauce.

Before starting his pudding, William pushed the Victrola from across the room next to the table. He put on a recording of arias sung by the famous tenor Giuseppe Ruscello. They listened as *Recondita Armonia* from Puccini's *Tosca* played.

They sat eating their bread pudding and listening to the ancient recording with its romantic phrasings and lush accompaniment. Emotions expressed in song and pressed into wax more than 100 years ago were sending vibrations through the room and through each person sitting there. Barbara stopped eating and listened, as did Garrett and William. The profound power this aria has over all that heard it was awesome, whether it was recorded long ago or today. It has the ability to silence large audiences and hold the attention of people who did not even like opera. That was the power of this amazing art form and of course, Puccini. Once the aria had stopped, Barbara brought her plate into the kitchen and retrieved Thomas Moore's diary off the small bookshelf. She laid it on the table and pushed it over to Garrett who pushed it back to her. "It's your turn."

Barbara looked over to William who nodded in agreement. William got up and pulled the needle from the edge of the recording, closed the lid and rolled it back against the wall.

Barbara opened the diary and leafed past the pages they had read. Some of the pages were slightly damaged by brown water marks and the writing was somewhat obscured. After about ten pages she stopped. Pressed between the pages were the remains of three violets. Carefully she slid them toward the bottom of the page so she could read.

April 5th 1871

The air has become scented by early spring blossoms and the surrounding mountains are dotted with blooming Sarvis trees. The apple and cherry trees are in full bloom which has caused some concern. We are all holding our breath hoping it won't frost again, but I'm afraid it's bound to happen as we haven't had a spring this early for as long as I can remember. I am starting my third painting of Mrs. Lilly and am happy to say the sweet Spring air and warmth have brought a blush of color into her cheeks that I haven't seen all winter. Her baby boy is walking and she and her servant chase him from room to room. Her husband, Viscount LeClaire, has been away a good deal and we have had many visitors from Washington stay here, giving Mrs. Lilly a chance to sing and socialize.

Today, she was dressed in a pale yellow gown with beautiful lace around her shoulders and a string of pearls around her neck. There is a vase of apple blossoms and golden forsythia at her side and flower petals at her feet.

We are painting in the theater which has become Lilly's sanctuary. I hope her happiness continues as it has illuminated every corner of the house. T.M.

Simultaneously they looked over at the painting over the fireplace. Barbara was the first to walk over. She turned on the main light and stared at the painting. A feeling of amazement went through her as she took a closer look. On the pedestal was the vase of flowers described in the diary, she was wearing the yellow dress, the string of pearls and the blush of color in her cheeks was quite apparent. Barbara put her hands to her mouth and shook her head from side to side. Garrett and William joined her in front of the painting and looked at it with a renewed interest.

"I feel so much more connected to Lilly now. I mean it's as though we were there when he painted it."

As they stood in front of the painting, the smell of linseed filled the room. Barbara whispered to William and Garret, "Smell that?"

They both nodded yes in silence. Then looking up, the painting took on a freshness of contrast and color. Garrett reached to touch it, pulled back his fingers and looked to see wet paint on them. William reached up to touch the painting too, but before he could touch it the electric lights in the room started to flicker and finally went out. The only lights left in the room were the candles on the table and the fireplace and they both seemed to dim simultaneously. The room got very cold. Barbara reached for William and Garrett, who huddled close to her each holding one of her hands.

A blue light shone in front of the main entrance to the house. In this light three figures started to materialize. There were two women and a small child. One of the women wore a bonnet and seemed to be talking to the other woman. They watched as the woman wearing the bonnet hugged the other woman. She then picked up the child, hugged him, put him down and left through a doorway. The child tried to run after the woman in the bonnet, but the other woman held him back. She picked him up and rocked him back and forth wiping tears from the child's face. Holding the child, she waved and as she did, the scene faded from view.

The room had become extremely cold now and an unnatural silence seemed to suffocate the sound of the crackling fire, the kitchen clock and even the sound of their own breathing.

Barbara was frozen with fear and started to shiver. Garrett moved his arm around her shoulder and leaned closer to her. From upstairs they heard a door open. Then they heard someone slowly come down the stairs. A robed figure stopped at the bottom. It was Parker, the man who had come into the kitchen earlier. He looked over at them with a blank expression on his face then passed in front of them and up to the front door. He then spoke in a loud whisper, "She's gone to Washington to sing for the President. She must come back before her husband, the Viscount returns. If he finds out that she has disobeyed him, he will never let her sing again and if Mrs. Lilly isn't allowed to sing, you may as well kill her."

Parker turned and looked into Garret's eyes, then turned and walked slowly back up the stairs and as he did, the shroud of heavy air slowly lifted and the room came back to life. The flames in the fireplace grew bright. They cracked and popped, sending hot embers onto the hearth. The flames on the table candles grew tall and fat and the overhead light and surrounding lights blinked on, flooding the room with light. The sound of heavy rain falling on the old tin roof filled the house with a soft sweet rhythmic hum, but Barbara, William, and Garrett all stood silent.

Barbara, leaning into Garrett, was still clutching both William's and Garrett's hands. From the kitchen, the chirping cuckoo broke the spell. William released Barbara's hand, bent down to put a log on the fire and then swept the embers from the hearth and threw them back into the fire.

Garrett was still holding onto Barbara who was only just starting to feel the circulation come back into her hands. She pulled away and sat down in the wingback chair in front of the fireplace. Garrett grabbed a throw from the hall tree and placed it around Barbara's shoulders, then retrieved one of the Windsor chairs from around the dining table and pulled it next to Barbara. "I can't be sure," he said as he sat down, "But I think I just heard my great, great grandfather speak to us."

William sat down in the other wingback chair and stared into the fireplace along with Barbara and Garrett for several moments before Barbara spoke.

"Why do all ghostly messages have to be so cryptic? Couldn't she just tell us what she wants us to do? She looked over at Garrett who was caught off guard by what she said, but at the same time nodded his head in agreement. William leaned his head into his hand, and turned to look at Barbara. "You make a good point, however, let's remember that Lilly is an actress and singer. It would be out of character for her to just tell us what she wants us to do. As an actress, she wants us to understand what she went through, emotionally and physically. Besides, don't you find yourself compelled to find out more?"

William straightened himself. "No, I think we must be patient and clever and appreciative of the fact that we were 'chosen' to help her."

At that, William rose out of the deep wingback chair, stretched, turned, and headed to the dining room table to clean off the dishes from the bread pudding.

Garrett slowly followed suit, rose and stretched. "I'll pick you up around 9, o.k?"

Barbara held up her hand to Garrett who pulled her slowly up from the low wingback chair. As she rose up, he pulled her to him and held her. His chin rested on top of her head which fit perfectly and snugly against his chest. He tenderly stroked her hair and took a deep breath whispering, "As far as I'm concerned, Lilly can take her time."

Barbara pulled back and looked up at Garrett, smiling. Still holding his hand, she walked toward the kitchen to the back door where Garrett had hung his coat. "Well, I'll see you in the morning."

Barbara opened the door and Garrett walked outside onto the back porch. "Good night, Barbara."

Once again, he walked backward off the porch, he smiled

and waved then turned and headed around the house and into the dark, rainy night. Barbara closed the door and leaned against it. Feeling warm and euphoric she closed her eyes and relived Garrett's embrace, remembering his clean cedar-like smell and his warmth.

"Love is a many-splendored thing, Barbara."

Barbara opened her eyes and found William standing in front of her. She couldn't wipe the smile from her face. "Is that what you think this is, love?"

William returned her smile, "Well, I can't be sure, but you do seem to be floating rather high right now."

Barbara laughed and gave William a hug and kiss on the cheek. "Oh William, there is so much going on right now. I don't know whether it is love or not, but one thing is for sure. I haven't felt this alive since I discovered you were my brother."

William smiled and walked into the great room to turn off the lights and stoke the fire. Once back in the kitchen he pulled a large flashlight from the pantry shelf, grabbed his coat and headed out the kitchen door with Barbara in tow, up to the garage apartments. Just as Barbara opened the door to her room she looked over at William and said, "What am I gonna do if this really is love?"

William replied in a brotherly voice, "Don't worry about what you're 'gonna' do. If it's love, and the right love for you, then nothing you can do will change the way it is to be."

Barbara tilted her head, looking at William, "What?"

"Never mind. Just get some rest."

Hot Spiced Apple Juice

Servings: 16

Easy and so wonderful when it's cold out. You can do the same with apple cider.

When you entertain, you can leave the large pot of spiced juice on my stove. Turn off the heat from time to time so it doesn't get too hot but am careful to keep it warm. You could also use a crock pot.

1 gallon apple juice
2 sticks cinnamon, whole
20 whole cloves
1 medium apple, any kind

- Pour the gallon of apple juice into a large non-reactive pot, like stainless steel. Save the jug it came in case you have some left over.

- Heat over medium flame until the juice starts to steam.

- Meanwhile, stick the cloves in the bottom of the apple around the base so it floats with the clove sides down.

- Place the apple into the juice and add the cinnamon sticks. Do not allow juice to boil but continue heating over low heat until ready to serve. Juice should heat for at least 15 minutes before serving so cloves and cinnamon can contribute flavor.

Serve in mugs.

Serving Ideas: This hot apple juice goes great with apricot brandy. About 1/2 shot per cup of apple juice.

Brandied Pear Bread Pudding with Whiskey Butter Sauce

Servings: 10

Wonderful texture and flavors.

The whiskey sauce is optional, delicious but high in calories. For a lower calorie option, pour the canned pear juice into a small pan. Add equal amounts of low-fat milk and heat 'til just hot. Spoon over your pudding.

1 pound whole grain bread, cubed
1/2 cup sugar
1/4 cup brandy
4 cups canned pears, 1 large can drained and cubed or fresh, (see note)
1/2 cup raisins
2 eggs
1/2 teaspoon salt
1 1/2 cups evaporated milk
1/2 cup sour cream
1 tablespoon vanilla
1 teaspoon cinnamon

- Place raisins in a cup and pour brandy over and allow to soak.

- Cube the bread and place in a bowl large enough to mix

all without spilling.

- In a medium bowl mix sugar, salt, evaporated milk, sour cream, eggs, vanilla and cinnamon. Stir to dissolve the salt and sugar and blend all together.

- Pour raisin and brandy mixture into the egg mixture and pour all of this over the bread.

- Add the chopped pears and stir to mix but don't over stir as this will turn the bread to mush.

- Butter a large 9x13 baking dish. I like to use glass or stone so edges don't get burned. Place in a 400 degree oven for 35 to 45 minutes. Check the middle to be sure it is not too mushy. It should be a little moist. Remove and serve warm.* (See note for pear juice concoction.)

NOTE: If using fresh pears, peel and core. Place 2 pears in a small pan of 1/2 cup water. Add 1 tablespoon brown sugar, cover, and cook until just tender, about 5 minutes. Remove pears from pan and cube.

WHISKEY BUTTER SAUCE
4 tablespoons unsalted butter
1/3 cup sugar
1 large egg
1/4 cup heavy cream
1/4 cup bourbon whiskey

- Melt butter in the top of a double boiler set over simmering water.

- Beat the sugar and egg in a small bowl until well blended.

- Stir the egg mixture into the butter.

- Add the hot water and stir until the mixture coats the back of a spoon, about 7 minutes.

- Remove from the double boiler and let cool to room temperature.
- Stir in the cream and whiskey using a whisk.

RAINDROP CONCERTO

Barbara was awakened by the sound of rain coming down hard on the tin roof above her room. On the floor near the door stood a small oscillating space heater which was glowing red and blowing hot air to little effect. The room was freezing cold and Barbara had already stacked every blanket in the closet on her bed.

The clock on the nightstand glowed brightly in the dim morning light. It was after 8am. There was a light tapping on the door, then William called out. "Barbara, you better get up or you won't have time for breakfast."

Barbara answered, "I'm up, I'm up."

She moved the small heater to the bathroom and shut the door. It should at least be able to warm up that little space. Barbara pulled a silk undershirt and a turtleneck shirt from her drawer. Then, from the closet she retrieved a beautiful knit vest that had different birds embroidered in yarn down the front panels. It was a long vest that hung half way down to her knees. This, and thick corduroys would help to keep out the cold. She dashed into the now-warm bathroom, washed, dressed, and pulled her hair out of the previous day's braid and brushed it. It was full of waves and hung just below her shoulders. Barbara stepped outside onto the small porch and put on her rain jacket, pulling the hood over her head. She carefully climbed down the slick wooden stairs and made her way around the front of the house to the side kitchen entrance where she found William pulling a large baking pan of cinnamon rolls from the oven. Barbara removed her coat and hung it on a hook in the pantry, "Man it's cold!" She poured herself a cup of coffee adding cream and sugar and walked over to the fire William had built in the kitchen. She stood with her back to the hot blaze and watched as William inverted the hot pan of rolls onto a large square stone platter that looked like a throwback to the sixties. Hot, melted sugar and cinnamon poured from the pan and oozed down the sides of the sticky rolls. A heavenly fragrance filled the kitchen making Barbara crazy for a taste.

William picked up the tray and headed to the dining room. "Hey, where you going with those?"

Just before William entered the great room he turned and said, "Not to worry, there is another large pan in the oven, I'll pull it out in a minute."

Barbara could hear the oo's and ah's from the people at the table. William certainly was giving them their money's worth. She peered in from a discreet corner of the kitchen. She could see Parker sitting among his peers, none the worse for wear.

"He probably has no idea what happened to him last night. Probably thought it was just some dream. In truth, it kind of was."

Barbara heard a light tapping at the kitchen door and turned to see Garrett standing there getting drenched by an intense downpour. She motioned for him to come in and in so doing gave away her hidden position. Parker looked over from the table and waved. Barbara waved back and moved toward the oven to check on the progress of the cinnamon rolls. Garrett, like Barbara, helped himself to coffee and stood by the fire with his back to it and watched as Barbara opened the oven. A cloud of grey smoke rose from the oven that smelled of burning sugar.

"Uh oh! These are starting to burn!" She frantically looked around for oven mitts finding them only just as William came back into the kitchen.

"Where are the pot holders?"

"They're behind you hanging off the island." William reached down and handed the mitts to Barbara who pulled the hot pan from the oven and onto the island behind her. She looked at the rolls, then back at the oven.

"I don't actually think they burned, I think some of the sugar ran over the edge of the pan and landed on the bottom of the oven."

The sweet fragrance of the cinnamon covered the burning sugar, making Garrett crazy for a sample. He sat on a stool at the island. "I sure hope you burned them so you can't give them to the guests."

William chuckled, "Better than that, these are for us."

Within the hour, Barbara and Garrett were heading toward Bickersburg in his Jeep. The rain had subsided and Barbara noticed that the creeks alongside the roads had risen quite a bit and most of the trees that were so brightly colored yesterday had been stripped by the heavy rains, giving the forest floor a brilliant multi-colored carpet. Garrett looked over at Barbara as she looked at the rain-washed landscape. "We really needed the rain."

Barbara turned to him, "Everywhere you look is like looking at a painting. I'm surprised you don't paint more landscapes."

Garrett replied, "I've tried painting landscapes, but never really felt the passion I feel when I paint portraits." He reached up to a CD holder above his head, pulled down a compact disk and put it into the player. It was Chopin's *Raindrop Prelude*.

Barbara listened to the delicate music for a moment, then she turned to Garrett again. "See, to me this piece is written about a beautiful landscape. I can see the stream, the golden fields, the rain."

Garrett, listened and nodded, then started the track over again. "Close your eyes."

Barbara closed her eyes and listened to the music and to Garrett's voice.

(Track 13 starts over.)

"Picture a lady with raven black hair and alabaster skin sitting near a window."

The music of Chopin laced between Garrett's words as he spoke slowly with the ebb and flow of the music. "Beams of gold-flecked sunlight pour down upon her. She radiates love and warmth. Gazing at her and not fearing for looking too long, I see her face as only he has seen her face. The sharp angle of her cheeks, the soft roundness of her lips, the weave of the eyebrow, the length of her lash. By just looking, I know the smoothness of her long neck and the softness of her earlobes where a ruby earring dangles. Lingering longer my eyes follow under her stubborn chin, down to her soft and full…"

Garrett was interrupted by the ringing of Barbara's cell

phone. She had been entranced by his words and the music and jumped, opening her eyes when it rang. She answered it. "Hello?"

"Barbara? This is Chef George."

"Ah,… hello Chef."

"Are you on your way?"

Barbara was coming around now, but starred at Garrett as she spoke. "Yes, I am on my way and should be there on time."

"Listen, I need you to work late today. I will of course pay you for your time. I'm not going to be there when you get there, but Doris will tell you what you need to do."

Barbara snapped, "Oh, hey listen, I don't think I can. I have a friend picking me up and…. Hello? Hello? Damn it! I mean, darn it."

She folded up her phone and put it back in her purse and looked forward at the road trying to regain her composure. Garrett had turned the music down and waited for signs of revival from Barbara who was in deep thought. She looked over at him with a deep intensity. "What?" he said, feeling her gaze. She looked back at the road. "I couldn't ask you to wait all day for me to get off work. You had better just head back after your errands. I can call William to pick me up."

"I don't mind picking you up."

Barbara looked back at Garrett who smiled at her. "No, I'll be o.k., I'll call William."

Garrett turned to her again, "Look Barbara, if it's all the same to you, I'd really like to pick you up, if that's o.k.?"

Barbara wasn't sure she wanted Garrett to pick her up. Listening to his intimate description of Lilly made her feel as though she was intruding. It made her feel like "the other woman."

They drove in silence for about 10 minutes before Garrett spoke. "I sense something is wrong. I'm sorry if I've upset you."

Barbara was moved by his sincere tone of voice and felt compelled to speak her mind, "I'm o.k. Garrett, but I must be honest, your description of Lilly has made me feel like an intruder in an intimate relationship and I'm not really sure how to respond."

There was more silence, then Garrett reached over for Barbara's hand. "Please, just know that you are the only person, well, you and William, to know me for who, or rather why I am the way I am." He held her hand tightly as he spoke. "I have been under the influence of a beautiful, but long-dead, opera singer my entire life."

"I have never been able to be totally honest in a relationship because of this. You, Barbara, know everything." He released her hand and looked forward. Barbara felt sorry she had spoken so abruptly, she reached over for his hand and held it the rest of the drive. As they pulled up to the Stone Hill, the sun broke through the clouds and brightened both their moods and the surrounding scenery. Garrett got out with Barbara and walked with her into the restaurant. Doris was standing at the hostess podium drinking her juice and reading the paper. She looked up at Barbara then at Garrett. "Good morning, Barbara."

"Good morning, Doris. I'd like you to meet my friend Garrett."

Doris smiled for the first time Barbara had seen and reached to shake Garrett's hand. "Very nice to meet you. Are you from around here?"

Barbara smiled as Garrett answered Doris. He was very handsome and so friendly and down to earth that women immediately "crushed" on him.

Barbara reached for Garrett's hand and headed toward the dining room. "Listen Doris, before I start, I want to show Garrett the painting in the main dining room."

Doris got up from her stool, "Which painting?"

"The singing woman."

Doris sat back down, "Oh, well, I'm sorry, but it's not there anymore."

Both Barbara and Garrett stopped dead in their tracks and turned to Doris, "What do you mean it's not there anymore?" Barbara walked up to Doris.

"Chef George took it down."

"Why?"

At this Doris lowered her voice and came closer to Barbara, "I think Chef George is losing his mind."

"What? Why?"

Garrett had moved closer as well, causing Doris to re-evaluate telling why. But his good looks brought him into her favor. She looked around, then whispered, "He says she is haunting him."

Barbara and Garrett looked at each other then back to Doris, who took their exchange the wrong way,

"Look, I'm sorry, I probably shouldn't have told you that. Chef George has been under a lot of pressure this past week. He took it down last night and I'm not sure where he put it."

Garrett looked concerned, "Did he mention selling the painting?"

Doris looked at Garrett with suspicion. "Are you an art dealer or collector?"

Garrett grinned his captivating grin and reassured Doris that he was not an art dealer. He spoke honestly and told her he had always wanted to see the painting. He told Doris of the other painting at Whippoorwill Ridge. Doris looked over at Barbara, "You didn't tell me there was another painting."

"I'm sorry Doris, it just never came up."

Doris looked at both Barbara and Garrett, "I think Chef George would want to know about the other painting, don't you?"

Garrett and Barbara looked at each other then at Doris, "Why would he want to know?" At this there was a loud clanging sound coming from the kitchen causing Doris to run to investigate.

Garrett looked at Barbara and walked to the door. "I am picking you up tonight. He opened the door and turned, "Just call me an hour before you get off work."

Barbara smiled and through the front window watched as he walked back down the sidewalk to his jeep.

William's Cinnamon Rolls

Servings: 24

A wonderful complex dough. Chewy, and perfect for cinnamon and butter.

ROLLS
2 packages dry yeast
1/4 cup lukewarm water
1/2 cup sugar
1 teaspoon salt
3/4 cup milk, scalded
2 large eggs, beaten
1 teaspoon grated lemon rind
4 cups all purpose flour, pre-sifted
1/2 teaspoon mace or cardamom, ground
1/2 cup butter

FILLING
1/2 cup butter, melted
1 cup sugar
3 tablespoons cinnamon

TOPPING
2 cups powdered sugar
1/2 teaspoon vanilla or lemon extract, your choice
3 tablespoons milk

- Pour water into a medium-sized bowl and add 1/2 teaspoon of sugar from the 1/2 cup sugar called for in this recipe. Whisk and place in microwave for 15 seconds. Water should be warm, but not hot.

- Add yeast to water and whisk to incorporate.

- Heat milk in a small saucepan over a medium high heat. Watch as milk creeps up the side of the pan, but shut off before it reaches the top.

- Pull from heat and add the butter, lemon rind, sugar, cardamom or mace and salt. Allow this mixture to cool for about 10 minutes, until you can touch the side of the pan comfortably. While waiting, find a deep mixing bowl. I like to use clay or ceramic. Apply butter to the walls of the bowl and set aside.

- Add the yeast mixture to the bowl of an electric mixer.

- Add the beaten eggs to the lukewarm milk and whisk to incorporate.

- Add this to the yeast mixture start to mix using a dough hook attachment.

- Add the flour one half cup at a time until you get to the last cup. If dough is still very sticky still, add another 1/2 cup of four. Check dough again. If it is still sticky add more flour a tablespoon at a time. The key is to have a moist dough but not too dry. If it's dry it won't rise the way you want it to. You may use less flour than the recipe calls for, or you may need to add a tablespoon or two more. Once dough is at the right consistency continue mixing for one minute. If you were making the dough by hand you would be kneading for 10 minutes.

- Once dough is mixed, pull from the mixing bowl and place into the buttered clay bowl. Turn dough once to coat top with butter.

- Cover with plastic wrap and place in a draft-free area.

- Allow dough to rise for 1 1/2 to 2 hours. Dough should double in bulk. Grease two (9 x 1 1/2 inch) round baking pans.

- Once dough has risen, punch down, remove from bowl and place on a lightly-floured board or counter top.

- Cut dough in half and place half back into the bowl, cover.

- Using a rolling pin, roll remaining dough on floured surface to a thickness of just under 1/4 inch.

- In a small bowl mix together the sugar and the cinnamon.

- Use a pastry brush to apply melted butter to entire surface of dough. Be sure to brush butter out to the edges.

- Evenly sprinkle the buttered surface with the cinnamon and sugar. Starting at the end closest to you, fold the edge over and continue rolling until all the dough has been rolled into what looks like a rolled up rug.

- Cut into one and one half inch slices and place into the greased round baking pans.

- Repeat with second half of dough until both pans are filled.

- Allow to rise for 30 minutes. 5 minutes before this time is over, preheat oven to 350 degrees.

- Place both pans on the top or middle rack, one slightly back and the other forward and bake for 30 minutes. Rolls should be a light golden brown.

- Remove from oven and place on cooling rack.

- While cinnamon rolls are cooling, in a medium bowl, mix together the powdered sugar, vanilla or lemon and milk. Should be a thick syrup.

- Use a spoon to drizzle over the cooled cinnamon rolls.

  STICKY BUNS VARIATION: If you want to have very

sticky rolls, start by greasing your pans, then line with parchment paper.

- Top this parchment with a mixture of 1/2 cup butter and 1 teaspoon cinnamon and nuts if you like.

- Place the unbaked rolls onto the parchment and into the melted butter, cinnamon and nut mixture.

- Once pan is full, allow to rise for 30 minutes.

- Bake as directed above on either top rack in oven or middle, but never bottom.

- After 30 minutes remove from oven and allow to cool for 10 minutes.

- Using a butter knife run blade around the edges of the pan to loosen rolls from sides.

- Place a plate on top of the baking pan and invert. The rolls should come right out onto your plate.

- Remove the parchment and watch as the gooey syrup drips down the sides of these amazing rolls.

This is decadent and only recommended at special occassions! NOTE: You may want to place a cookie sheet under the baking pans as sometimes sticky buns run over the edge and burn at bottom of oven.

Serving Ideas: A good strong cup of coffee or tea.

ƒAVE THE BEAUTIFUL NIGHTINGALE

William had cleared away the morning dishes and was alone at Whippoorwill Ridge. The guests would be gone most of the day, as they had left for a scenic train ride that would take them along the Potomac River and deep into the West Virginia woods. They would see pre-Civil War homes and rare and beautiful bald eagles soaring above the river. There would be photo opportunities, as this particular train ride would be stopping at several scenic locations.

William had been up since 5:00am and was starting to fade. He stoked the great room fire, added another log and sat down in one of the two leather wingback chairs in front of the fireplace. He was attempting to put together a menu and wrote ideas down on a small pad of paper. The leather chair was warm from the fireplace and enveloped William who was losing the battle to stay awake. His heavy lids closed and he felt himself drift into sleep.

A scene unfolded within his dream that placed him outside of the old shed where he found so many of Lilly's things, only the shed was intact. The roof was not caved in and on the side of the shed stood a large carriage that gleamed with polish and craftsmanship. William was drawn by a rhythmic sound of metal being struck. He followed the sound and found himself inside the shed, not in the cellar of the shed, but the ground floor. It was a livery where the horses were stabled. Two men stood there watching as one man hammered a red-hot horse shoe on an anvil. Using large tongs, the man dipped the hot shoe into water where it hissed and sputtered.

The oldest of the three men rubbed his rough leathery hands and shook his head in disapproval. He pointed outside to the skies and became very animated. The youngest of the three seemed to be challenging him and proceeded outside carrying large leather harnesses. The surrounding trees and grasses were green like spring, but fog poured from each man's mouth as he spoke. It was cold and starting to rain. Every time the young man would strap on a part of the harness, the older man would remove it. The young man pushed the old man away in a defiant move. The older man just shook his head and walked away.

The dream shifted and William was sitting on a wooden bench in a garden. It was just before sunrise. The air was laced with the sweet smell of honeysuckle and large teacup-sized roses in pinks and yellows hung heavy with dew. Music and singing filled the air. It was Lilly. She was singing *Bailero* from Canteloube's *Chants d'Auvergne*.

For the first time in a lifetime of dreaming of her, he was able to call her by her name. "Lilly…"

He called her again and again, and her song became louder and closer. Then, as the first rays of morning broke through and hit the ground at William's feet, Lilly materialized from the ground up. As the light grew stronger, her image became brighter and more solid. Looking up into her eyes, William's heart overflowed with joy. It was in this blissful state her words passed to him. "You and I can never be, William, for I live on the other side and cannot cross over. And for you there is someone else just beyond the horizon."

Lilly extended her hand to William who stood up. He took her hand and held it. Her fingers were like ice and William could feel the cold penetrating his hand and move up his arm. He looked into her face and no longer saw a golden glow, but a bluish hue. Her eyes were saddened and hollowed and her words became thin and icy, "You must save her, William, or she will die, just as I died. Save the beautiful Nightingale."

William woke up shivering violently. He knelt down on the hearth and stoked the fireplace, adding several more logs as it had burned very low.

Still cold, he wrapped a blanket around his shoulders and stared into the fire as it hissed and popped from the still-damp firewood he had brought in that morning.

William kept thinking about the dream, afraid he would forget some important detail. He leaned forward placing his hands over his face and rubbed his eyes. He looked up at the painting of Lilly, "You know it would be a lot easier if you would tell me who it is I'm suppose to save."

He listened hoping to hear a response, but all he could hear was the hiss of the fire. "Fine, be that way." William rose from his chair and headed to the kitchen. He had slept for two hours and was going to have to hustle to get the appetizers made.

It was half past four and Barbara had been put to the task of peeling yams, Granny Smith apples and russet potatoes then slicing them very thin. It was a break from yesterday's smelly task, but was still tedious. At least today she was allowed to use a food processor to slice the potatoes and apples, making it go fairly quickly. After she was finished, she watched the sous chef assemble the first gigantic gratin in a large copper and nickel-plated square baking pan with large aluminum handles. First he layered the bottom of the pans with hot butter. Then came the layering of the potatoes. Like an efficient artist, Sous Chef Lawrence layered the yams on the bottom of the pan in a spiral. He sprinkled the first layer with sea salt, pepper and nutmeg. He then added a layer of apples in the same way, placing the slices in a spiral on top of the yams. He topped the apples with browned pork sausage and sprinkled freshly chopped sage over the sausage. Now, he layered the russet potatoes onto the sausage and with a pastry brush coated them with a thin layer of butter, salt and pepper. The last layer was be yams spiraled and on top he added a mixture of butter and orange juice, then a tablespoon of orange liqueur, a dash of salt and ground pepper and a handful of chopped pecans. Sous Chef Laurence asked Barbara to do as he did and between the two of them they completed the other two gratins and placed them all into the hot oven.

Barbara was starting to feel very tired and told Doris she was taking a break. "It's about time. You were starting to make us look bad." Doris guided a wealthy-looking couple back to their table.

Barbara needed some fresh air. She stepped outside and walked to the parking lot. It was pleasant outside, but it smelled like rain and felt like it too. She walked around the side of the Stone Hill to the parking lot in back where she had seen Chef George park a few days earlier. As she walked toward the lot, an old rusted-out Chevy drove slowly past her spewing noxious fumes.

Barbara saw the back stairs to the kitchen. She headed up the rickety wooden steps and was nearly to the top when a young girl with long dark hair walked quickly beside her then passed her, up the stairs and into the kitchen. Barbara slowed and watched as the girl passed her. She looked kind of familiar.

There was a small wooden deck at the top of the stairs and a rusted bar with an ashtray full of cigarette butts and a wine glass. Barbara sat on a stool next to the wooden railing and looked out over the lot and the beautiful meadow beyond. It felt good to sit down, but there was the danger that she wouldn't want to get up again. Within five minutes, the door to the kitchen opened and the same girl who had come up before, was standing speaking French to someone inside. Barbara could not understand a word, but could tell by the girl's body language that she was in a hurry to leave. Within seconds, the girl had shut the door, looked over at Barbara and headed back down the stairs and back to the old rusted car which was still running. Barbara knew she had seen this girl before but was confused as to where. She got up and was just about to go into the kitchen door when something caught her eye. Leaning with its front against the wooden rail of the landing facing outward, was the painting of the singing woman. It was completely soaked from the earlier rain. She pulled the large frame toward her so she could get a better look and sure enough, there was Lilly, out in the elements.

Barbara could not believe he would do this. "He must have really been scared." She thought, "But why is Lilly haunting him? What part does he play in all of this?" She laid the painting back against the railing and headed into the kitchen.

There was a feeling of frenzy in the kitchen because half the restaurant had been reserved for a private party. One hundred guests were coming and the staff seemed stressed by the absence of Chef George. Sous Chef Lawrence signaled for Barbara to uncover the chilled appetizer platters that had been prepared earlier. In a way, it was a blessing to be so busy, it made the time pass quickly.

When Barbara looked at the clock she was surprised to see it was nearly 7 pm and still no Chef George.

The large party kept the kitchen quite busy and the dessert was just about to be served when out of the corner of her eye, Barbara saw Chef George. He had come in the back door to the kitchen and walked into his office.

Barbara moved closer for a better look. She pretended to be picking something up from under a shelf in front of his door when she saw him reading a letter. His hands trembled as he read and he muttered under his breath. Barbara had stood up and was looking right at him when he violently crumpled the letter up and threw it into the trash. He picked up an empty wine glass and threw it right out his door. It smashed against the block wall near where Barbara was standing. She let out a yelp and ran from the door. For the next hour, Barbara didn't set foot near Chef George's office. She helped clean the counters and bus the tables.

It was nearing 9 when Doris told her she could go. "Oh shoot," she said as she looked at her watch, "I forgot to call Garrett to pick me up, It'll be 45 minutes before he gets here."

By now the restaurant was empty. The bus boys were turning chairs upside down on the tables for cleaning. Barbara walked into the bar near the entrance and ordered a glass of red wine, helping herself to a platter of miscellaneous appetizers left over from the large party. There were herbed crab cakes with a tangy caper sauce and cold sliced cucumbers with a smoked salmon, creamed cheese piped onto the tops and decorated with delicate dill leaves.

Barbara was so busy working that she had forgotten to eat and was stuffing her face quite efficiently when Chef George walked up to her.

"I see you like the crab cakes." He pulled up a stool and sat beside her.

Barbara's mouth was too full to answer so she brought her fingers to her lips and kissed them as if to say, "Magnifique!"

Doris brought in a bottle of wine, opened it and poured it into two glasses, offering Barbara one and the other to Chef George. She looked over at Chef George and said something in French which surprised Barbara, as she didn't know Doris spoke French. Their conversation was brief but enough to irritate Doris.

And while Barbara didn't understand French she did pick up the name Sarah. It was then it dawned on her that Sarah was the girl she saw on the landing earlier and that she was their waitress when she, William and Gertrude, ate there more than ten days ago. Doris walked off muttering what sounded like French obscenities and Chef George took a drink from his glass. "You should try this. It is one of my favorites."

Barbara sniffed her glass and rolled it around. Thin strands of wine clung to the side of the glass as she did this, indicating what William would call a touch of "character." She took a small sip and with it pulled air in through her teeth to oxygenate the taste, which turned out to be incredible. She raised her glass to him, but did not say a word.

The second sip Chef George took essentially finished his glass and he poured another one right off.

He took another drink and turned to Barbara, "So, my sous chef tells me you are quite a quick learner." He pulled a crab cake from the platter and put the entire cake in his mouth. Still chewing he said, "I appreciate your staying so long. As I'm sure you noticed, we were quite busy this evening."

Barbara again found herself with no words but this didn't seem to bother Chef George.

"Do you have children, Barbara?"

Barbara nearly fell off her chair at this one. "No, Chef, I don't have children."

"Well, you're lucky. I have a child, an ungrateful child who doesn't know what is good for her."

It was becoming obvious to Barbara that this was going to be a one-way conversation. She sat and sipped as he continued. "I am prepared to give my daughter an amazing culinary education. I have already enrolled her in one of the best culinary schools in New York and what does she do? She refuses to go. She tells me that she never wanted to be a chef and that I would know this if I listened to her."

He pulled out a pack of cigarettes and started to light one. At this Barbara stopped him. "I would really appreciate it if you wouldn't smoke around me." Chef George threw the cigarette down and drank more of his wine.

"Let me tell you something." He was very close to Barbara now, "I have listened to what she wants to do with her life and all I have heard for the past five years is indecision. She is nearly 22 years old and all she does is flit around town and sing in silly little shows that she puts on."

Barbara looked over at him. "What shows?"

"I don't know! Little programs that she puts on. She sings!"

In a flash Barbara realized who Sarah was. Sarah had been their waitress, but she had also been the girl she had heard sing with Garrett.

Barbara became defensive and flushed with anger. This time it was she who pushed herself into Chef George's face. "Have you heard you daughter sing?"

"Of course I have." He turned and faced his glass.

"When? When was the last time?"

"I don't know, it has been a while," he laughed, "She told me she wants to audition for the Washington Opera." He turned toward Barbara, "Where does she get off thinking that she can just go off and audition, and for what? They probably wouldn't even let her in the chorus. And even if she got in, then what would she do?" He pulled a cucumber slice from the tray and shoved it into his mouth, "No, she has to be realistic. She is not getting any younger."

Barbara's blood started to boil. She got up and stood on the other side of Chef George. "You are a fool, a chauvinistic fool."

Chef George fired back, "What do you know about it?"

Barbara held her ground and in a calm voice said, "I'll tell you what I know about it! I heard your daughter sing not three nights ago, and let me tell you she was amazing! The audience gave her a standing ovation!"

"Where did you hear her? Why didn't you tell me?" Chef George's eyes twitched with anger.

"I didn't know she was your daughter! I only just now made that connection."

Chef George raised his voice, "Well, it doesn't matter how she sings, she is going to culinary school!"

At this Barbara took the last sip from her glass, and again in her calm voice said, "It must be lonely hearing nothing and no one else but your own voice."

Chef George did not move but looked straight ahead.

Barbara moved back to where she was sitting. "You're gonna lose the only family you have because you won't take the time to listen, to hear what she wants, to help her to achieve her dreams. God knows it's hard enough to follow one's dreams, but without the support of her family, it's got to be hell!"

"Enough!" Chef George turned to her, "You don't know what hell is! I have worked my way from bus boy to executive chef. I had nothing when I started. I had to fight for everything I had! She doesn't have to go through that if she goes to school. She will come out on top and have a place to work!"

Barbara gathered up her things and headed toward the door.

"Why did you become a chef, huh? Was it the only choice you had? What did your father want you to be? Your daughter has a great gift, an amazing gift and passion enough to stand up to her stubborn father who is making it so much harder than it has to be. Shame on you, Chef George!"

Barbara pushed open the door and quickly walked down the sidewalk. Just as she reached the parking lot, both Garrett and William pulled up in the Jag. Garrett got out and held the door to the front open for her. She did not even look at him, she just got in. Garrett, sensing something, closed her door then opened the back door and got in.

William looked over at her as she stared through the front windshield. "What's wrong?"

Barbara was still filled with anger when she got in the car but did not want to take it out on either William or Garrett. "I'm o.k, I just need a moment to pull myself together."

At this Garrett became alarmed, "Why, what happened? What did he do to you?"

William looked at Garrett in the rear view mirror, "Hang on Garrett, just give her a minute and I'm sure she'll tell us."

Barbara had tears streaming down her face, "William, pull around to the back of the restaurant."

Without question, William pulled around to the back. Barbara got out and walked up the stairs leading to the back door of the kitchen. She picked up the painting and carefully brought it down to the car. William and Garrett got out and opened the trunk. "Are we art thieves now?"

"No." She said as she loaded the painting face up in the car trunk, "Now, we are preservationists."

They drove in silence for several minutes before Barbara could bring herself to speak and when she did, tears rolled down her cheek. "Well, I'm happy to tell you that I won't be working for that jerk anytime soon."

William opened the glove box and handed her a tissue.

Barbara took the tissue, wiped her eyes and blew her nose. "That guy is such a chauvinist! So pig-headed!"

Barbara told them everything. How Sarah, the girl who waited on them when they first arrived was the same girl she had heard sing at the Coriander Café when she was with Garrett. That Sarah was Chef George's daughter and he in no way supported her dreams to sing. William himself became enlightened as he remembered his brief encounter just the day before. "I remember Sarah, I saw her in town yesterday when I was waiting to pick you up."

Barbara turned to William, "Sarah is going to audition for the Washington Opera."

William looked briefly away from the road and at Barbara. "Does that mean she is coming to Whippoorwill Ridge this weekend?"

Barbara unclenched her purse and sat it on the floorboard near her feet. "I don't know, he just said she was auditioning for the Washington Opera and what made her think she could actually get in?"

This time it was Garrett who spoke from the back seat. His voice came slowly, but cut through the engine noise, "Sarah must be a part of all this. I have been consumed with wanting to paint her. Every time I see her, I see Lilly and when she sings, I feel as though I am standing in Lilly's presence." Garrett's voice became strained. "I have spent so many years trying to forget about Lilly, and then I heard Sarah sing and was right back at square one." The engine's quiet hum filled the car as they took it all in.

"Well, I don't know about you two, but I'm looking forward to this weekend's auditions." William's words broke the spell of tension in the car and they chattered more freely the rest of the way.

When they arrived back at Whippoorwill Ridge, William pulled the painting from the trunk of the Jag and brought it into the house. The wooden frame was soaked through, but the canvas remained undamaged. He placed it on the mantel next to the other painting of Lilly and all three looked in silence for a long time.

Garrett was the first to speak, "I will call my sister in the morning, I think we should bring all of the paintings together. Perhaps it will give Lilly the strength to tell us what she needs us to do."

He walked to the front door opened it and turned to Barbara.

"I am going to be finishing that portrait of Martha tomorrow morning. I would love it if you could come with me."

Barbara looked over at William who nodded, "I'll be fine." She nodded to Garrett and watched as he got into his Jeep and drove up the hill.

Once inside, she and William sat at the kitchen table and spoke over a hot cup of herbal tea. William told Barbara about his dream of Lilly. His hands shook as he recounted how cold Lilly was and how like death she looked. Barbara reached over to steady William's hands. "The nightingale? Who is the nightingale? And did she really say there was someone for you just around the horizon? More cryptic clues. Well, I am at a loss and emotionally spent. Maybe it will come to us in our dreams."

At this, William looked up at Barbara, "I sure hope not."

Yam and Apple Gratin
with
Sausage, Potatoes and Pecans

Servings: 8

Full flavored, complete meal or holiday side dish. For vegetarians, replace sausage with more pecans.

3 large yams, peeled and sliced thin
2 medium Granny Smith apples, peeled and sliced thin
3 medium russet potato, peeled and sliced thin
1/2 pound ground pork sausage
1 teaspoon dry thyme
1 teaspoon fresh sage or half as much dry, chopped finely
1/4 cup orange juice (or juice from 1/2 orange)
1/8 cup butter, melted
1 tablespoon Grand Marnier, or brandy
1/2 teaspoon salt
1/2 teaspoon ground black pepper
1/2 cup pecans, chopped

- Brown sausage in large iron skillet, breaking up with a spatula into little granules. Once fat has rendered and sausage is no longer pink, but browned, scrape onto a paper towel and allow to drain.

- Drain oil from pan till there is only a thin coating remaining.

- Place butter in a small pan and add the thyme and orange juice. Keep over low heat so it is melted for use.

- Preheat oven to 400 degrees. Layer bottom of iron skillet in a spiral with yam slices until the entire bottom of pan is covered.

- Sprinkle with a little salt and pepper.

- Top this layer with apple slices, spiraled in the same manner.

- Top the apple slices with the browned sausage and add the chopped sage.

- Top the sausage with a layer of russet potatoes, layering them in a spiral.

- Coat this potato layer using half the butter and thyme mixture and a light sprinkle of salt and pepper.

- Top with a final layer of sweet potatoes, spiraling once again, then coat with remaining butter mixture.

- Add salt and pepper and sprinkle with the chopped pecans.

- Sprinkle the top with the Grand Marnier, cover with foil and bake for one hour.

- Remove cover and bake for 10 minutes more to brown the top. If it is not sufficiently browned, turn broiler on and broil for one to two minutes. Watch carefully so as not to burn.

- Remove from oven and allow to sit for 10 minutes before serving. Cut into wedges

  Serving Ideas: This dish can be served as a main course or a side dish at Thanksgiving.

  Suggested Wine: Chardonnay

Herbed Crab Cakes with Tangy Caper Sauce

Servings: 12

Preparation Time: 30 minutes

Light and wonderful, full flavored, a meal in itself. You can make bread crumbs using a food processor. Take French bread, slice it up and put slices through chute. If you don't have a food processor, you can use your coffee grinder. Just be sure to first run several pieces of bread through to clean out any residual coffee grounds. Makes great bread crumbs quickly.

CAPER SAUCE
1 cup mayonnaise
1/2 cup capers, drained
1/2 cup fresh parsley, chopped
1/2 cup fresh chives, chopped
2 tablespoons olive oil
1 tablespoon lemon juice

- Whisk all ingredients in medium bowl. Cover and refrigerate until ready to use. Can be made ahead.

CRAB CAKES
1 1/2 pounds crab meat
3 cups fresh bread crumbs, from French bread
1/4 cup fresh parsley, washed, dried and chopped very finely
1/4 cup spicy brown mustard

1/4 cup mayonnaise
1 large egg
1 1/2 teaspoons Old Bay™ seasoning
1/2 cup olive oil

For Crab Cakes:

- Combine crabmeat, breadcrumbs, parsley, mustard, mayonnaise, egg and Old Bay seasoning into a bowl. Mix until well blended. Form into small round cakes.

- Heat 1/4 cup olive oil in heavy large skillet over medium heat high heat. Working in batches, fry crab cakes until brown, adding more oil to skillet as needed, about 4 minutes per side. Place cooked crab cakes onto a paper towel to drain.

Serve cakes on a round platter, on a bed of curly kale, with caper sauce in a small bowl in the center.

Cedar Smoked Salmon Spread

Servings: 20

Preparation Time: 45 minutes

You can use leftover salmon grilled on a cedar plank. However, leftover baked salmon would work too.

If you want a fancy presentation, use a cake decorator icing bag and a large star tip. Fill the bag with the spread and place one star shaped "kiss" onto each cracker or cucumber.

1 cup sour cream
1 package cream cheese
8 ounces cooked salmon, grilled on a cedar plank is best
1 tablespoon lime juice, fresh
1 tablespoon horseradish
1 dash worcestershire sauce
1 dash black pepper
1 dash salt, to taste
1 dash paprika, for color
1 package fresh dill, for garnish
1 tablespoon capers, smaller berries
2 large cucumbers, peeled and sliced 1/4 inch thick

- Combine all ingredients, except the capers, dill, paprika and cucumber, in a food processor and blend until creamy. If your spread is very smooth, you can use a large icing decorator tip to pipe spread onto cucumbers (or) just smear on with a spreader. Sprinkle with paprika and a few capers then a sprig of dill. Beautiful and delicious.

Serve cold.

Serving Ideas: Serve rolled inside a small dill crepe. Pipe into a pea pod or into a celery rib.

MARTHA TELLS A STORY

The next morning when Barbara headed down from the apartment above the garage, she had to be especially careful as the stairs were covered with a heavy frost.

She could see where William had walked earlier and tried to stay within his footsteps. Looking out, the entire front lawn looked as though it was covered with snow. Barbara saw Garrett's jeep parked in the driveway. She walked around to the kitchen entrance and saw Garrett standing at the stove stirring a pan filled with local country sausage.

The fragrance pulled at Barbara's appetite making her mouth water. "I didn't know you could cook."

Garrett continued stirring, scraping the bits of dark brown sausage from the bottom of the thick cast-iron pan. "Oh, I don't do much cooking but I can keep food from burning if asked nicely."

Barbara stole a few crumbles from the paper towel where the cooked sausage was draining.

"Man that's good."

"Of course it's good, it's as fresh as it gets."

He turned the stove off and scraped the rest of the cooked sausage onto the absorbent paper. "Where's William?"

Garrett poured two cups of coffee. "He's helping in the theater. Guess the auditions are today. Phone's been ringing off the hook since I got here."

"Ah ha! I knew it was going to be a bigger deal than he let

on. What's he doing in there?"

Garrett headed over to the table with the sausage in one hand and coffee in the other. Already there was a tall stack of buttered raisin toast in a basket lined with a red and white checkered cloth.

"Dunno." He bit into the crunchy toast and looked over at Barbara who had joined him.

"What time do we need to be at Martha's house?"

Garrett looked at his watch and with his mouth full said, "Now, you better eat something."

Within minutes they were headed into town. The skies were clear and the sun had reached above the mountain ahead causing great shafts of light to illuminate the tops of the surrounding mountains. The fields that were riddled with rows of corn stalk stubs sparkled with the heavy frost that had fallen. It was crisp and clear and smacked of the approaching Thanksgiving holiday.

They crossed a large blue-painted steel bridge that was suspended over a narrow part of the south branch of the Potomac River and headed up the final rise into town. Barbara looked over to see a hillside studded with very old looking headstones. "What's that?" she asked.

Garrett looked out through her window. "That's Indian Mound Cemetery and those stones are probably from the Civil War." He slowed the jeep down considerably. "Speed trap," he said as they crept past the elementary school and into town.

It was Saturday morning and this normally quiet town was bustling with folks doing their weekend errands.

In front of a row of shops were whiskey barrels overflowing with mums and pumpkins. They stopped at one of two stoplights in town. Looking right, Barbara saw the shop William had mentioned earlier, Anderson's Corner. Its windows were warm and inviting, filled with beautiful home décor, gifts and wine. Just outside the entry hung a colorful autumn flag and a hand-painted sign swung back and forth over the sidewalk. There were people going in leaving the door open just far enough to capture Barbara's attention.

Garrett looked over at the shop, too. "That's a great little shop. Have you been in there yet?"

"No, but William told me about it. I definitely want to go before I head back." Barbara felt a pang of regret at these words and looked over at Garrett who did not respond.

The light turned green and they headed east through town ,passing buildings that were nearly as old as the B&B. In front of the courthouse stood a large plaque. Barbara could only make out the name Robert E. Lee.

"So much history here," she said as they approached the West Virginia School for the Deaf and Blind. It looked like an old plantation with great buildings and graceful trees. Garrett pulled down a narrow street lined with elm and maple trees, most of which had lost their leaves by now. About three blocks down he pulled up to a dilapidated-looking Victorian home.

"You know, while I was growing up here, no one ever mentioned the history much. This was a thriving farming community. It sparkled with American pride and shiny new tractors. We had a movie theater, a Montgomery Ward and two car dealerships. But now, it's the history of the place that brings in the tourism. Don't get me wrong, there are still lots of successful farms here. Why there's a fellow who raises beef with no hormones, or antibiotics. He only lets the cows feed from fields that have had no pesticide sprayed on 'em. He does real well, but it's the history that has been the big money maker these past few years.

"They have a big annual festival called Hampshire Heritage Days that takes place every fall, with Civil War reenactments and many old home craft demonstrators. You could watch someone make a cane-bottom chair or tool leather. All the shops in town celebrate with open-houses and there's a train that takes folks through many historic sites. It's a great time to be here and you are right, it's all about history."

Garrett got out and headed to the back of his Jeep where he pulled out a well-used painter's easel and a stool. Barbara joined him there and he handed her the stool and what looked like a large tool box. Then he grabbed a tripod and headed up two wooden steps and across a side porch that lead to a side door. Barbara followed behind and stood at the door with Garrett who had rung the bell and was starting to knock loudly.

Barbara started to laugh, "You have the thing about pounding on doors, huh?"

Garrett set down the tripod replying, "Hey, she's over 100 years old." He went back to the Jeep to bring in his light and diffuser, but before he returned the door opened up and Barbara found herself looking down into the bluest eyes she had ever seen.

"Can I help you?"

"Oh, hello, my name is Barbara, I'm here with Garrett." Barbara smiled hoping she understood. "Well, why don't you come on in, it's a little cold out here for me." Barbara picked up the box and followed Martha into her kitchen. Barbara quickly glanced around and immediately fell in love. There was a very old electric cook stove that looked like new sitting in one corner and across the kitchen an equally old refrigerator. In the center of the kitchen was a metal-framed table with Formica top. It was surrounded by four matching chairs with shiny vinyl seat cushions and back padding. An old AM-FM radio sat on the counter and next to it a large "Elsie the Cow" cookie jar.

"Can I get you some tea?"

Before Barbara could answer, Garrett came bustling in carrying his tripod and light.

"Good morning Martha!"

"Good morning Garrett, you know I expected you an hour ago."

"I know Martha, I'm sorry, but I couldn't get Barbara to move any faster."

Barbara shot Garrett a look that was not lost on Martha.

"Well, no matter, I'm not going anywhere today."

Garrett picked up his things and carried them down the hallway out of the kitchen. Martha looked over at Barbara, "I know it wasn't your fault. Garrett's always an hour late. As a matter of fact, I count on it."

She walked over to her sink, filled a kettle with water, and sat it on her stove where it immediately started to whine and labor as the water slowly heated. Barbara watched Martha pull three cookies from the cookie jar and place them on a small saucer. She couldn't have been more than four and a half feet tall. Her braid of white hair hung down her back to her waist. The dress she wore was much like the appliances in her kitchen, very old, but in perfect condition. It hung loosely over her very thin body.

Once again, Garrett came in, carrying the easel and stool. "I'm almost ready Martha, give me five minutes."

Martha didn't respond but turned to Barbara and invited her to sit with a gesture. "Can I help you with something?" Barbara got up from her chair. "No, no, 'deed no, I need to keep moving. You don't move it you lose it you know."

Barbara sat back down. Within minutes, the kettle came to a whistle and a steaming pot of tea sat on a tray with the cups, sugar, cream, and cookies.

"Now you can help," she said to Barbara and pointed toward the tray. She then headed down the same hallway Garrett had gone down.

Barbara picked up the tray and followed her. The door at the end of the hall stood open and a bright golden light poured from it.

Barbara stood at the entryway holding the tray and looked into the room, which was quite large and formal with high ceilings. Old family portraits hung suspended by long cables from the beautifully crafted crown molding. There was a large, white-manteled fireplace with exquisitely detailed pillars on each side at the far end of the room and on its hearth stood a tall brass vase filled with dusty peacock feathers.

The walls were covered with a floral wallpaper and the furniture was all Victorian. A red-velvet couch with a dark carved wood frame and tightly bound upholstery sat prominently in one corner of the room and two enormously tall windows draped with luxurious damask and sheers sat opposite the wall where stood the chair Martha would sit on while Garrett painted her. It too was Victorian and matched the couch perfectly. To the right of the chair stood a three-legged Victorian tilt-top table with small claw feet strewn with a round lace doily, two ancient tintype pictures and several small books. "You can set the tea down over there." She indicated a wide bookshelf that stood between the two windows. Setting the tray on the bookshelf, Barbara couldn't help but notice the ancient books within.

She poured a cup of tea and brought it over to Martha who had already sat down. "Would you like cream or sugar?"

"'Deed no, but thank you dear."

Barbara placed the cup on the table next to Martha. Garrett was sitting on the stool in front of his easel before his canvas squeezing paint from his tubes onto his palette. Barbara walked over to look at the nearly-finished painting.

She was captivated by how realistic the painting was. Garrett had captured the blueness of her eyes and her delicate pink cheeks. Every strand of hair was lovingly painted and even the translucence of her white skin was perfect. Garrett pulled his stool closer to the easel. "Do you like it?"

She looked up at him, "It's wonderful, Garrett!"

He pulled drops of linseed oil onto his palette and started to blend it into a beautiful deep red with his palette knife. Within minutes, Garrett became quite focused and started adding detail to the unfinished areas of his painting.

Barbara watched in awe as he brought the room around Martha to life. His use of color to create the illusion of light was stunning. Barbara was pulled from her trance by Martha's voice, "So, I hear you're staying at Whippoorwill Ridge."

Barbara came from where Garrett was working and pulled a chair near to Martha. "That's right, my brother and I are taking care of the place until Gertrude gets back."

"I haven't been out there for years. There used to be wonderful dances out there."

"Really?"

"'Deed yes, before I was married, I attended several of them with my family. Half the town would be there. They would move the furniture in the great room out of the way, roll back the rugs and we would dance 'til all hours of the night to fiddle, guitar and even piano. Oh, that was a very long time ago."

Martha sipped from her cup and looked dreamily ahead. "It used to be owned by a governor back then. Does the portrait of Miss Lilly still hang over the fireplace?"

Garrett looked at Barbara who returned his glance replying; "Yes, she still hangs over the great room fireplace."

"Oh, I remember that painting. She is dressed in a brightly colored dress and she is singing. 'Deed I do remember now. Poor Miss Lilly." Martha pulled her cup from the saucer and took a sip looking head with an expression of trying to remember. "Why do you say that?" Barbara asked in a soft voice so as not to startle Martha.

"Say what?" Martha looked at Barbara now.

"Why did you say, 'poor Miss Lilly?' "

"Well now, that's an old house and like most old houses there are stories. Doesn't make them true stories mind you, but they typically contain a little bit of truth." Martha carefully got up and crossed the room to the bookcase where the tea tray stood. She pulled open the glass door to the bookcase and from the lower shelf she pulled a very old-looking notebook-sized portfolio held together by a long piece of leather. There were mildew blossoms around its top corner and bits of brittle paper crumbled out as she sat back down in her chair.

Garrett had stopped painting and gotten up to get a better look. "What have you got there, Martha?"

Martha was fiddling with the knot trying to untie it with no success. Garrett knelt down and tried to untie the dried out leather strap with no success.

"I'm afraid if I pull too hard it's gonna snap, Martha."

"I don't care if it snaps, I'll find something else to tie it shut, just open it."

Garrett pulled out a small pocket knife and slid it under the strap. It snapped as he pulled the knife through and fell to the floor in a permanently square shape. Martha opened the album and immediately started shifting through yellowed newspaper clippings and very old photos. She pulled out a folded piece of paper, unfolded it and handed it to Barbara who got up and stood under Garret's bright light. She read it aloud:

"Lovely Miss Lilly sang her sweet song from the dark of night 'til the break of dawn.

The word went out of her great voice, but her husband dear gave her no choice.

You will stay where you're required, no matter that your song's admired.

Then one day she stole away to sing for the president's birthday,

Upon return she became quite lost, They didn't find her 'til the very last frost.

There's them that say they still can hear, on cold dark nights with skies so clear,

Miss Lilly's singing sad and long.

Still singing till the break of dawn."

Barbara examined the piece of paper the poem was written on. It looked like it had been torn from a book. "So, she got lost and must have run off the road."

"Where did you get this Martha?" Barbara folded the letter back up.

"'Deed, I really can't remember." She kept riffling through her ancient scrapbook. "I have always loved Lilly's story. You see, she died just before my mother was born, so I grew up hearing about her story from both my parents. Most folks these days probably don't even know who Miss Lilly was."

Barbara was interested in finding out more. "Would you mind if I made a photocopy of this poem? It's really quite marvelous."

Martha resumed her search through her scrapbook when she stopped suddenly. "Ah, here it is," she held up a yellowed photograph. "These are my parents. Look how young they are. And those two folks to the left of my parents are Garrett's great-grandfather and grandmother. As I recall, this man was the son of Thomas Moore, the man who painted Miss Lilly so many times. He was an artist too, but couldn't make a living at it. I think he became a teacher."

Garrett returned to his painting. The room became quiet except for the sound of Martha carefully pulling together the papers and photos she had been looking through. She closed the album and handed it to Barbara.

"Martha, would you mind if I looked through your album?"

"'Deed no, go right ahead, but before you do will you go get my crossword puzzle, it's on the kitchen table?"

Barbara returned, handing the puzzle and pencil to Martha who smiled contentedly and immediately started writing. Barbara picked up the album and sat down on the large velvet sofa at the far corner of the room. She used the large cushion as a table and started to sort through the photos and papers. While she didn't find anything more about Miss Lilly, she did find several clips from an old newspaper called the Hampshire Review. One dated 1908 appeared to be a birth announcement for Martha herself. Another clipping boasted a large affair happening at the Century Hotel and another, a wedding announcement that was illegible with the exception of the headline. Barbara gathered all the photos and clippings together and placed them back into the album and onto the bookshelf.

Martha was immersed in her puzzle and Garrett in his painting. Looking up, Garrett smiled. "You bored?"

"No, not really." She walked over to see his progress.

"You know, we're only four blocks from town. You could go and have a look around. Garrett wiped his hands on a well used rag. "Make sure your cell phone is on and I'll call you when I'm done, which should be about an hour."

Barbara didn't want to be rude, but at the same time, was very interested in seeing this town during the day. "O.K., you talked me into it." She walked over to Martha. "It was nice meeting you, Martha."

Martha looked up from her puzzle. "Are you leaving?"

"Yes, I'm going to walk into town."

"Oh, well, it was lovely meeting you, please stop by anytime, I love company."

Barbara bent down and gently hugged her and kissed her on the cheek. "I'll definitely come to see you again, Martha."

Garrett got up and walked Barbara to the door. "I'll be done in about an hour."

This time it was Barbara who walked backwards down the walk smiling.

A LOVELY LAVALIERE

Barbara headed down Martha's boxwood-lined sidewalk and out to Birch Lane. The sun peeked through white voluminous clouds and a light breeze whistled through a 100-foot tall blue spruce near the road. She turned left at the spruce and headed up the lane. There was a mixture of homes on this street. Grand Victorians with gingerbread trim sat right next to brick ranch homes probably built in the '50s or '60s.

She passed flowerbeds overflowing with golden brown mums and homes bedecked with cornstalks and pumpkins. After about two blocks, Barbara stood next to Main Street and headed west toward the town. She could see for at least a quarter of a mile down the road.

Both sides of the streets were lined with shops and in the distance she could see a white church steeple gleaming in the diffused light of the sun.

Looming up in the west was a large mountain. Not like a mountain you would see in Colorado, but a tree-covered blue-ridge mountain, the top of which was covered with rows of orchards. The fragrance of boxwood and cedar followed Barbara as she walked further into town. She passed the bank and glanced across the street. Hanging above a door on the side of large office building was a sign that read, "The Hampshire Review."

"Well, I'll be," she thought to herself as she jaywalked across Main Street and over to the door of the newspaper. Just as she was about to open it, someone opened it for her, saying hello then walking away.

She stepped into a small reception area. A tall counter sat off to one side. A display of old cameras and old framed newspapers hung on the wall behind the counter. Barbara waited patiently for about five minutes, then was just about to ring the service bell when a disembodied voice from behind the counter called out, "Please don't do that, I'll be right with you."

Startled, Barbara peered over the counter to see the owner of that voice bent underneath her desk behind the counter. "Gosh darn it!"

Barbara watched as an arm came from under the desk and hit a button and moved the computer mouse on the keypad.

"Stupid computer!"

The young lady came out from under the counter and quickly rose to Barbara's level, smoothing back her hair. "Can I help you?"

Barbara smiled, "Computer trouble?"

The young girl gave her an impatient expression. "Now what gave you that idea?"

"Perhaps I can help." Barbara continued smiling.

"No. Thanks anyway, it's probably me." The young woman, sat down in her desk chair. "Is there something I can help you with?"

"Well to be honest, I'm not sure. Does this paper allow the public to access its archives?"

"Yes. Do you know what edition you want to see?"

Barbara shifted from one foot to the other, "Well, not exactly. I'm not even sure what year."

This time it was the girl grinning at Barbara. "You're on a wild goose chase, huh?"

"Kind of. Do you have access to editions of your paper from 139 years ago?"

Barbara had sparked the young woman's attention. "We

do. We have every paper ever published on microfiche and are starting to scan some of those into our computer database. Maybe we have your edition on the computer already. Can you give me any search parameters?

Barbara thought for a moment. "Well, start by looking in either 1871 or 1872 and I think the winter months."

"O.K., let me see what we have."

Barbara watched as the girl's hands whirled over the keypad. Within seconds she looked up. "You're in luck, we scanned through 1900. O.K. let's see, winter months. Now what?"

"I'm looking for a story on an accident."

Again, the young lady's eyes brightened, "What kind of accident?"

"A carriage accident."

The young woman paged through the editions with expertise. "Do you have any names?"

Barbara had not wanted to give a name, but knew it would be the only way to truly find out. "Lilly LeClaire."

Again, the young lady scanned for a few moments. "I have found three carriage accidents, but none involving Lilly LeClaire. Wait, I'll check 1872." After several minutes the girl looked up. "Boy, I really hate to admit this, but I'm coming up with zilch. Can you tell me more about this accident?"

"Well, no, I'm hoping you can tell me."

Are you sure it was in the winter? She punched at her keypad, flipping back and forth through editions. Finally, she looked up. "I have looked through all the winter months for both years and have found nothing."

Barbara had hoped there would at least be a mention of the accident. She pulled the folded piece of paper that Martha had given her to read and laid it on the counter. She audibly sighed and rested her head on her hand and elbow on the counter.

The young lady stood up and picked up the delicate paper reading the poem aloud. "This is what we are researching?"

"Well, partly."

"Did it really happen, or is this just whimsy?"

"I believe it really happened."

"Which president?"

Barbara looked confused.

"This poem says she sang for the president's birthday so, which president?"

Barbara looked at the poem again. "You know, I don't know which one. Can you look it up?"

"Yes, but it will cost you."

Barbara pulled her purse onto the counter and started rifling through for change. "I was only kidding." The young girl made a copy of the poem and handed her the original and the copy. "You should put the original in an envelope or something." She pulled out a small envelope, handed it to her and plopped down at her computer. In less than a minute she called out, Ulysses S. Grant, April 27th.

"Fantastic, thank you for all your help. My name is Barbara, what's yours?"

Just as she was about to answer, Barbara's phone rang causing her to jump. "Oh my gosh, I nearly forgot I was supposed to call Garrett.

She dug through her purse for her phone and finding it, she flipped it open. "Hello?"

"Hi Barbara, it's William."

"Hi William, how are things going?"

"Well, it's been interesting. The competitions are scheduled to start at 3:00. When are you coming back?"

"I'm not sure. Garrett is still with Martha and I'm downtown walking around."

"Great! Isn't it a nice little town?"

"Well, I haven't seen very much of it, but what I've seen is very nice. The people are especially nice." She smiled at the young woman who was on another search. "Listen William,

Garrett and I will probably eat lunch downtown, so don't worry about feeding us. Would you like me to pick up something for you?"

"Yes, that's why I'm calling. Bring me three bottles of Ridge Runner Red. We're having Rosemary Beef Stew tonight."

"You've got it! I'll call you with an e.t.a. as soon as I have one. Bye William." She folded her phone and placed it in her purse. The young woman handed Barbara an envelope, "Give this to Patty Anderson at the shop, it's the proof for this week's ad."

Barbara gave her a confused look. "What?"

"You're going to pick up some wine from Anderson's Corner right? Well, bring this envelope with you and give it to Patty Anderson, she is the owner there."

"Oh, sure, no problem." Barbara took the envelope and placed it in her purse.

"Give me your cell phone number and I'll call you if I find anything on that carriage accident."

"That would be great, but don't you have other work to do?"

"No, it's slow on Saturdays, not much goes on here."

Barbara wrote down her cell phone number and her number at the Inn and handed it to the young woman. "Thanks again. She left the Review's office and headed back toward Main Street. From where she was, she could just see the sign for Anderson's Corner just up ahead. As she approached the shop, she saw a sign in the window advertising a book signing. She pushed open the door and was immediately greeted.

"Hi," a handsome young man smiled at her from behind the counter. He was polishing a piece of jewelry with a small piece of moleskin fabric. "You here for the reading and book signing?"

"Actually no, I'm just here to look around and buy some wine."

"Well, the wine is through that door there, but you'll need to wait a bit. They're in the middle of a reading. Should be over in about 15 minutes."

Barbara looked at her watch and checked her phone. Anderson's Corner was primarily a family-owned jewelry store. The small front room had two large oak and glass display cases and one smaller one near the register. Beautiful jewels shone from the cases. Diamonds in many colors: yellow, pink, and even black were held tight in gold and platinum settings. Earrings, rings, bracelets, were placed on dark velvet fabric. It was the picture of opulence.

Moving over to the smaller case, Barbara looked down and saw a display of antique jewelry. Brooches, hat pins and bejeweled lockets rested on folded satin. Toward the front coming out of a small, black-velvet box was a very old looking pendant. Barbara bent down to get a closer look.

The young man at the counter came up from behind her. "Would you like me to pull anything from the case for you?"

Barbara stood up, "No, I'm just looking."

Just then a woman came from the adjoining room. "Tim, your mom needs some help in the back."

Barbara watched as he passed through the doorway. She peered into the room and saw nearly 25 people sitting and listening as a young bearded man read from a book. One of the men sitting nearest the door beckoned her to come sit. Shaking her head no, Barbara smiled and retreated back into the front room of the store and back to the counter where the antique jewelry was.

She loved old things and she stared deep into the case. In amongst the jewelry were intricately designed demitasse spoons, delicate golden pill boxes, a silver brush and mirror and two tintypes framed in embossed gold metal and held together with a leather cover. She looked at the two solemn faces and wondered to herself. "These must have been taken near the time Lilly was alive."

Deeply entranced in the case, Barbara didn't notice when a middle-aged, brunette woman with blond highlights came in and stood behind the counter. She wore many beautiful rings and diamond earrings. In a sweet genuine voice with a lovely West Virginia drawl, she commented, "Aren't they lovely?"

Barbara looked up into a pair of pale blue eyes and a smiling face. She couldn't help but smile back, "Yes, there are some very nice pieces in there."

The lady turned a key at the back of the display and slid open the door. "Would you like to see something a little closer?"

Barbara still hadn't heard from Garrett, and had found herself once again drawn to the pendant. "Actually, yes, I would like to see that lovely pendant."

"Isn't that a pretty piece? It came from an estate here in Hampshire County. It's a Victorian lavaliere."

She pulled the necklace from the case and set it on a piece of velvet on top of the display case. She pulled a hinged magnifying glass over the piece and started pointing out the fine detail etched into the rose gold. "See the tiny sapphire in the center? And look at the clasp holding the teardrop pearl. The filigree is so delicate."

Barbara was curious about the piece, but was not one to buy on impulse. "How old would you say this is?"

The lady picked up the lavaliere and turned it over studying it as she did. "I would say it's probably from the late 1800s. Try it on."

"Oh, I couldn't."

"Sure you can." The lady had already unclasped the necklace. Barbara lifted her hair out of the way as the lady pulled it around her neck and fastened it. There was an antique gilded mirror to Barbara's left she turned and stared at the lavaliere. "It's beautiful on you."

Barbara placed her hand onto the pendant's smooth surface and held it. She knew she had to have it, and without another word, pulled her wallet from her purse. Just then one of the sales clerks came from the other room. "Patty, they're nearly finished in there. How do you want me to ring up those books?"

Barbara interrupted, "You're Patty? Patty Anderson?"

The fair-haired lady smiled, "Yes, I'm Patty,"

Barbara reached into her purse and pulled the envelope from the Hampshire Review out and handed it to her. "The girl at the Review gave me this for you."

Patty laughed, "Thank you, for the special delivery. Michele, will you please write up this transaction for our lovely delivery lady!"

"Sure Patty." The young woman pulled a beautiful velvet jewelry box from below the case. "Do you want to wear it out or shall I box it?"

Still holding it in her hand, Barbara decided she would wear it.

From behind her, Barbara could hear the shop door open with the clink of a little bell. She turned and saw Garrett step in. Michelle, the sales clerk called over to him, "Hi Garrett, you here to buy something pretty for one of your girls?"

Garrett smiled at Michele, and walked right up to Barbara putting his arm around her, "No Michele, apparently, my girl buys her own jewelry."

Both Michele and Barbara laughed as she put her wallet back into her purse. "Did you pick up the wine?"

Barbara looked up at Garrett. "How did you know I was supposed to buy wine?"

"William called me first. Oh, and you should check your phone, I've tried to call you twice."

Barbara pulled her phone from her purse. It had turned itself off. "The batteries must be dead. I'm sorry Garrett, but am glad you found me."

He faced her now and looked down at the lavaliere she had just purchased. His face became quite serious as he picked it up and turned it over in his hand.

"Isn't it beautiful?" Barbara was beaming, "I'm not typically an impulse buyer, but I just had to have it."

Garrett withdrew his hand from the pendant and Barbara returned her hand to it. "I can't seem to keep my hands off it."

He looked at her and back down at the pendant. Michele watched the exchange from behind the counter.

"It's very fitting." He said as he smiled coyly

The sales girl laughed and handed Barbara a receipt and a small bag. "Fitting? Come on Garrett, you can do better than that."

People started coming from the other room with books in hand. Barbara and Garrett squeezed past them and into the other side of the shop.

This room was much larger and held many beautiful hand-crafted gifts. There was a large antique cupboard filled with blue and grey salt pottery. Hand-dipped candles, stained glass, framed photography, decorative hand-blown glass wine goblets and delicate Christmas ornaments.

From the ledges, she could see authentic Tiffany lamps of every type and below the ledge were hundreds of bottles of local West Virginia wines.

After picking up three bottles of Ridge Runner Red and two bottles of Mountain Mama Merlot, Barbara and Garrett grabbed a bite to eat and headed back to Whippoorwill Ridge to see if William needed help. It was after 2 pm when they returned and already there were cars parked in the driveway. They walked in through the front door to see a couple of people looking up at the paintings of Lilly and a couple of people sitting on the two wingback chairs.

Barbara unloaded the wine and asked if anyone had seen

William. A demure looking woman pointed her to the theater.

Garrett and Barbara walked back down the hall toward the theater. Barbara and Garrett could hear laughter spilling from the slightly-opened door. They looked in and saw William leaning on the piano while Parker played.

"Hey! Look who's returned!"

Barbara and Garrett walked in. The theater gleamed with care and the finish on the grand piano shone like glass. The stage lights were on which made the mural on the back walls look three-dimensional.

There were a few people sitting on chairs while others stood pacing and holding music.

Barbara looked at her watch, "What time is it supposed to start?"

William straightened, "Not till four."

"Why are they here so early?"

"Oh, I figure they wanted to be sure they got done early. First come first heard."

Garrett, walked over to William, "Do you have any ideas how you want them to park outside?"

William smiled, "I'm glad you asked that Garrett. How does Gertrude have folks park when there are a lot coming?"

"How many is a lot?"

"Well now, that is the ultimate question isn't it? I have no idea how many will be here at once."

"Well, I'll park my Jeep over on the west lawn, probably should pull the Jag over there as well."

William handed Garrett the keys, "Thanks, Garrett."

Barbara sat down in the front row of chairs.

Parker looked over at her and smiled, "We've had more than 100 calls."

"Oh, my gosh! You guys are gonna be busy."

Within half an hour the house started filling with people.

Numbers were given out to the singers as it was first come, first served. William had set some light refreshments on the dining table along with literature on the theater and B&B.

Barbara could see Garrett directing the cars through the great room windows. It was starting to rain once again and Garrett looked drenched. She walked outside and called to him. "Garrett, come in out of this weather. They'll find their way."

The auditions started out with a quick speech from one of the judges. Then it started right off. There were easily a hundred people there, most to listen and support those auditioning.

ABSOLUTELY HANDS DOWN!

Barbara and Garrett sat in the kitchen drinking hot tea. From there, they could hear the piano start to play and then a nervous voice chime in. William walked into the kitchen, poured himself a cup of tea and pulled up a stool from the island to the table. Barbara put her cup down and looked over at him. "Any special talents been displayed so far?"

William laughed, "Well, yes, I'd say there are many very special talents."

Barbara threw him a look, "You know what I mean."

"Well, it has only just begun." William looked up at the cuckoo clock. Barbara looked into her tea then over to Garrett. "Do you think Sarah will audition?"

Garrett had been wondering the same thing himself. "I don't know for sure, but you said in the car that she told her father she was auditioning for the opera, so she must have meant this audition."

William walked over to the long kitchen windows and looked out. The rain was steady and it was nearly dark. He walked across the great room and down the hall leading to the theater. No one was singing. He leaned into the open door and looked into the theater. People were standing at the sides and every chair was full. Already one small group was gathering their things to leave and another singer was about to start. William scanned the room looking for the dark-haired Sarah, but she was not there. He walked back to the kitchen where Garrett and Barbara sat.

"Any sign of her?

"Nope, I thought maybe she might have snuck in, but she is not in there."

Garrett pulled the drawer from the book shelf open and pulled out Thomas Moore's diary. He leafed through it. The last entry they had read was from April. He leafed beyond this page and found nothing but mildew and water damage. There were no other entries.

It was nearly 6pm when William started to cook. He placed a medium saucepan on the stove. From the refrigerator, he pulled a large leek, four medium-sized russet potatoes, some garlic and butter. He placed a cutting board on the island and started trimming and cleaning a leek. He sliced it down the middle and muddy drops of water dripped from its center. He ran the leek under a trickle of running water until the mud was flushed out. He then rinsed off the board, placed the leek halves onto it cut side down and chopped off the root portion. From that end, he started slicing the leek until he got to the tough green leaves. He pulled away and discarded the outer layer of dark leathery leaves and continued to chop the lighter more tender leaves until all were chopped.

Barbara and Garrett both moved over to the stools around the island and watched as William turned the flame up under the pan and added butter. Once melted, he added the chopped leek and garlic, sautéing them until they started to turn brown. To this he added chicken broth and a bay leaf. He covered it with a lid and returned to the island to peel and slice the potatoes.

They sat and watched William slice as they listened to a young man singing Scarlatti's *Gia il sole dal Gange* from the other room. His pitch was very good, but his sense of timing was terrible as he kept missing his entrances.

William rinsed off the peeled potatoes and added them to the boiling broth. He removed the lid, turned the heat down to medium and cooked the soup until the potatoes were tender. At this point, William added a cup of whole milk from the refrigerator and stirred until it was well incorporated. The soup took on a creamy golden color and steam rose in lovely curls as William shut off the flame underneath.

Barbara got down from her stool and pulled several pieces of rosemary sourdough bread from a bag on the counter and started to toast them. "I thought you were going to make the Rosemary Beef Stew?"

"Yea, I was, but I ran out of time." William ladled the soup into three shallow bowls and sprinkled freshly-ground black pepper onto each bowl. He went to the refrigerator and pulled a bottle of Chardonnay from the side door, uncorked it and poured each of them a glass.

Within minutes they each crunched on their toast and sipped their soups until every last drop and crumb was eaten.

Garrett got up and cleared his bowl and bread plate off then returned to the table where Barbara thoughtfully sipped the last of her wine. Garrett sat down and leaned back, "So, what do you call that soup you made?"

William was brushing the crumbs of toast off the table and into his hand and into his empty bowl, "That was a French recipe called vichyssoise. It is typically served cold, but I like it warm especially when it's cold outside."

It was nearly 7:30. The auditions were still going on but were scheduled to be over by 8:00pm.

Barbara, William and Garrett headed into the theater which was nearly empty now. There were about 20 people sitting there, but still no Sarah. The judges were speaking to one of the singers and another was speaking to Parker, the accompanist. Just then, from the great room someone called out, "Hello?"

William looked over at Barbara and Garrett, got up and headed into the room. Within moments, a smiling William returned with Sarah following behind him. She looked pale and somewhat drawn. Her dark eyes scanned the room stopping at once when they came to Garrett and Barbara. With an unbelieving expression, she placed her notebook and bags on a seat in front of where they were sitting.

Garrett stood up. Smiling, he bent forward to give her a hug. She smiled back and lightly embraced him back with the traditional French greeting of a kiss on each side of his face. "Hello, Garrett."

"Hello Sarah. We're so glad you came to audition. We have been waiting for you."

Sarah looked at Barbara and William with a look of unfamiliarity. "I'm sorry, I can't seem to remember your names but you both look very familiar."

Barbara smiled and introduced herself, "Hello, Sarah. I was with Garrett last weekend and had the pleasure of hearing you sing at the Coriander Café."

Sarah smiled in recognition, then looked over at William who impishly said, "I'm the guy who likes Divas, Damsels and Donuts." He held out his hand and in his best French said, "Enchante."

At this, Sarah blushed and smiled, causing both Garrett and Barbara to give William a funny look.

Parker started to play the introduction for the next singer and at this, Sarah sat down, and William found his seat next to Barbara. They watched and listened as a very young looking girl started to sing *Vergin Tutto Amor*. This was another of a series of antique art songs they had been hearing all evening.

The girl's voice was lovely but not quite developed. It was a short piece and within moments, the girl finished and several of the people left in the room applauded. The girl stepped off the stage, gathered her music from Parker and returned to her seat. Half the people in the room had stood up and were preparing to leave.

One of the judges called Sarah up to where they were sitting and had her fill out the audition application.

Within moments, eight people had picked up and left the theater leaving Barbara, Garrett, William, Sarah and one other woman who was sitting several seats to the right of Sarah. She did not look like she was one of the singers; she was a little too old and had an air of sophistication about her, but she kept looking over at them paying special attention to Sarah, who had returned to her seat.

Sarah turned to Garrett, "Is there anyplace I can warm up? I have been on the road for more than an hour."

Before anyone could answer her, the judge called her up. "Sarah, you're up."

She looked back again at Garrett, William and Barbara and shrugged her shoulders. "I guess I'll just have to make do."

She handed her music to Parker who raised his eyebrows when he received it. She climbed the stairs and stood in the center of the stage looking out.

"Could you please state your name and what you are going to sing?"

Sarah nodded her head and facing her three fans said, "My name is Sarah LeClaire Rossignol, and I will be singing a piece from *Gianni Schicchi* by Puccini called *Oh Mio Babbino Caro.*

"Excuse me young lady." Parker called from the piano, "Did you say LeClaire?"

Sarah turned to him and smiled, "Yes, LeClaire."

At this, Parker looked over at Garrett, William and Barbara, who responded with a look of enlightened shock. Parker started to play the piece, filling the theater with an adlibbed introduction.

Then, as before, Sarah's voice streamed unfettered, filling the theater with the voice of a daughter pleading for her father's consent.

The aria she chose to audition with could have been a disaster, as it is considered a standard and sung almost too often, usually by inexperienced singers with no clue of its meaning. But within moments it was clear that Sarah had a complete grasp of the piece. Using the colors of her voice she whined, whimpered and threatened to throw herself off the Ponte Vecchio if she didn't get her father's blessing. With or without his blessing she will go, but she begs for peace. Her final words, "Babbo pieta...pieta" were sung in an exquisite, spinning pianissimo. When she finished everyone in the room remembered to breathe and tried to comprehend the rare gift they just witnessed. Then, with full abandon, they applauded her long and fitfully. The lights in the theater flickered during the applause and when it subsided, they stopped flickering. Sarah rose from her bow and smiled at Barbara, Garrett and William, then over to the judges who returned her smile. The woman who had been looking at her from a few rows over was beaming as well and applauding with the same exuberance. Parker shouted, "Brava!" got up from his piano and approached the judges. Sarah came down from the stage and joined her three fans that shook her hand and hugged her.

"That was just wonderful, Sarah!" Barbara was so happy to see Sarah do so well.

"I think she was the best one this evening don't you?" William turned to Garrett and Barbara.

"Absolutely! Hands down!"

Sarah put her music in her bag and was putting on her coat to leave when the judges called her up.

"Ms. Rossignol, that was just marvelous! We are very excited to have heard you and must ask you a few questions. If you are chosen to be a part of this production, will you be available evenings for about three weeks at the end of June and into July? And will you be able to participate in two matinees and three evening performances?

"Before you answer, please know that this is a great opportunity for anyone, and we must be certain that whoever we pick will be completely committed to this project."

Without hesitation, Sarah, answered, "I can think of nothing or no place I'd rather be than in whatever part I'm offered in your program. However, to be realistic, I will need a place to stay and a job."

The judges exchanged looks and smiled, "Indeed, a level head. Excellent! We will let you know within a week whether you are chosen, but know this. You demonstrated great promise this evening and we are very happy you came to audition."

They each shook her hand and handed her a large manila envelope. She walked back to her chair and started picking up her things.

"Oh, do you have to run off? Won't you stay for some tea or something warm?" Barbara looked over to Garrett and William for support.

"Yes, Sarah, won't you please stay for a few minutes?" William smiled warmly.

"I would really love to, but I need to head back. It's getting late and I have to work in the morning."

"Where are you working?" Barbara was worried she would say at the Stone Hill.

"I started a new job about a week ago at the Free Trade Coffee Shop in Bickersberg."

Sarah was heading toward the door of the theater. "I have to be at work at 7am, which is killing me, but beats the late hours at the Stone Hill. Plus, I don't have my father screaming at me."

They followed her down the corridor and into the great room when the lights in the living room started to flicker. Barbara, William and Garrett looked around the room but Sarah did not seem to notice. She walked to the front door and turned to say goodbye when her eyes widened. "Why is my father's painting here and where did you get this other painting?"

Barbara spoke, "I found your father's painting out in the rain and felt it would be damaged if it remained, so I rescued it."

Sarah looked at Barbara in disbelief. "My father would never leave this painting out in the rain. It has been in our family for more than 100 years."

Barbara and William parted as Sarah walked up to the paintings and looked in wonder. "I don't even know who she is, but I have gazed upon her face my entire life." She held her hand up and touched the other painting moving her hand as far as she could reach on the canvas. "All my life I wanted sing because of how beautiful she looked in this painting."

William stood beside her now and looked up at both paintings. "You don't know who this is?"

Sarah looked over at William, "Do you?"

Barbara stood on the other side of her, "Sarah, this is Lilly LeClaire. She lived and sang in this house more than 130 years ago."

"LeClaire? Did you say, LeClaire?"

William looked over at Sarah, "We think you are somehow related to Lilly LeClaire."

Sarah turned to each of them and started to laugh, "Is this

some kind of a joke?"

"This is no joke, Sarah." Garrett moved next to Barbara. "Each of us in this room has been inspired in some way by these paintings. And what's more, we feel that Lilly has been trying to…"

At this Barbara interrupted Garrett. "Garrett, I'm not sure now is the time."

"Where did you get that necklace?" Sarah was looking at Barbara's lavaliere.

Barbara, who had developed a habit of holding it in her hand and rubbing it, looked back at Sarah and followed her eyes up to the painting of Lilly that came from the Stone Hill Inn. There around Lilly's neck was the very same necklace.

Barbara looked at her lavaliere and back to the painting. "Oh, my goodness, it's the same!"

She turned to Garrett. Smiling, Garret replied. "Did you know it was the same?"

"I suspected it when I first saw it, but wasn't sure. Obviously, she wanted you to have it."

Sarah gave Garrett a wide-eyed look "You guys are starting to freak me out a little. I know my middle name is LeClaire, but I don't think we are related."

William sat down on one of the two wingback chairs in front the fireplace. "I don't understand why you would think that. You yourself said this painting has been in your family for more than 100 years."

Sarah shifted on her feet, "Well yes it has, but it is not a member of our family, it's just an antique. Ask my father, he will tell you. He has put it up in every restaurant he has ever had. As a matter of fact, he said she brings him luck. So why would he put it outside in the rain?" Sarah nervously looked at each of them and was starting to clutch her things more tightly.

Barbara stepped back, "Look Sarah, I would be happy to

give this painting back to you tonight, but you must promise you won't give it back to your father just yet, o.k.?"

Sarah gave Barbara a confused but relieved look as Barbara and Garrett pulled the large frame off the mantel.

"Garrett, will you carry this out to Sarah's car?"

As Garrett turned the painting around Sarah could see the wet splotches on the back side of the painting where it had not yet dried. Sarah walked toward the door.

"I cannot understand why he would leave it out in the rain." She opened the door and stepped onto the porch with Garrett, William and Barbara following right behind her.

"It's freezing out here." Barbara watched as Garrett walked with Sarah out to her old, rusted-out car. "Be careful Sarah, it may be slick out there."

Sarah started her car as Garrett loaded the painting into the back seat. He shut the door and said a quick goodbye and joined Barbara and William on the porch. They all three watched as she pulled out onto Route 50 and sped away.

Vichyssoise (French Potato Soup)

1 leek - roots removed, split and rinsed
4 medium russet potatoes – peeled and sliced
1 garlic clove – sliced – peeled and sliced
2 tablespoons butter
6 cups low-sodium chicken broth (no msg)
1 bay leaf
1 cup whole milk – warmed

- Using a medium saucepan, melt butter.

- Add leeks and sauté until lightly browned.

- Add garlic and sauté a minute more.

- Add the bay leaf, broth and potatoes and cook over medium-high heat until tender, about 15 minutes.

- Turn off heat and add the warm milk and stir until well incorporated.

This easy and delicious soup is traditionally served cold, but it's also good served hot, especially on cold winter nights. Serve with your favorite buttered toast, especially a good rye with caraway or rosemary sourdough.

A LITTLE BIRD TOLD US SO

Barbara, William and Garrett quickly went inside and headed once again to the kitchen, only this time it was not tea that warmed them, but warmed apricot brandy.

William stoked the fire in the great room, adding logs and within minutes it was blazing brightly. Four of the six people from the opera had gone upstairs. Then, the woman who had been watching Sarah from the audience walked with Parker into the great room.

"Now, this looks cozy, a little brandy and a blazing fire."

Barbara got up, "Hello Parker, would you like some brandy?"

Parker laughed, "Now you wouldn't be trying to bribe one of the judges would you?" Parker laughed again causing them all to chuckle.

"Forgive me Parker, but somehow, I don't think a bribe would be necessary. I'm sure all of your judges are capable of identifying real talent when they hear it." William sipped his brandy and looked up at Parker.

"Indeed William, indeed. Oh, let me introduce my friend. Mrs. Copeland, this is William, Garrett and Barbara. They are caring for this inn while the owner is away. Mrs. Copeland is the reason we were able to hold this audition. She wants to find a young talent and help them to achieve their dreams."

"What a wonderful thing you are doing, Mrs. Copeland."

Barbara offered her a glass of brandy, which she declined. "Thank you. Your little theater was the perfect place to hold these auditions. Really wonderful acoustics. It must have been designed to sing in." She looked at her watch, "Well, I'm tired. It's been a wonderful evening and was very nice meeting you all, goodnight."

Parker took the brandy glass from Barbara's hand and gulped it down with a wink, handing her back the empty snifter. "Me too, I'm totally spent. If I had to play one more art song I think I'd go crazy."

"Well, goodnight."

They listened as the doors closed at the top of the stairs.

Garrett got up from his chair, "I better be heading home too, it's been a big day." He walked over to Barbara, "I'll call you tomorrow."

Barbara, who was spinning her teardrop lavaliere in her hand, smiled up at him. "Good night Garrett, see you tomorrow."

After Garrett left, Barbara and William sat by the fire and allowed the brandy to seep into their tired muscles rendering them useless. Barbara's glass was empty and her eyes were starting to close when she was suddenly awakened by the phone in the kitchen.

William jumped up startled and walked to the kitchen to answer it. "Hello? Yes. Who may I say is calling? O.K., just a minute. Barbara, it's Betsy from the Hampshire Review."

"At this hour?" Barbara slowly got up and walked to the kitchen the light over the island was too bright, causing Barbara to walk to a nearby stool with her eyes squinted shut. "Hello?"

Barbara unconsciously reached for the lavaliere necklace and spun it in her hands. "Ms. Kinder? This is Betsy from the Review. I think I may have something for you on that carriage accident you wanted me to look up."

Barbara started to come out of it, "You mean to tell me you've been searching all day?"

There was silence at the other end, "I'm slightly obsessive-compulsive, o.k.? In my line of work it's a good thing, right? "Anyway, you know how you had me looking in the winter months? Well, I scanned five years worth of winter months and found nothing. Then, I went into the Spring issues and that was where I found it. That carriage accident was a result of a freak ice storm and a sharp curve in the road."

Barbara looked over at William, "Betsy, would you mind if I put you on speaker phone?"

"No, that would be fine." She continued, "Apparently, they had an early spring, record breaking in fact. The temperatures were in the 50s and 60s all through March, so much so, that all the orchards in the area were starting to bloom. Folks were worried about losing all their fruit.

Anyway, they found her carriage just outside of Winchester. Said the driver probably lost control as it was found down a bank at a famously dangerous curve in the road. They didn't find the carriage for two days. There were two fatalities, Countess Lilly LeClaire and her driver, Thomas Moore. The article says they both suffered head injuries and essentially froze to death. It was quite a story. Apparently, this countess was a famous singer of the time."

Barbara was stunned into silence.

"Ms. Kinder? Are you there?"

"Are you sure it said Thomas Moore?"

"Yes, Thomas Moore was the name of the driver."

"Wow Betsy, good work! Can I get a copy of that article?"

"Yes of course, but it'll cost you."

Barbara could hear Betsy laughing, "Not to worry Betsy, it's worth paying for."

"One thing Ms. Kinder, I am just wondering why you are so interested in this story."

"Oh, Betsy, I would love to tell you and perhaps I will very soon, but not tonight. Thank you very much for your diligence. Good night."

Barbara hung up the phone and walked over to the island across from where William was sitting. "That was Betsy from the Hampshire Review."

She walked over to her purse and pulled from it an envelope. "When I was at Martha's this morning she showed me a poem. Barbara handed the brittle paper to William. "This poem caught my attention. Sometimes history is written in poetry and songs."

William read through the poem and looked up Barbara who continued, "Most of the newspaper clippings in Martha's album were from the Hampshire Review. So, when I walked into town and saw the paper's office, I thought perhaps I could find out more and well, you heard her. Apparently it was true, but I had no idea about Thomas Moore, did you?"

William was looking past her now searching his mind for some indication of Thomas's inclusion in this, other than that of his being the artist who painted her. He shook his head, "Well, it was Thomas's diary we've been reading. And, it was Thomas who told us she was going to sing for the president, but I had no idea he was the driver of her coach."

William continued to search his thoughts. Barbara pulled a stool around and sat across from him. He remembered the last dream he had with the stableman. "In my last dream, I saw them ready her coach for this trip. There was an older man who seemed to be against it, he kept taking off the harness as the one man was trying to put it on. I thought it would come to blows, but the older man just shook his head. Maybe the old man was the driver and wouldn't take her."

Barbara listed intently, "Maybe the young man was Thomas Moore. Tell me more about this last dream."

William shivered, "Well, I told you about the second part

already, remember? She touched me with her frozen hands and said, 'I must save the nightingale,' or she will suffer the same fate as she did."

At this, he looked over to Barbara, and she back at him, "The same fate as she did? So the nightingale will die in a carriage accident?"

William looked off into space again, "Well, maybe not a carriage accident, but a car accident." He got up and walked to the window. A thermometer was attached to the outside sill.

The temperature had dropped dramatically and was now sitting at 30 degrees. He looked over at Barbara. "It's gonna turn to ice out there."

Barbara was still sitting at the island with her chin resting in her left hand and the teardrop lavaliere spinning in her other.

Absent-mindedly she said, "I sure hope Sarah doesn't have any problems getting home." Then she turned to William who was still looking out the window.

Suddenly, the lavaliere became ice cold in her hands. She held it in her palm and looked as the sapphire glowed. "William! Something's happened to her! Something's happened to Sarah!"

He turned to her in immediate acknowledgment. "Call Garrett, we're going after her."

The lights in the house were flickering madly as they both grabbed their coats and went out to look for her. Garret pulled up and they all jumped into his four-wheel-drive Jeep. The roads were not frozen yet, but there were patches over the bridges that were very slick.

They drove in silence for about 15 miles when they approached a very sharp turn in the road.

"There, there! I see a light coming from over that bank. Oh, my God, William! Do you see it?"

Garrett slowed down and carefully pulled up to the bank

where he too could see a light. They jumped out of the car and looked over the bank. There, about 100 feet down, they saw the headlights from an indiscernible automobile.

William took off over the bank and yelled back to Barbara, "Call 911!"

Garrett had a winch at the front of his Jeep which he put into action. He pulled the cable with him down the hill and caught up with William. "Can you see her?"

"I can see her, but I can't get the door open, it's wedged between these trees. "

Garrett attached the winch cable to the front bumper of her car and ran up the bank to his Jeep where he engaged the winch. It groaned as the cable slowly pulled the car from between the two trees.

Just as it was pulled clear, William pulled open the door and found Sarah hunched over the steering wheel. He pulled her out, carried her up the hill and laid her out onto a blanket that Barbara had found.

"How is she?" Barbara placed another blanket over Sarah and watched as William pressed a towel against her forehead.

"She's losing a lot of blood! Did you get through to 911?"

"Yes, but they said it would take probably 20 minutes to get here."

Just then they could hear the sound of the approaching ambulance siren. Within 10 minutes they were loading Sarah's small body into the back of the ambulance and heading into Romney.

Barbara, William and Garrett followed behind the ambulance and waited at the hospital to hear how Sarah was doing. William called Chef George and told him what had happened.

Within an hour the emergency room physician came into the waiting room and approached them. William was the first to speak, "How is she?"

The doctor smiled, "She is a lucky lady. If you hadn't found her, she probably would have bled and frozen to death. Oh, she'll wake up with a terrible headache, but thanks to you three, she'll wake up."

There was not a dry eye between them as they smiled and hugged each other.

The doctor watched as this went on. "I have to ask. How did you know she was in an accident?"

They each exchanged looks, then Barbara piped up, "I guess you could say a little bird told us."

DON'T GO

It was nearly 10:00 am when Barbara and Garrett walked into Romney Hospital to visit Sarah.

William had gone to Winchester to pick up Gertrude, as her surgery and physical therapy had gone well. She was nearly fully recuperated and ready to return home. Carrying a bouquet, Barbara pushed Sarah's hospital room door open and there on his knees at the foot of Sarah's bed was Chef George. His face was wet with tears when he looked up and saw Barbara. "You! it was you who saved my Sarah!"

Barbara started to back up and nearly stepped on Garrett's toes in the process.

Chef George quickly rose, walked up to Barbara, grabbed her hands, pressed them to his forehead and kissed them. "I am so grateful to you, to all of you." He looked up at Garrett and then back at Barbara. "I have been so foolish. To think I almost lost the most important person in my life and over such a stupid thing." He embraced Barbara holding her very tightly. "I don't know what I would have done if I had lost her. Thank you."

Tears continued to stream down his cheeks. He wiped them away on his shirt sleeve then returned to Sarah whose eyes were starting to open. Chef George reached for her hand and held it as he pulled her hair away from her eyes. "Look mon petit choux, you have company."

Sarah drowsily looked over at Barbara and Garrett and smiled. She then motioned for them to come closer.

They were standing on the other side of where Chef George was standing.

"I wanted you to know that she was with me."

Chef George looked up at Barbara and back at Sarah, "Who was with you ma cherie?"

Sarah smiled at her father and looked back at Barbara and Garrett, "She told me you were coming. She sang to me. She said she would not leave me alone until you came."

Chef George looked at Barbara and Garrett. "Who was with her?"

Sarah turned to her father, "Lilly LeClaire was with me Papa, my Great, Great, Great, Grandmother."

At this, Chef George looked out the window as yet more tears streamed down his face. He dropped to his knees and cried into her bed. Garrett came closer to her side, "We know she was with you, she led us to you. Perhaps now she will rest. Perhaps now, we can all rest."

Eyes glassy with tears, Barbara held Sarah's hand.

Garrett's words resounded in Barbara's heart. She knew Garrett was finally free of his obsession with Lilly. She was at peace now and Garrett was free to live a normal life, without obsession and perhaps, without her. Sarah smiled and stroked her father's curly hair as he cried into her mattress. "She told me I must sing for her, for both of us."

Barbara looked at Garrett and back to Sarah, "You will sing and we will all be there to hear you."

She stepped away from the bed and toward the door with Garrett at her side, "Well, you need your rest. We'll be in touch. Remember, we are your biggest fans!"

Garrett and Barbara drove back toward Whippoorwill Ridge in silence. The brooding skies added to the weight on Barbara's heart. She looked out her passenger window and into the deep forests wishing she could escape what she felt was inevitable.

Garrett reached his hand across the seat and held hers and quite automatically, she pulled her hand away. Then, without warning, Garrett pulled off the main highway, onto a dirt road and up a winding hill to a historic Civil War site that overlooked Mechanicsburg Gap. He drove up to a large gravel parking lot, came to an abrupt stop and turned off the engine. They sat for moment in silence before Barbara spoke.

"Things are going to be different for you now, Garrett. You'll no longer be consumed with painting Lilly. You have a chance to live a normal life."

Without saying a word, Garrett got out of the car, walked around to her side, opened Barbara's door and extended his hand to her. The cold air flooded the car, but Barbara was compelled by his intense expression. She took his hand and allowed him to lead her along a wooded path and down a hill. There at the bottom of the hill was the majestic Potomac River, shimmering with the dull light of the cloudy sky and moving slowly along. In the distance, the sounds of rapids echoed off the sides of the mountains. Out of the corner of her eye, Barbara saw a large bird fly overhead and land at the top of a tall dead tree across the river.

"That's a bald eagle."

Barbara watched as the bird flew away. "I didn't know there were bald eagles here."

Garrett pulled her closer and placed his arm over her shoulder. They looked across the river in silence for a while before Garrett spoke. "There is so much beauty here Barbara, so much that remains unspoiled and untouched by man."

He turned to her, holding both of her hands. "This river bank is just one of a multitude of beautiful spots where a person can go to think and to receive the peace that exudes from the forests and lands here. Is it like this where you live?"

Barbara knew it was not. Urban sprawl had eaten up so much of the open lands around her, the night skies were diluted with light and there was always a plane overhead. No, it was not like this where she lived. Garrett looked down at their joined hands and moved his thumbs back and forth across the top of Barbara's. He whispered, "I don't want you to go." And with those words, he pulled her close and pressed his lips to hers, kissing her deeply and passionately.

ROSSIGNOL

It was half past five when Garrett pulled into the driveway in front of the Whippoorwill Ridge Bed and Breakfast. The blue skies were fading into night and the stars were starting to shine. It had snowed a couple of inches, making the house and surrounding trees look like a Currier and Ives painting. Golden light poured from the great room windows and reflected onto the snow in the front lawn. It was that and the heavenly smell of the feast being prepared inside which drew Garrett up to the front door where a beautiful juniper and spruce wreath hung.

As he opened the door, the warm air from William's bright fire welcomed him. The house was alive with people and music streamed in from the hall leading to the theater. Looking over above the fireplace he saw three paintings of Lilly all looking more vibrant than ever.

He walked down the hall and peeked into the theater.

Sarah was at the piano standing next to Parker, singing while he played. Not wanting to disturb them, Garrett walked back to the great room and over to the doorway to the kitchen, where the bright kitchen light flooded past him and spilled onto the great room floor. From the doorway, Garrett watched as Gertrude fired off orders to William who was smiling from ear to ear as he pulled a large pumpkin lasagna from the oven and sat it on the wooden island next to two rustic cranberry tarts. Barbara and Cathy, her friend from home, were walking down the stairs into the great room.

"Hey Garrett, I'd like you to meet a friend of mine. Cathy, this is Garrett, Garrett, Cathy."

Cathy held out her hand to shake his then looked back at Barbara, "Does he have a brother?"

Garrett flashed his charming smile and blushed slightly. "No, only a sister."

The girls both laughed and walked into the kitchen where Gertrude immediately put them all to work setting the table. Within the hour, the table sparkled with freshly polished silverware and flickering candles. Large red and white china bowls held green beans with almonds and steamed carrots laced with nutmeg and brown sugar. The pumpkin lasagna sat in its original baker and right smack in the middle of the table on a large round-rimmed platter, sat a crown roast, stuffed with wild rice and currants. Along its outer edge were small apples and sprigs of bay and rosemary. Cranberry tarts held the promise of a perfect finish to this feast. William tapped his glass and stood up. "A toast."

Everyone held their glass up. "To friends and family, to those who are here, and those no longer with us, and to our futures. May they be filled with love and joy."

"And music!" Barbara piped up. Everyone laughed and responded, "Here, here! Here, here!" They clinked their glasses together and drank the fine French wine Chef George had brought with him. They sat snugly around the large dining room table, Gertrude at one end and William at the other. Next to William, Garrett was sandwiched between Barbara and Cathy. On the other side sat Chef George, Sarah and Parker.

There was laughter and love and an unspoken feeling that a great weight had been lifted from each one.

After dinner they gathered in the theater where Sarah was going to sing a short program. Parker stood up from the piano bench and introduced her.

"Ladies and gentlemen, I would like to introduce to you a fresh young talent all the way from Bickersburg. She has just been awarded a summer scholarship with the Virginia Opera where she will be given a major roll in… what ever opera they will be putting on. I don't think they have decided yet. Anyway, … I give you, the lovely Sarah LeClaire. At that they all applauded, well, all except Chef George, who cleared his throat and said, "Rossignol."

"What?" Parker didn't quite understand. Chef George spoke again, "Her name is Sarah LeClaire Rossignol."

From the piano bench Parker said, "Sorry, that's right, Rossignol. Um…. Rossignol? What exactly does Rossignol mean in French?"

Sarah, standing in the curve of the grand piano turned to Parker, "It means nightingale."

At this William tilted his head back and laughed, Barbara understanding his reason for mirth, laughed as well. Parker started playing the introduction to the first aria, which was fast and filled with an anxious feeling only to slow down just before the singer's entrance. Just as Sarah opened her mouth to sing, another voice was heard emanating from the walls and carried with it a feeling of great joy. It was Lilly, and this beautiful song would be her last aria.

The name of the song?

Pace, Pace by Verde.

It means Peace, Peace.

Fin

Green Beans with Marjoram and Almonds

Servings: 8

2 pounds green beans, fresh, snapped and trimmed,
  cut into 2 inch pieces
1 tablespoon butter
1/2 teaspoon dried marjoram
1/2 cup slivered almonds
1 dash salt, to taste

- Fill a medium soup pot half full of filtered water and bring to a boil. Once boiling, add washed and trimmed green beans and allow to cook for 8 minutes. Don't over cook. Beans should not be limp when done.

- Once cooked to your preference, drain in a colander over your sink.

- Return to pot and add the butter, marjoram and slivered almonds. Stir until butter melts and starts to bubble add the salt, marjoram, and almonds. Stir til well incorporated.

- Add the beans and toss til beans are coated. Pour into your favorite serving dish and serve immediately.

Serving suggestions: roast pork, alongside stewed apples. Excellent with meatloaf too.

Balsamic Glazed Carrots with Pistachios, Nutmeg and Orange Peel

Servings: 8

Preparation Time: 30 minutes

This tastes best when the carrots are a little firm. If you like your carrots a little more done, continue boiling and test with a fork to determine your desired tenderness. Remember, they do keep cooking a little after you drain them. So, always stop cooking right before desired tenderness.

2 pounds baby carrots, farmers market fresh - not pre-peeled
1/8 cup butter
1 teaspoon balsamic vinegar, good quality
3/4 cup toasted pistachios
1/2 cup fresh orange juice
1 teaspoon orange rind, finely grated
1 teaspoon brown sugar
2 teaspoons orange zest
1/4 teaspoon nutmeg

- Peel and slice carrots. Cover carrots with water in a 2 quart saucepan Bring to a boil and then simmer for about 10 minutes or until just tender. Do not overcook. Drain and set aside.

- Melt butter in a large skillet. Add pistachios and saute for one to two minutes or until evenly browned, remove and set aside.

- To the same skillet, add balsamic vinegar, orange peel, juice, sugar and zest and heat until bubbling. Add the carrots and saute until heated through and glazed.

Serving Ideas: Excellent with any roasted fowl.

Crown Roast with Jeweled Basmati Rice Filling

Servings: 18

A feast fit for a king. Ask your butcher to "French" the ribs meaning to remove the meat from between the bones of the ribs about 1 1/2 inch down. This gives the "crown" a traditional look.

If you are having 18 guests, you will need 18 ribs. Also, because each roast is slightly different in how lean it is or how much water it may be holding, an exact baking time cannot be given.

SMALLER ROAST. You can make a standing rib roast by ordering only a few ribs. Using 8 ribs you might bake it for 1 1/2 hours. Bringing temperature to 160. It's delicious and juicy.

> 2 crown (bone in rib) pork roasts, totaling 10 to 12 pounds. You will get two racks.
> 1/2 teaspoon salt and pepper, or more if needed to lightly cover entire roast inside and out.
> Butcher's twine

GARNISH
1 bunch rosemary sprigs, washed and left whole
6 small apples, rubbed to a fine shine
1 cup fresh cranberries, washed
1 branch California laurel or bay, washed and dried to a shine

- Preheat the oven to 350 degrees. Remove one metal rack from oven and set aside. Bring remaining rack to bottom or second to bottom shelf so there is enough height for roast to stand without hitting the top of the oven.

- Rinse ribs and pat dry using a paper towel.

- Lightly sprinkle salt and pepper on both sides of the roast. You can ask the butcher to tie the two racks into a crown or do it yourself. To tie the ribs together bend them in a circle so that the ribs curve out and the meat is on the inside of the roast. Tie them by wrapping the butcher's twine twice around the two racks like a belt, then knot.

- Place the roast on a wire rack and place the rack in a large baking pan with at least 2 inch high sides.

- Bake for 2 hours, then remove from oven and insert meat thermometer into the thickest part of the roast without hitting a bone. You want the roast to measure 160 degrees. While you are waiting for the temperature reading, use foil to individually cover each bone ending so they don't scorch or blacken. If the roast has not yet reached 160 degrees, put it back into the oven and check it again in 20 mintues. Repeat after another 20 minutes until it measures 160 degrees.

NOTE: While you are roasting the pork prepare your rice. Cook rice according to directions on package. Be sure not to over cook rice. Should be tender but firm. Place in a strainer and rinse off excess starch.

BASMATI RICE FILLING

10 cups basmati rice (measures 5 cups before cooked), cooked to al dente
2 tablespoons unsalted butter
1 medium onion, chopped fine
1 large clove garlic, chopped fine
2 tablespoons capers
1/2 cup golden raisins
1/2 cup pistachio nuts, roasted, chopped fine
1/4 cup flat leaf parsley, chopped fine
1 dash salt and pepper, to taste

- In a large skillet, melt butter over medium-high heat.

- Add the onion and garlic and saute for five minutes till soft.

- Stir in the capers, raisins, and pistachios and cook for 5 minutes more over medium heat.

- Add the cooked rice one cup at a time and stir between additions until all the ingredients are well blended.

- Add the parsley and salt and pepper to taste. Set aside and allow to cool. The rice can be made well in advance then reheated just before putting it into the crown roast center.

- When roast is done, pull from oven and allow to sit on the counter. Take the temperature, it should measure 160. As it sits the themometer should and likely will rise to 165 to 170 which is what you want. Remove roast from rack and place on a serving platter. Surround with the rosemary sprigs, apples, cranberries and bay leaf branch. Put the hot rice into the cavity of the crown and serve.

- One rib equals one serving. Slice roast between ribs and using granny fork place meat on each plate. Then place a rounded spoonful of the rice along side the chop.

Curried Pumpkin Lasagna

Servings: 16

Fantastic flavor and texture. You will love the savory pumpkin taste.

Baking this dish in a clay baker works very well. You may want to have extra lasagna noodles depending on the depth of the pan you use. Make as many layers as your pan will accomodate.

3 tablespoons unsalted butter
1 large shallot, finely chopped
1 1/2 teaspoons ginger, finely grated
2 medium garlic cloves, minced
3 teaspoons curry powder
1/2 teaspoon ground cinnamon
1/2 teaspoon salt, rounded measure
32 ounces pumpkin puree, one large can
2 1/2 cups ricotta cheese
1 1/2 tablespoons brown sugar
1 medium onion, sliced into rings
1/2 cup dry white wine, such as Pinot Grigio
1 large Pippin or Granny Smith apple, peeled/cored sliced
   and sliced 1/8 inch thin
1 1/2 cups walnuts, chopped
2 cups vegetable broth or chicken stock
1 package lasagna noodles, uncooked
2 tablespoons heavy cream
1 dash fresh ground black pepper
1 cup mozzarella cheese, freshly grated
1/4 cup asiago or parmesan cheese, freshly grated

Preheat oven to 400 degrees and use a 12" x 8" lasagna baking dish.

LASAGNA FILLING

- Melt 2 tablespoons butter in a small saucepan over medium-low heat and saute shallots for 3 minutes, or until soft.

- Add ginger, garlic, curry powder, cinnamon, and salt and saute for 2 minutes.

- Add the pumpkin puree, stir to thoroughly incorporate ingredients and cook another 3 minutes.

- Remove from heat and cool. Add ricotta cheese and sugar and blend well.

WINE SAUCE

- Melt remaining 1 tablespoon butter in a medium saucepan over medium heat and saute onions until translucent, about 4 minutes.

- Add wine and vegetable broth and simmer for about 2 minutes.

- Remove from heat and set pan aside, add cream and stir. Add salt and pepper to taste.

- Coat the bottom of a large lasagna pan with olive oil.

- Pour 1/4 cup of the wine sauce into the lasagna pan.

- Put one layer of lasagna noodles on the bottom.

- Top this with 1/ 2 inch layer of the pumpkin-ricotta mixture.

- Add a layer of apples then sprinkle on half of the chopped walnuts.

- Place another layer of lasagna noodles on top of the walnuts.

- Pour 1/2 cup sauce onto noodles and coat with 1/2 inch coating of the pumpkin-ricotta mixture.

- Top with sliced apples and walnuts. Place another layer of noodles over apples.

- Pour the remaining sauce onto these top noodles.

- Sprinkle liberally with asiago and mozzarella.

- Coat a large sheet of foil with butter or olive oil and cover the lasagna.

- Place in hot oven. Bake for 40 minutes. Remove the foil and allow to bake for 10 more minutes or until the top is brown and bubbly.

- Allow lasagna to sit for 20 minutes before serving. Cut and serve lasagna on a large dinner plate.

  Serving Ideas: If serving for brunch, serve with fruit. If serving more as a dinner, serve with a fresh garden salad.

Old World Cranberry Raisin Tart

Servings: 6

Preparation Time: 1 hour

A rustic tart with an intense holiday flavor. Remember this is not a pie but is a freeform tart that needs no pie plate.

TART FILLING:

3/4 cup light brown sugar, firmly packed
1 tablespoon tapioca
1 teaspoon orange zest
1/2 cup fresh orange juice
2 cups cranberries, fresh or frozen
1 cup golden raisins
1/8 cup whiskey
1/4 teaspoon salt

Make the filling:
- In a saucepan stir together the brown sugar, the tapioca, the zest, and the juice and add the cranberries, the raisins, and the salt.
- Bring the mixture to a boil, stirring, and simmer it, stirring for 5 minutes, or until the berries have just started to burst.
- Add the whiskey, stir and shut off heat.
- Transfer the filling to a bowl and chill it covered until

cold. Can be made two days in advance.

DOUGH:

1 1/4 cups all-purpose flour
3 tablespoons sugar
1/4 teaspoon double-acting baking powder
1/8 teaspoon salt 3/4 stick unsalted butter, cut into bits
1 large egg
1 tablespoon cold water

Make the dough:

- In a bowl stir together the flour, the sugar, the baking powder, and the salt, add the butter, and blend the mixture until it resembles meal.

- In a small bowl whisk together the egg and the water. Add the mixture to the flour mixture, stirring with a fork until the mixture forms a dough. Dust with flour and chill it wrapped in wax paper for 1 hour.

- Preheat the oven to 425 F.

- Roll out the dough into a 12-inch round on a lightly floured surface and transfer it to a baking sheet.

- Spoon the filling onto the center of the dough, spreading it into an 8-inch circle, and fold the edges of the dough over it leaving the center of the filling uncovered.

- Brush dough with the egg wash and bake the tart in the middle of the oven, covering the exposed filling loosely with foil after 10 minutes, for 15 to 20 minutes, or until pastry is golden.

Serving Ideas: Serve with vanilla frozen yogurt or fresh whipped cream. Serve hot so that the frozen yogurt or vanilla ice cream will melt over the tart.

ABOUT THE AUTHOR

Author Elizabeth Podsiadlo is a mother, wife, chef, musician, teacher, producer and entrepreneur. She grew up in the woods of West Virginia, and later in the suburbs of Chicago. She currently lives in San Diego with her husband of 16 years, her ten-year old daughter, and two dogs.

Chef Elizabeth is a charismatic speaker. Much of who she is today shines through during her cooking classes, public appearances and musical performances, where she shares her "small town" wisdom on life, love and music. Chef Elizabeth produced and sings on the companion recording to "The Last Aria," where she is joined on that recording by three talented friends.

Elizabeth continues to develop her singing voice through the teachings of Maestro Pandeli Lazaridi, whom she has studied under for nearly six years. She works weekly with pianist John Danke, who plays on the companion recording, to expand her operatic repertoire of arias and to keep her performances fresh.

As the "Opera Singing Chef," Elizabeth has been interviewed for KPBS's "These Days," and appears several times a year on local television stations such as San Diego 6, NBC 7/39, KUSI and programs on both Time Warner and Cox Cable, where she shares recipes and promotes her books, upcoming concerts and cooking classes. She is always asked to sing and is always asked back, which has helped build her reputation in San Diego County and soon in Los Angeles.

Chef Elizabeth teaches cooking classes in many San Diego County venues including San Diego Botanic Gardens, San Diego's Natural History Museum and through OASIS, a nationwide senior education program.

To learn more about Chef Elizabeth, her classes and performance calendar, visit her website at: www.theoperasingingchef.

POJTJCRIPT

Barbara and William stayed on with Gertrude for a week after Thanksgiving. William wanted to be sure Gertrude wouldn't over-exert herself, although trying to slow her down was like trying to slow down a freight train. During that week Garrett would come and steal Barbara away for hours. They would hike lofty ridges during the day then spend their evenings together at Garrett's rose-covered cottage where they would make plans on when they would meet through the year.

William's dreams of Lilly ceased but he could not get her out of his mind so he decided to write about her. He and Barbara collaborated and pieced the entire experience together in a journal much like the journal Barbara created after she met William. It was just after the completion that Barbara told William she was going to write a book of how they met. She felt compelled to share their story and it was this compulsion that motivated William. He too decided to write a book. Only his would be about Lilly. After about a year, both books were complete and both had agreed to share authorship of each other's book since the experience in both cases had been shared. They were published together and promoted as a set. It wasn't long before calls started coming in from all over. Folks wanting to share their own ghost experiences and folks wanting Barbara and William to help them with their own. Now, William and Barbara had no intention of becoming "ghost whisperers". They felt their experiences were personal and could not be duplicated in a strange situation. After all, they had had a connection with both of their experiences.

No, it wasn't until more than a year after the books came out when that fateful call came in. The message left on the answering machine was garbled, yet there were a few words and two voices that held Barbara captive. She replayed the message over and over again picking up words and sounds here and there, writing them down, trying to make sense of it. William, too, was curious. It was a distorted message, yet almost orchestrated. After hours of listening and writing Barbara came up with this: "Must come, must be written, must come... come soon." Barbara had a feeling about this one that she couldn't shake. William felt it too, but it was Barbara who became obsessed with it. It would be three days before the related call came in. The call asking for their help.... A little town in the Russian River Valley had a house with a haunt and wouldn't you know, it's right in the middle of a working vineyard so poor William would have to cook and sample his way through this next adventure.

3750008

Made in the USA